Praise for Falguni Kothari's
My Last Love Story

"A profound and deeply emotional twist on the classic love triangle, *My Last Love Story* is a provocative tale of lifelong friendship tested by fate. Poignant and satisfying, *My Last Love Story* is ultimately the type of celebration of love and life that reminds us why we read in the first place."

—Jamie Brenner, *USA TODAY* bestselling author of *The Forever Summer*

"At once heartbreaking, delightful, and completely unexpected. A must-read!"

—Sonali Dev, award-winning author of *The Bollywood Bride*

"[A] love triangle that defies all expectations and crosses all boundaries...and moved me to tears."

—Julia Tagan, author of *A Question of Class*

"Kothari transcends the expected.... A deeply affecting story about what it means to love."

—Kathryn Craft, award-winning author of *The Far End of Happy*

"Equally heartwarming and heartbreaking, *My Last Love Story* takes you on a complex emotional ride that will have you examining the heart's capacity for love long after the book is done."

—Farrah Rochon, *USA TODAY* bestselling author

"Ms. Kothari's writing is beautiful, lyrical and full of surprises."

—K.M. Jackson, author of *Romancing the Fashionista*

"Smart and moving.... Falguni Kothari has written a tender novel with a passionate heart."

—Soniah Kamal, award-winning author of *An Isolated Incident*

"[G]et ready to fall in love."

—Megan Hart, *New York Times* bestselling author

"Darkly poignant, beautifully written, and heartbreaking.... As emotionally raw and demanding as the characters that inhabit its pages."

—Nalini Singh, *New York Times* bestselling author

My Last Love Story

FALGUNI KOTHARI

GRAYDON
HOUSE

**GRAYDON
HOUSE**

Recycling programs
for this product may
not exist in your area.

ISBN-13: 978-1-525-81139-5

My Last Love Story

First published by Phalguni Kothari in 2016
This edition published by Graydon House Books, 2018
Copyright © 2016 by Phalguni Kothari

For questions and comments about the quality of this book, please contact us at
CustomerService@Harlequin.com.

GraydonHouse.com
BookClubbish.com

Printed in U.S.A.

To Pinky,
a gentle warrior to the end.

And to all the warriors cancer has drafted. You amaze me.

1

Love is a dish best served naked.

As a child, those oft-quoted words of my father would have me rolling my eyes and pretending to gag at what I'd imagined was my parents' precursor to a certain physical act.

At thirty, I'd long ago realized that getting naked wasn't a euphemism for sex.

Neither was love.

It wasn't my father invoking the expression just now, though, but my husband. Nirvaan considered himself a great wit, a New Age philosopher. On the best of days, he was, much like Daddy had been. On the worst days, he was my tormentor.

"What do you think, Dr. Archer? Interesting enough tagline for a vlog? What about Baby in a Petri Dish?" Nirvaan persisted in eliciting a response from the doctor and/or me for his ad hoc comedy, which we'd been ignoring for several minutes now.

I wanted to glare at him, beg him to shut up, or demand that he wait in the doctor's office like he should've done, like a normal husband would have. Khodai knows why he'd insisted on holding my hand through this preliminary checkup. Nothing of import would happen today—if it did at all. But I couldn't perform any such communication, not with my eyes and mouth squeezed shut while I suffered through a series of uncomfortable twinges along my nether regions.

I lay flat on my back on a spongy clinic bed sheeted with paper already wrinkled and half-torn. Legs drawn up and spread apart, my heels dug punishingly into cold iron stirrups to allow the fertility specialist's clever fingers to reach inside my womb and check if everything was A-OK in there. We'd already funneled through the Pap test and stomach and chest checks. Like them, this test, too, was going swell if Dr. Archer's approving happy hums were anything to go by.

"Excellent, Mrs. Desai. All parts are where they should be," he joked only as a doctor could.

I shuddered out the breath I'd been holding, as the feeling of being stretched left my body. Nirvaan squeezed my hand and planted a smacking kiss on my forehead. I opened my eyes and focused on his beaming upside-down ones. His eyelids barely grew lashes anymore—I'd counted twenty-seven in total just last week—the effect of years of chemotherapy. For a second, my gaze blurred, my heart wavered and I almost cried.

What are we doing, Nirvaan? What in Khodai's name were we starting?

Nirvaan stroked my hair, his pitch-black pupils steady and knowing and oh so stubborn. Then his face rose to the stark white ceiling, and all I saw was the green-and-blue mesh of his gingham shirt—the overlapping threads, the crisscross weaves, a pattern without end.

Life is what you make it, child. It was another one of my father's truisms.

Swallowing the questions on my tongue, I refocused my mind on why we were here. I'd promised Nirvaan we'd try for a baby if he agreed to another round of cancer-blasting treatments. I'd bartered for a few more months of my husband's life. He'd bartered for immortality through our child.

Dr. Archer rolled away from between my legs to the computer station. He snapped off and disposed of the latex gloves. Then he began typing notes in near-soundless staccato clicks. Though the examination was finished, I knew better than to sit up until he gave me leave. I'd been here before, done this before—two years ago when Nirvaan had been in remission and the idea of having a baby had wormed its way into his head. We'd tried the most basic procedures then, whatever our medical coverage had allowed. We hadn't been desperate yet to use our own money, which we shouldn't be touching even now. We needed every penny we had for emergencies and alternative treatments, but try budging my husband once he'd made up his mind.

"I'm a businessman, Simi. I only pour money into a sure thing," he rebuked when I argued.

I brought my legs together, manufacturing what poise and modesty I could, and pulled the sea green hospital gown bunched beneath my bottom across my half-naked body. I refused to look at my husband as I wriggled about, positive his expression would be pregnant with irony, if not fully smirking. And kudos to him for not jumping in to help me like I would have.

The tables had turned on us today. For the past five years, it'd been Nirvaan thrashing about on hospital beds, trying in vain to find relief and comfort, modesty or release. Nirvaan had been poked, prodded, sliced and bled as he battled aggressive non-Hodgkin's lymphoma. I'd been the stoic spectator, the supportive wife, the incompetent nurse, the ineffectual lover.

And now? What role would I play now?

As always, thinking about our life left me feeling even more naked than I was in the open-fronted robe. I turned my face to the wall, my eyes stinging, as fear and frustration bubbled to the surface. Flesh-toned posters of laughing babies, pregnant mothers and love-struck fathers hung from the bluish walls. Side by side were the more educative ones of human anatomy, vivisected and whole. The test-tube-like exam room of Monterey Bay Fertility Clinic was decorated in true California beach colors—sea-foam walls, sandy floors, pearl-pink curtains and furniture—bringing the outdoors in. If the decor was meant to be homey, it wasn't having such an effect on me. This room, like this town and even this country, was not my natural habitat, and I felt out of my element in it.

I'd lived in California for seven years now, ever since my marriage, and I still didn't think of it as home, not like Nirvaan did. Home for me was India. And no matter the dark memories it held, home would always be Surat.

"All done." Dr. Archer pushed the computer trolley away and stood up. "You can get dressed, Mrs. Desai. Take your time. Use whatever supplies you need. We'll wait for you in my office," he said, smiling.

Finally, I can cover myself, I thought. Gooseflesh had erupted across my skin due to the near frigid clinic temperatures doctors tortured their patients with—like a patient didn't have enough to suffer already. Medical facilities maintained cool indoor temperatures to deter inveterate germs from contaminating the premises and so its vast flotilla of equipment didn't fry. I knew that. But knowing it didn't inspire any warm feelings for the "throng of professional sadists with a god complex." I quoted my husband there.

Nirvaan captured my attention with a pat on my head. "See you soon, baby," he said, following the doctor out of the room.

I scooted off the bed as soon as the door shut behind them. My hair tumbled down my face and shoulders at my jerky movements. I smoothed it back with shaking hands. Long, wavy and a deep chestnut shade, my hair was my crowning glory, my one and only feature that was lush and arresting. Nirvaan loved my hair. I wasn't to cut it or even braid it in his presence, and so it often got hopelessly knotted.

I shrugged off the clinic gown, balled it up and placed it on the bed. I wiped myself again and again with antiseptic wipes, baby wipes and paper towels until the tissues came away stain-free. I didn't feel light-headed. I didn't allow myself to freak. I concentrated on the flow of my breaths and the pounding of my heart until they both slowed to normal.

It was okay. I was not walking out with a gift-wrapped baby in tow. Not today. No reason to freak out.

I reached for my clothes and slipped on my underwear. They were beige with tiny white hearts on them—Victoria's Secret lingerie Nirvaan had leered and whistled at this morning.

Such a silly man. *Typical Nirvaan*, I corrected, twisting my lips.

Even after dressing in red-wash jeans and a full-sleeved sweater, I shivered. My womb still felt invaded and odd. As I stepped into my red patent leather pumps, an unused petri dish sitting on the workstation countertop caught my eye.

The trigger for Nirvaan's impromptu comedy, perhaps?

Despite major misgivings about the direction my life had taken, humor got the better of me, and I grinned.

Silly, silly Nirvaan. Baby in a petri dish, indeed.

One thing I'd come to love and respect about doctors was their ability to remain unruffled in the most bizarre circumstances.

A large mahogany work desk headlined the length of Dr. Archer's office. I took my seat before it, my stomach twisting like Twizzlers. Nirvaan sat on my right, gregarious and talkative like always, as if all was right in his world, as if he had every right to reweave the very fabric of my existence forever and ever.

But there was an animation in him today that I hadn't seen for some time now, and I let it wash over my qualms. If I overlooked the thinning hair, the tired curve of his spine and the melting muscles beneath his shirt, he almost looked like the man I'd married.

For better or worse, Simeen. I can't say no to you.

He'd always been there for me. Always. No matter what I'd asked of him. Did he not deserve the same courtesy in return?

My husband caught me staring at his profile. He winked, grinning wolfishly, and my lips responded to his charm with a helpless smile.

Dr. Archer cleared his throat and began his spiel. He skimmed over our options—from the cost-effective natural fertilization via intrauterine insemination to the more expensive intracytoplasmic sperm injection, or ICSI. That method involved injecting a single sperm—Nirvaan's—directly into my extracted egg in order to fertilize it. Dr. Archer explained how my eggs would be extracted and the zygote reintroduced into my womb for gestation.

I loved that he spoke directly to me. He addressed Nirvaan only sporadically. Childbearing was a woman's prerogative, after all. Though, in my case, I'd hardly use the word *prerogative*. *Coerced* would be more apt.

My fingers hurt as I gripped the armrests of my chair. I wasn't ready to be a mother. Not yet. Maybe I'd never be. The thought of being responsible for another person's health and security scared me like nothing else. Nirvaan knew that—or he ought to know it.

I'd thought of children as waves crashing over a distant horizon. I'd discussed—or, no, we'd never discussed having a baby, Nirvaan and I. Not before we'd gotten married. Not after. Not until Nirvaan had been diagnosed with cancer, and the option of freezing his sperm before his first chemo had come up—a treatment that had left him irreversibly sterile.

I didn't want to deny my husband his wish. But I did not want a baby. Not now. Not when our lives were in flux again.

"You have a good chunk of information to sort through." Dr. Archer wound down at last. The walls in his office weren't the calming colors of the Pacific Ocean. They were the no-nonsense white of his doctor's coat. "Meanwhile, we'll start monitoring your cycle. You need to come in for a detailed consult next week, Mrs. Desai. We'll do blood work and a preliminary ultrasound. Narrow down the best route for you. Prescribe medications for maximum ovarian stimulation and so forth." He glanced at his desktop monitor. "I have Monday afternoon and Thursday morning open. Or you can call my assistant for later dates."

"Monday's great," replied Nirvaan while I pretended to scroll through my largely appointmentless phone calendar.

Monday was only three days away. I could be pregnant by the end of the month.

My husband would be dead this time next year.

My breath turned to stone in my lungs. The white walls of the doctor's office shrank. I thought I'd finally scream.

"Call whenever you're ready." Dr. Archer's words were kind. His pale blue eyes were kinder. "Call if you have questions or any doubts. Your youth really is in your favor, and it's not infertility we're dealing with in your situation but extenuating circumstances. Even though we have a limited amount of your husband's sperm to work with, we have an excellent success rate, Mrs. Desai. Rest assured."

Hysteria bubbled up in my throat. He thought I was worried that this wouldn't work. How do I confess to him—*to anyone*—that I was petrified it would?

2

On the drive home, Nirvaan jabbered inside the car while the rain played a harmonica on the Jeep's roof—fast, then slow, loud and then soft.

Since I commanded the steering wheel, I was exempt from input on the baby-making plans beyond a well-placed hum or an indistinct nod. Normally, it took about twenty minutes to get home from the clinic in Monterey, but the downpour hampered our speed today.

By home, I meant the beach house we'd rented for the year in Carmel-by-the-Sea. We'd moved in barely two weeks ago, and we were still feeling our way around the resort-town community. We weren't complete strangers to the area. Being so close to San Jose, where we'd lived for the first two years of our marriage, both Carmel and Monterey had been our favorite spur-of-the-moment getaways. We'd often discussed buying beachfront property as an investment or retiring to a seaside town in our winter years—all this, of course, before the cancer had forced us to move to LA and in with Nirvaan's parents. We were living our dream now, in a fashion, as part of Nirvaan's Titanic Wish List—the list so dubbed because of the magnitude of its scope and theme.

The beach house was ideally located for our needs—twenty minutes from the fertility clinic and a scant five-minute drive from one of the best cancer hospices in the country. The Bay Area boasted a temperate climate throughout the year, getting neither super hot or insanely cold. With Carmel Beach as a backdrop, Nirvaan truly had chosen the perfect place to die.

"Why didn't you make the appointment, Simi?"

I'd expected the question, yet I flinched when Nirvaan asked it.

"Your treatment starts next week. Let's concentrate on one thing at a time, honey," I replied, collecting my wits.

"You're trying to wiggle out of our bargain."

"No, I'm prioritizing the important stuff." I kept my eyes peeled on the rain-slick California highway. If I looked at him, I'd melt or say something I'd regret.

"The IVF is important. You promised we'd try, Simi." His words were matter-of-fact, but I heard the accusation hidden in their folds well enough.

"We will. *We are.*" My voice wobbled, and I struggled to moderate it. "Once the radia—"

"No." He cut me off, reaching over to rub my thigh.

I hadn't realized my body was clenched so tight.

"Both procedures together. Whatever we do, we do together, like always or not at all," he said in a tone that would not countenance an argument.

I wanted to scream at him for being such a bully, but I couldn't because I had promised, and I'd never broken a promise to him in my life. I might lie to him—had lied to him many times about many things. I wouldn't deny manipulating him, but I'd never broken a promise.

When the parish church loomed up like a stone beacon on the right, I eased my foot off the accelerator and took the exit onto the local roads, driving around the church building. A backlit signpost stood, water smudged, on the front lawn. Every single day, the pastor—an austere-faced though jolly man—would put up a new adage for the world to pontificate on.

Today, it simply read, "Trust in God. He knows what He's doing."

My face tightened at the patently false advertisement. Khodai didn't know what He was doing any more than Nirvaan and I did.

Trust in God? The God who'd inflicted cancer on a fun-loving young man? The God who'd orphaned children and would leave a wife as a widow? The impotent God who'd done nothing while my eighteenth birthday turned into my worst nightmare?

Thank you, but no. I could never trust God as His executive decisions had failed to impress me so far.

And Nirvaan wanted to produce another soul for Him to torture.

The rain began to pelt down in fat musical drops as I zigzagged through the streets, filling the obstinate silence inside the Jeep. I was glad for the sound. It allowed me a reprieve from all words, emblazoned or spoken or thought.

At the tip of a quiet long road with nowhere left to go, I eased the car over a pebbled driveway and parked as close to our slate-blue craftsman-style home as I could. Ahead of us, a strange black truck with monster tires blocked the front of the detached carriage house, the rear covered in blue tarpaulin.

Before I could utter a word, Nirvaan chortled, "He's *back*," in a bizarre falsetto.

"So I gathered. But what's he brought back?"

Instead of answering the question, Nirvaan unbuckled his seat belt in one fluid motion, grabbed my face between his hands and smooched my lips, as if our recent tense moments had never happened.

It was typical of him. Nirvaan stubbornly refused to let bad

moods win. I approved of the quirk with great gulps of grati-
tude, as one moody bitch per household was quite enough.

"Happy birthday to us, baby." He grinned from ear to ear
as our noses eskimo-kissed.

I squinted at my husband. Our birthdays weren't for another three weeks. Mine fell on May 31, and Nirvaan's was
on June 1. I wondered what kind of present had gotten him
even more excited than the visit to the fertility doctor.

Nirvaan spilled out of the Jeep before leaping up the three
steps onto the thick wraparound deck where our longtime
friend, the third Musketeer of our pack, Zayaan Mohammed
Ali Khan, stood under the aegis of the front porch. He, too,
grinned like the Cheshire cat high on cream.

I'd steeled my nerves before looking at him, but even then
a gasping ache speared my heart. Zayaan was the living reminder of all that was wrong in my life, all Khodai had taken
from me as part of His grand plan to keep me in line.

Astoundingly, Zayaan and Nirvaan shared their birthdays.
The fact was the deciding factor in their friendship that had
been founded one summer on the streets of Surat, the year
they—we—turned fifteen. Same birthday, same street address,
same damn–the–world temperaments, where could they—
we—go wrong, really?

But we'd gone wrong. Like a roller coaster plunging off its
tracks, our world had splintered apart one awful night, and
I'd been left bleeding and alone, as always.

Stop wallowing in self-pity. Control yourself, and get out of the car.

Nirvaan gestured at the truck and said something. Zayaan
nodded in reply, still grinning. He held a nonalcoholic beer in
one hand, a hand towel in the other. His thick mop of poker-
straight hair stood up in glossy spikes, like he'd vigorously
rubbed it with the towel, while the rest of him was drenched
from shoulders to sandaled feet. His cotton shirt was soaked

through and plastered against his torso, delineating every muscle beneath it.

My throat went dry. I was a sucker for broad shoulders and washboard abs, and Zayaan's were quite deliciously on display right now.

Cursing the paradox of emotions he always spawned inside me, I pulled the red hood of my raincoat over my head, as much to serve as blinkers for my wayward vision as to protect my hair from the rain. With a tight grip on my nerves and my purse and the tote bulging with a dozen medical files, I got out of the car and dashed up the wet whitewashed steps.

Nirvaan grabbed the towel from Zayaan to mop the splashes of water from his own face and arms. Not so long ago, those arms had been thicker than Zayaan's, the shoulders broader, the bulk of Nirvaan's body heavier and stunningly sculpted. I'd not lied when I compared Nirvaan to Michelangelo's *David* during our monthlong honeymoon in Italy.

I dropped my burdens on a rickety porch bench. Then I removed my raincoat and hooked it over a rocking chair to dry. I wished that my anxiety could be stripped off as easily as the raincoat.

"Those had better not be the death traps I expressly forbade you to ride." I flicked a telling glance at the truck.

Nirvaan might not care if he died today or a year from now, but I bloody well did.

"Damn it, Zai. You don't have to give in to every harebrained idea he jots down on that stupid Titanic Wish List. He's not supposed to drive a car even, much less ride a motorbike." It felt good to blast someone even if he wasn't the target of my anger or worry.

For a second, it seemed Zayaan would chuck me under the chin, like he used to when I shrieked. My voice had an unfortunate nasal quality to it and a tendency to become shrill when I got excited or upset. But the hand moving toward me changed direction and gripped the banister instead.

Zayaan did not touch me anymore, not if he could help it. Zayaan had stopped touching me the day I asked Nirvaan to marry me.

Shattered Dreams was the title of an oil painting I'd seen in an art gallery in Mumbai once. The artist had rendered a perfectly featured, golden-hued portrait of a person. It was androgynous in composition, as you couldn't tell if it was a man or a woman staring out of the canvas. What had struck me—the observer—the most about the painting was that the artist had worked in a tornado through the beautifully daubed face, as if one had birthed the other.

Zayaan's face had been a tornado of shattered dreams when Nirvaan and I had told him of our engagement on Skype, more than seven years ago.

It should've brought me relief, his aversion to touch me even after all this time. Instead, his solicitude left me empty and cold and slightly afraid.

"They're not what you think, Simi." Languid dark eyes snared me in their net, wary but not without humor beneath a fringe of sooty thick lashes.

I wanted to look away, but I didn't. *Take control.* "Really? Those aren't motorbikes?"

For years, I'd zoomed around Surat in a yellow Vespa scooter, and I felt confident that the vague T-bar shape under the tarpaulin was a bike. Two massive bikes, in fact.

"Last week, I physically barred you from walking into a Harley-Davidson showroom, so you enlisted his help?" I groused at Nirvaan.

How things had changed. When had I turned into a party pooper? A dozen years ago, I would've hurdled over the guys and staked my claim on the biggest, baddest bike available.

Now I couldn't even address my deepest fears to myself, much less voice them to my husband.

Zayaan's lips curved upward in a smile that still had the power to devastate me. He looked at Nirvaan, and the smile broadened, turned wicked. My breath soughed out in a huff.

"Not bikes. Jet Skis!" the guys hollered in unison, slapping high fives above my head.

"Fucking A, I still can't believe we won them." Nirvaan whacked the towel on the bench and stabbed a finger in the air, just shy of Zayaan's chest. "You were right to stick to our price. Fucker, you're always right. Luck of the fucking devil." He grabbed the thick wooden banister with both hands, seemingly ready to leap over and verify the rightness of the purchase with his own eyes, rain be damned.

Zayaan stopped him with a casual press of his hand on Nirvaan's shoulder, saving me the trouble of lecturing my husband on the inadvisability of getting soaked with his weak constitution or falling and breaking his bones by vaulting willy-nilly over banisters dewy with rain. I threw Zayaan a grateful smile, but he'd turned his attention elsewhere. As had Nirvaan.

The truck and its marvelous contents held both men utterly rapt. Then, with raucous laughter and an F-bomb-sprinkled explanation, they described the events leading up to this momentous occasion.

Apparently, my thrill-seeking husband and his idiot best friend had bid on the Jet Skis in an online auction. Zayaan had spent the morning fetching the prize—our birthday surprise—from San Francisco. I refrained from pointing out that I was the only one surprised here, and I wouldn't quite use the word *surprise* for what was roiling in my nervous system.

After a point, the dialogue turned bilingual, as it often did with us. The guys' absolute favorite Gujarati curse word, *chodu*, made its appearance, replacing *fucker* intermittently.

While Gujarati was our collective mother tongue, all three of us spoke it distinctly, apropos to our individual ethnic backgrounds. Nirvaan's dialect was harsh and guttural, even diluted by his strong American accent. He was a bona fide *Gujjubhai*, a typical man from Gujarat. Mine, due to my Persian Zoroastrian ancestry, was the softer, fancier Parsi Gujarati. Zayaan's was softer, too, idiomatic to his Khoja or Aga Khani Muslim roots and flavored by the accent he'd acquired from the dozen or so years of living in London.

Having known the guys for half of my life, I'd become immune to their rough talk even though I rarely blasphemed myself. My mother, Feroza Batliwala, had been a true lady and had been determined to raise one. So, while I'd failed in the etiquette department as a teenager, I tried hard to emulate my mother as much as I could now in honor of her memory.

When Nirvaan exclaimed, "To hell with the fucking weather. Let's test the bikes right now," I drew on every ounce of self-control I had and kept my mouth shut.

If I brought up his health, it would only make him mad and more determined to throw caution into the rain. I couldn't be sure that he wouldn't jump on a water bike and ride it to Hawaii just to prove fate wrong. I honestly didn't know which scenario scared me more—Nirvaan trapped under a motorbike, bleeding to death on a highway; Nirvaan getting *Jaws*-attacked in the Pacific after flying off the Jet Ski; or Nirvaan catching deathly pneumonia right before his scheduled chemo-radiation.

I placed my hands on my hips and glared—first at my husband and then his cohort. Even in my heels, I had to crane my neck to look at them. Both men were taller than average. Nirvaan was over six feet tall, and Zayaan was just shy of six feet. I was a hobbit compared to them at five foot three and slim as a beanpole.

Our heights and widths hadn't matched even when we'd first met, but in every other way, I'd been their equal. No, I'd been their boss because I was older—a full ten hours older than Zayaan and close to twenty hours older than Nirvaan. Hence, I was a cougar in my husband's delightfully twisted mind. Anyway, I'd been a budding teenage girl with promising girl-powers, and they'd been hormone-driven idiots. Of course I'd led them down a merry path. I still would when I plucked up the courage.

"I claim dibs on one and want mine painted periwinkle pink. The two of you can share the other one," I declared cleverly.

This way, I'd command my own ride, and Nirvaan would be chaperoned by default. The cherry on top? I did not come off as the world's naggiest wife.

Two masculine faces crinkled with confusion. The looks poured dread into my belly.

"Please don't say you bought three Jet Skis." *How much money did they blow?*

Zayaan took my statement as a personal affront, but Nirvaan laughed outright.

"No stinting, remember? Of course we bought three. Baby, are we or aren't we the Awesome Threesome?" So saying, Nirvaan grasped me by the waist and hauled me up in the air. He spun us around and around until I was sure we'd fall and break our necks, all the while singing, "Happy birthday to us," like a demented Donald Duck.

"Put me down, you idiot," I shrieked, swatting at his shoulders.

He didn't simply set me down. He slid me down his body, kissing me all through my descent. I felt dizzy, unsteady from his kisses, from the spins, and I wrapped my arms around him until the world righted itself. His heart beat strong and steady under my cheek.

Thud, thud, thud, thud.

I closed my eyes and burrowed into his chest. I didn't want to let go, not just yet. *Not ever,* I vowed, tightening my hold on my husband.

He moved then, not to disengage us, but his body went taut, as if he were reaching for something and—

Oh, crap. I realized too late what he intended and wasn't nimble enough to pull away in time.

Just breathe, I told myself. *It's only Zai. You know him. It's okay. You know him.*

"You're insane, *chodu*," Zayaan muttered right before I became the sandwich filling between two hard, half-wet, male bodies.

I couldn't help the shiver that coursed through me.

The Awesome Threesome.

A long time ago, we'd been that and more to each other, and in the coming year, we'd probably draw on that bond like we'd never done before. We needed to become a well-oiled machine again, working in tandem to fulfill the promises we'd made to Nirvaan, trying to live a normal life when our situation was anything but normal.

I, Simeen Desai—a plain-Jane rebel, the mad Parsi chick—was living in a ménage with two gorgeous men, the twin knights of my life.

I concentrated on that fiction. In my mind, I perpetuated the fantasy we'd once imagined for us because to think about the truth of our situation, about the inoperable metastatic tumor inside my husband's brain, was anathema to me.

3

The late spring drizzle didn't let up for the whole day, leaving the guys and me housebound.

Personally, I didn't mind it so much. Trips to doctors' offices often left me sore, sour and in frantic need of my comfort zone.

I changed into a simple top and a pair of knit shorts. Then, too restless to just sit around playing video games with the guys, I started on my chores. I did two loads of laundry and vacuumed every square inch of the house, preparing it for Nirvaan's parents, who were set to visit over the upcoming Mother's Day weekend.

The beach house had come fully furnished and comfortably so. The furniture, if not new or color-coordinated, was made of sturdy cedar wood and wicker that had withstood the water-heavy ocean air and deposits of inadvertently smuggled-in sand for decades. There was enough storage around the house that I didn't need to worry about clutter when bombarded by our constant weekend guests, and the carriage house with its own bathroom was a bonus even if in disrepair. Zayaan wanted to quick-fix it up—spray-paint the walls, polish the furniture, or replace it with cheap new pieces—and move in there, so we might all have some breathing room. But Nirvaan wouldn't hear of it. He wanted the three of us together at all times, space or no space. And what Nirvaan wanted, Nirvaan would get.

He'd say, "Jump."

We'd ask, "How high?"

He was dying. We were not. It was that simple.

It wasn't that space was an issue when it was just the three of us. The house was sufficiently large with an inviting open layout. The front door led directly into the living area, two bedrooms and a master bath fell to one side of it, and a third bedroom, a tiny den, and another bathroom crowded the other. None of the rooms had any doors on them, except the two bathrooms. Thick damask curtains acted as doors to the rooms, giving one a vague sense of privacy when drawn.

I could go for hours without bumping into Zayaan, if I wished. The house was that spacious. The thing was, I didn't seem to want to. I was getting used to him again. And no matter how resistant I still was about our living arrangement, my devious husband had counted on just that. Nirvaan wished I'd overlook Zayaan's inadvertent transgressions—meaning, I should look more kindly toward his religion and his infamous Pakistani family, including his obnoxious mother. I'd perpetuated those lies for a long time, and I would continue to flame them. It was better the guys thought of me as a paranoid bigot than suffer the truth.

The nonstop rain had triggered a drop in temperature, both outdoors and indoors, and one of the guys had thoughtfully built a fire in the living room.

My chores done, I decided to serve lunch in front of the cheery crackling fireplace. I'd put together a nutritious *bhonu* meal of egg *biryani* and a Greek yogurt-based vegetable *raita*—a simple dish but plentiful—keeping the guys' bottomless stomachs in mind. It'd taken Nirvaan a long time to rebuild his appetite, reawaken his taste buds that cancer medications had destroyed, and I dreaded the coming months that would leach it from him again. I was determined to spoil him as much as possible until then.

I wasn't a great cook. I wasn't bad, either, and could manage simple dishes well enough. But given a choice, I'd gladly surrender the kitchen to a more seasoned power, one of the reasons I looked forward to my in-laws' visits. No one indulged my husband's notoriously *Gujjubhai* palate better than his mother. My mother-in-law was the undisputed queen of the Desai kitchen, and I, her quasi apprentice.

That reminds me...

"I should stock up on groceries before your mother arrives. If you guys have special requests, tell me now." I paused, a forkful of *biryani* dripping with yogurt poised before my mouth. "Don't make me or even yourselves run to the store twenty times for ingredients."

I exaggerated, but the guys did have a tendency to spring culinary demands when least expected. Like last week, Nirvaan had had a craving for Indian-style Hakka noodles in the middle of the night, and no Hakka noodle packets had been in the pantry.

Nirvaan chewed on his food and my question, when, suddenly, his face twisted into a frown, as if he'd tasted something bad. Or rather, he'd seen something unpleasant—my bun. I'd bunched my hair into a topknot, so it wouldn't get in the way of my chores.

I sighed, reached up and pulled the rubber band off, letting the weight of my crowning glory drop. "Happy?" I rubbed my scalp and fluffed my hair out.

Nirvaan had developed this hair fetish after his own had fallen off during his first chemo. I understood his obsession, sympathized with his apprehensions, but sometimes, he took things a bit too far—and not just with my hair.

"You know what I like, baby. I'll leave the satiation of my cravings in your skilled hands," he said, giving me a syrupy smile.

I rolled my eyes at the not-even-clever double entendre. I could've pointed out that we were discussing the satiation of his cravings through his mother's hands, but I thought better of it. The comment would no doubt trigger rebuttals, and I didn't want the conversation to slide into the gutter.

"And you?" I darted a look at Zayaan, or more specifically at the fringe of hair flopping over his eyes. I'd worked out a system to deal with him. I would not get too close, and I'd stick to minimum eye contact.

"Everything Mummy cooks is delicious. Just make sure there's enough left over to last until her next visit." He smacked his lips together, clearly anticipating the forthcoming delicacies.

"Not that we don't appreciate your cooking, baby. The *biryani* is orgasmic. No, seriously, I *love* it," added Nirvaan.

The patently fake, obsequious tone made me snort. I was proud of my strengths, and I'd learned to live with my weaknesses. Cooking was neither. I just didn't care about cooking enough to take offense that I wasn't a master chef in people's eyes.

"We can drop you at the market on our way to the marina," offered Zayaan, briefly smiling at me before jerking his chin at Nirvaan. "We should get the Jet Skis checked out—serviced, gassed up and whatever else. Daddy will want a ride first thing tomorrow."

"You're right," groaned Nirvaan. "Damn it. He'll hog one all weekend. Thank God Nisha's not coming, or between Aarav and her brats, we'd never get a turn."

He was joking, of course. Nirvaan loved his sister, got along famously with his brother-in-law, and doted on his niece and nephew, who adored their Nimo in turn.

For reasons slightly more serious than the sharing of Jet Skis, I, too, was glad my sister-in-law had postponed her visit. We'd hosted Nisha and her family last weekend, and we would see them at our birthday celebration at Nirvaan's parents' house in LA at the end of the month. So, it wasn't a huge tragedy to miss bonding this once.

I had no issues with Nisha, as such, but she'd started behaving a bit funny with me over the past few months, and I didn't know what to make of it. She was probably worried about Nirvaan, I'd concluded, and unable to express her feelings about the tumor and its ramifications. It might explain her stiff attitude toward me. It was difficult to find the right words of support and solace in our kind of situation, and Nisha and I had never been chums to begin with.

In truth, I'd never even tried to get friendly with her—or anyone else since my fifteenth birthday. I'd been so blinded by the guys, so wholly satisfied by our friendship and what it'd brought to my life, that I hadn't wanted any other friends. And after…after that night, I'd been too afraid to step out into the world. So, what would I have done with making friends, anyway?

Nisha and I had become passably friendly only after my marriage. But then, we'd had to, hadn't we, for Nirvaan's sake?

"Stop whining, *chodu*. I should be whining." Zayaan flicked an uneaten clove at Nirvaan.

The spice bounced off my husband's shoulder and landed on a white seashell embossed on the shrimp-colored fabric of the sofa. He pinched it up and popped it into his mouth. Nirvaan could eat anything remotely edible.

"You'll get out of playing golf by faking fatigue or the bubonic plague, and I'll be stuck on the greens with Daddy for hours or days. Fuck, I hate golf. It's such a tedious game." Shaking his head, Zayaan ambled into the open-style kitchen and dumped his empty plate and bowl in the sink. He twisted the tap on, running water over both.

It spoke volumes to just how entrenched Zayaan was in the Desai household that he addressed my in-laws as Mummy and Daddy. Even I didn't do that. I couldn't. Mummy and Daddy were honorifics reserved for my own parents alone even though I considered Nirvaan's in the same light. I'd addressed my in-laws as Kiran Auntie and Kamlesh Uncle since I was fifteen, and I continued to do so after marriage. Neither my in-laws nor Nirvaan had ever questioned me on it even though plenty of our relatives had. I'd usually smile and shrug in answer to such nosiness.

The thing was, as a Parsi daughter-in-law, I could get away with a lot of things in the Desais' predominantly Hindu household that another woman of similar faith would not have. Especially as we Parsis were known for our outspoken, eccentric attitudes. My own family hailed Freddie Mercury of Queen fame as a hero—a nonconformist outspoken Parsi, if there ever was one—and his hit song "I Want to Break Free" was the family motto. I sat on the fence regarding the hero worship even though I did love his music.

I cleared the remnants of our lunch onto a tray and took it into the kitchen, humming the catchy beat of Freddie's song under my breath. Nirvaan brought in the empty beer bottles and soda cans, tossing them into the recycling bin. From the fridge, he drew a tall glass of the mixed berry smoothie I'd whipped up for him earlier and glugged a quarter of it down along with his provision of meds. There were a few more pills in the mix than there'd been last month, as his medications were an ever-changing cocktail. I looked for signs of discomfort or pain on his face and relaxed when none showed. His head would hurt when he overdid things, and we'd already had an exciting day so far. Maybe I'd persuade him to take a nap before we ran our errands.

Zayaan brushed past Nirvaan to the squat new coffee machine by the fridge and programmed in a double espresso, his after-lunch special. "You sure you want them going back on Monday?" He looked askance at Nirvaan as the machine chugged out black-brown liquid in a swallow-sized cup. "They'll want to be here, Mummy especially, during the radiosurgery."

I stiffened and then quickly spun around to face the sink to hide my panic. The antiquated kitchen had no room for a dishwasher, so I soaped up a sponge and started washing the dishes by hand. I was furious with myself for reacting so badly, so typically. And I'd thought Nisha needed lessons on how to behave around Nirvaan. *Ha.*

"Nah. They're doing enough, man—driving up and down on weekends, Dad taking on my share of the business acrobatics—and…you know, Ba hasn't been keeping well, either. He needs to take care of his mother, too. She's getting old. Besides, the procedure won't even take half a day. No hospital stay and no side effects. Not a biggie at all." Nirvaan's words were all but muffled under the thundering beats of "I Want to Break Free" spooling around and around in my head.

What kind of a wife fears taking care of her sick husband? What kind of a person quakes to hold an ailing man's hand?

I could handle death—the finality of it, the suddenness of it. I'd lost my parents when I was fourteen, and while it had changed me forever, it hadn't broken me. I could face death. What I couldn't face was sickness. What I couldn't bear was the corrosive odors of a hospital and the utter helplessness one experienced in the face of trauma. That was why Nirvaan and

I had moved in with his parents when the cancer first tainted our lives. It was the reason Zayaan lived with us now.

I was a useless spouse.

If I was a poor example of a wife, Nirvaan was the epitome of an exceptional husband.

He forgave all my faults and loved me anyway. He didn't expect anything from me I wouldn't willingly give—or he hadn't until the baby. That he had my heart and my devotion was no secret. He'd had it since we were fifteen. He didn't try to change me, not in any way. Even when it had become clear he was my second choice, in love and in marriage, he had not faltered. Neither had he begrudged Zayaan's place in my life. In fact, Nirvaan had always encouraged the unconventionality of my desires. Later, when he could've walked away for all those reasons, he'd stayed beside me and become the Band-Aid for my wounded soul.

I'll tell you one thing for sure. It rocked to have Nirvaan for a husband.

Groceries, Jet Skis and a couple of other errands later, the guys and I made a night of it in town. By unanimous agreement and an available table, we drove to Hara Kiri, a Japanese steak house known for its gourmet teriyaki and teppanyaki menu. We parked the truck in a supervised lot down the street from the restaurant to ensure the Jet Skis would be safe.

It was still raining. Shallow puddles had formed in places where the earth was dented. The guys, as usual, were oblivious to the vagaries of weather, content with the deficient protection their unzipped hooded coats provided.

I was more circumspect. I cinched my raincoat about me and opened an umbrella large enough for a homeless man to use as a shelter. Without making a fuss, I hurried after Nirvaan and brought him under the red canopy and out of the rain. He shot me an amused grin and curled an arm around my waist, pulling me flush against his body, as we plodded forward.

Lately, life seemed to amuse him a lot. I guessed when one was about to lose his life, he had to choose whether to laugh or cry about it. I supposed the same could be said for anyone not about to lose his life, too. I recalled the Elbert Hubbard quote Nirvaan had printed out and stuck on the fridge at his parents' house some five-odd years ago.

"Don't take life too seriously. You won't get out of it alive."

Inside the restaurant, Nirvaan headed straight for the restroom while I tried to remove my coat, one-handed, while juggling my handbag and the dripping umbrella in the other. There were days when Nirvaan would experience moderate to severe incontinence due to a change in his medications or a reaction to some food. I hoped it wasn't bad. Maybe Hara Kiri hadn't been such a great idea...

"Here, give me those," Zayaan said, tugging my bag and umbrella out of my hand.

Unencumbered, I shrugged off my raincoat, and he took it, too, handing my purse back to me before heading to the coat check. After the exchange, we didn't speak or even look at each other as we waited for Nirvaan.

Sometimes, it saddened me that it'd come to this between us. This man was my soul mate, and through no fault of his, I couldn't stand to be near him now. I found no humor in our situation, no matter what Hubbard had quoted.

"Are you okay?" I asked when my husband rejoined us. "Would you rather go home for dinner? Or somewhere less exotic?"

Nirvaan shook his head, saying he only had to pee and was fine, so we followed the sleekly dressed half-Asian hostess to the hibachi grill in the middle of the restaurant. The space was packed, every seat taken, every table laden with food and sake.

I was glad I'd had the foresight to make a reservation through the restaurant's mobile app. The hostess took our drink orders once we'd settled in our seats and sauntered off to fulfill them.

"Pink Shirt and Fake Tits checking you out, *chodu*," said Nirvaan through the corner of his mouth. He had the menu open before him but clearly wasn't interested in selecting his dinner from the listed offerings, busy as he was with scanning other delights. "Baby, scoot hither." He conspiratorially leaned close. "Give those two lovely ladies a chance to corrupt our friend here. He deserves a reward for all his hard work today."

I followed my husband's line of vision to the women sitting on the opposite side of the massive grill. In the expanse between us, a quartet of Asian chefs danced about, flaming up masterpieces in the woks on the grills. Pungent garlicky aromas wafted up, making my mouth water and my stomach growl. Through the steam, I saw the women were indeed looking our way. A sideway squint showed Zayaan returning the favor with his signature mystery-man look—hooded eyes, calm but cocky expression, a hint of a leer curling his lips.

A flame of jealousy ignited in my belly. I wrenched my eyes away and looked down at the menu in my hands.

I didn't understand myself at all. I loved my husband. We were happy together. I didn't want Zayaan anymore—not in any capacity, other than as a good friend. I had pushed him away, locked up all memories of him for twelve years. I'd been very successful. But ever since our forced proximity, it had become impossible to maintain any sort of equanimity.

I didn't want those women staring at my guys—both my guys. I wanted to stake my claim on them in front of the whole world.

I could brand Nirvaan, claim his mouth with lips and tongue, and there would be no mistaking my rights. Then I could lean into Zayaan and run my hand down the pearly-white buttons on his shirt to his heart. A kiss here, a touch there. I wondered if the women would take my actions as a warning or an invitation.

Here was the thing about places like Carmel-by-the-Sea where half of the populace was of an artsy temperament and the other half was mega rich—no one cared about ménage à trois or even ménage à twenty. In such places, kinky was normal.

Not that the guys and I had ever been kinky outside of our childish fantasies. We weren't a sexual ménage. Had never been, would never be.

But our audience didn't know that, did they?

I wasn't drunk, truly. My sake bomb had only just been placed in front of me, so I couldn't blame my insane cogitations on its consumption—not that I ever blamed alcohol for anything. I preferred to take responsibility for my own thoughts and fancies.

I didn't know these women, but I did know how my guys would react if I actually gave in to my wicked desire. Nirvaan would guffaw if I made a spectacle of us. Probably egg me on to add a tabletop belly dance to the action. But Zayaan would bristle like an angry porcupine. He used to dislike public displays of anything. I didn't think he'd changed all that much.

Anyway, I decided not to test the theory.

"Do stop staring, Zai. They might think you're available." I raised an eyebrow. "Unless you want them to think you are? But then whatever will Marjaneh think of Nirvaan and me? Bad enough that we stole you away from her charms for a whole year. That we couldn't even protect her man from the big, bad California Barbies would be unforgivable. She'd never let you off her leash again."

Marjaneh Shahrokhi was Zayaan's girlfriend of two years and colleague of five. According to Zayaan's mother, the couple was a hairbreadth away from getting engaged. Marjaneh was smart, pretty, moderately religious and sensible—the perfect woman for Zayaan. We'd met her on our last trip to London. I'd hated her on sight.

"What's put your nose out of joint tonight?" remarked Zayaan, calling me out on the *Mean Girls* act.

It shut me up, as intended. I wrinkled my rather large Parsi nose with the inexplicable bump in the middle. The thing was an added insult on my plain-Jane face. I had a lovely peaches-and-cream complexion, courtesy of my mother, but no glamorous features to speak of, nothing to inspire a Leonardo to paint me as *Mona Lisa*.

No, that wasn't entirely true. Both Zayaan and Nirvaan, during our hormone-crazed teenage years, had composed love sonnets in my honor. Some of them had been absolutely filthy limericks extolling the virtues of my various body parts, but I'd found them enchanting regardless.

In turn, I'd penned praise of their sinewy beauty. Nirvaan was the classic tall, dark, lithe type of handsome while Zayaan was ruggedly good-looking and very fair. Zayaan, without his golden tan and face stubble, was almost as pale as me. Our common Persian heritage, we'd deduced, during one of our trillion and one profound midnight chats.

Sometime over the past millennium, to avoid persecution, first the Parsis and then the Aga Khani Muslims, a sect of the Shiite Ismailis, had fled Persia to settle down on the mildly distant but welcoming shores of Hindustan—the shores of the State of Gujarat, to be precise—setting the precedent for a religiously and ethnically diverse yet secular nation.

The undulations of history fascinated all three of us. But while Nirvaan's and my interest remained amateurish, Zayaan had studied the subject to death. He held degrees in world literature, sociology and Islamic studies from the University of

London and Oxford. He spoke Farsi, Urdu and Arabic as fluently as Gujarati or English. Add in a smattering of Hindi, Latin and French, and we had an *octolinguist*. Nirvaan had coined the word a while ago.

Currently, Zayaan was working on a dissertation that hoped to shed light on the cross-cultural relationship between Muslims and their neighbors from the time of Ishmael through now. Zayaan was a super nerd. It wasn't all he was, but it was the one quality that continued to stagger me. He worked for the Share Khan Foundation in several capacities, all mostly academic, and while it hadn't been convenient for him to apply for a sabbatical at this point in his career, he'd done just that to come live with us. Of course, his superiors in London believed he was pursuing his doctorate in earnest, which he was.

But the simple truth was, Zayaan had come because Nirvaan needed him, and that was all that should've mattered to me. I was doing all of us a disservice by my behavior. Zayaan was the third of our triad. He had every right to be here with us, every right to say goodbye to Nirvaan. So why had I begun to resent his presence, their friendship, when I'd always been glad that they had each other before?

Nirvaan kissed my bumpy nose, tugging me back from the side trip I'd taken into the extraordinary complications of my life. He always claimed my nose gave me character, a sort of distinction. With an unholy gleam in his eyes, he looked over my head at the man who was his soul mate as much as I was.

"Did I hear you insult my sweetie's nose? You must be punished for it, you infidel. Kiss her nose, or lose your head. *Oy!* Kiss her nose, *and* lose your head since kissing her did have that effect on you once," teased Nirvaan.

Then, out of the blue, he pushed me at Zayaan. I yelped, teetering unsteadily in my chair, finding balance against Zayaan's chest, our faces not two inches apart.

Again, why do I love my husband? I struggled to right myself, blushing furiously.

"People are watching, for fuck's sake." With a tight grip on my arms, Zayaan settled me back in my seat before I fell over, trying to get away from him. "What'll they think of us?"

Nirvaan put a hand on his cheek and gasped, "No! You pulled the LSKS card?"

LSKS was an acronym for, *Loko shu keh shey?* Or, *What will people say?*

It was the most common rhetoric *Gujju* parents—any parent, for that matter—badgered their children with.

My parents had plagued me with such questions in sigh-worthy regularity. *What will people say, Simi, if you dye your hair purple? What will people think, Simeen, if you fail your exams? Don't be rude to your grandmother's sister's grandniece's mother-in-law. Behave. Behave. Behave yourself in public.*

I started giggling. I was that flustered.

"Don't encourage him." Zayaan looked thoroughly disgusted with us.

We could do that to him. Only Nirvaan and I could ruffle Zayaan's feathers that easily. Any minute now, he'd start lecturing us in Farsi.

Nirvaan's arm snaked around my middle, pulling me back against his chest, as he sniggered like a college boy. His breath tickled my ear, making me whimper. Zayaan's eyes went dark and glittery as he glared at us—not angry, not envious, but something in between.

My face was probably scarlet by now.

"What I've learned with this time bomb ticking inside my head, *chodu*, is that life is too short to live in regret." Nirvaan's laughter faded, his voice went low and hoarse, and I stilled in my husband's arms. "Life is so fucking short, my loves. So, fuck the world and its fucking rules."

Like a maestro at the helm of an orchestra, Zayaan steered his ruffled feathers back to smoothness. "Easy for you to say, *chodu*. You'll be dead. We won't be." He broke off and clamped his jaw shut in an obvious effort not to say something regrettable.

There was a lot of that going around between the three of us—regret, broken words.

It wasn't the first time we'd had this conversation. It wouldn't be the last, not with Nirvaan trying to cram a whole lifetime into one year or less. Both men were right in their own ways, but Zayaan's point was undeniable. What Nirvaan expected from us would get tongues wagging, and they'd never stop. I didn't want to care what the world thought of me or how I'd chosen to live my life. But did I really have the luxury to be a part of this world and not care?

I frowned into my sake. Experience had taught me to care, to be careful and to be private. I couldn't change who I was, not even for my dying husband. *But dare I try?* I raised the sake cup to my lips and took a swallow.

And what of the child? The child who, if conceived, would be Nirvaan's and mine...and Zayaan's, too, in a way.

What would people say about such a child?

4

We got home earlier than expected. The guys' intense exchange hadn't ruined our dinner—we'd managed to slide the conversation back to a glossy, innuendo-filled level again—but it'd left us not quite in the jolly mood to go clubbing, like we'd originally planned.

I tucked the groceries away and then headed for the bathroom for a much-needed soak in the tub and some much-desired time alone. As my body relaxed in the warm pool of foamy water, I tried to do the same with my mind, immersing it in the historical thriller I'd downloaded on my e-reader. Every so often, I was jarred away from the intrigues of Napoleon's court by the sounds of laser guns and bombs exploding beyond the powder blue walls of the bathroom.

The guys were trying to obliterate each other via their gaming avatars. I winced at a particularly loud bomb blast, followed by a string of clipped curses and a bout of heated argument about the best way to circumvent land mines and storm alien territory without getting blown to bits. Whoever had penned the phrase "boys and their toys" had known the male yins of the universe well. I remembered my mother muttering something to the effect in reference to my father and brothers pretty much every day.

I had a pair of them—brothers, I meant. Surin and Sarvar

were both much older than me, and ever since the fatality that had taken our parents, they'd become more parents than siblings to me. I'd had a third brother, a sickly boy named Sam, who hadn't survived his first year in this world. I had him to thank for my existence. If Sam hadn't died, I wouldn't have been born, as my parents had wanted no more than three children.

When I was little, my brothers would tease me about being a replacement, the spare wheel, the girl who'd destroyed the manly kingdom of the three Batliwala brothers. I'd scream for them to take their hideous words back, sob as if my heart was breaking, until the day my mother had sat me down and opened my eyes to the bullshit that was the male psyche.

Mean to begin with or not, Sarvar had become the kind of brother every sister should have. He didn't hover or smother, but he was always there when I needed to pour my heart out. Sarvar was my anchor in the ocean of life, a safe harbor for tempestuous times. Lucky for me, he lived in San Jose, close enough to meet when we wished.

I have the Desais to thank for it. Ever generous and helpful, they'd somehow convinced Sarvar to move to the States right after my marriage. They'd sponsored his legalization documents and whatnot. They'd even offered him a managerial job at one of their motels, but he hadn't taken them up on it. These last six years, Sarvar had expanded our family's plastic business across the Americas, and so far, both my brothers seemed satisfied with the results. It'd been my father's dream to expand Batliwala Plastics outside of India, and I felt incredibly proud that my brothers had made it come true. I liked to believe, in a small way, I'd had a hand in it, too.

Surin, seven years my elder, still lived in Surat, close to the factory we'd almost lost right after our parents' deaths. The Desais hadn't been able to convince him to immigrate to California. To leave India would mean selling Batliwala Plastics or trusting someone else to run it, and Surin would cut off his right arm before he did that. He'd fought so hard to keep the factory, sustain it and make it prosper. He'd shed sweat, blood and youth for it. He'd never leave it in someone else's care. He couldn't even bring himself to take a decent holiday with his wife and kids for fear the factory would collapse in his absence.

I hadn't seen Surin in over three years because of that. He wouldn't come to California unless there was an emergency, and I couldn't go to India until...Nirvaan let me.

At times, I missed Surin as violently as I missed my parents. And then there were days when he'd cease to exist in my American reality. As if being out of sight, out of tangible reach, he'd become a ghost in my mind.

I stared at the words I held between my hands, unable to decipher them, as my mind slowly clouded with memories. My parents. My brothers. Surat. My life there. All I'd lost. All I'd gained. Nirvaan. Zayaan. My life here.

I leaned over the edge of the cast-iron tub and set the e-reader on the closed toilet seat. My movements upset the cooling water, and waves splashed against my breasts and back in protest. I pulled the plug, watched the water spool into the sieve and gurgle down the drain. If only I could rid myself of ghosts so easily.

I stood up and stepped out of the tub. Naked and shivering, I walked across the beige-tiled floor into the shower. Under a pounding hot spray, I soaped and loofahed my body. I can't pinpoint when I started crying or if I cried at all. When my eyes stung, I convinced myself it was the soap. My breath hiccuped, and my skin puckered, but I stayed under the shower until the Antarctic threatened to melt through it. I got out then and wrapped myself in a towel. I didn't look in the mirror, not even when I brushed my teeth and my hair. I refused to give my weakness a form, an image, another ghost to remember.

I slipped on a nightshirt and went straight to bed. I didn't wish the guys good-night. I couldn't. Nirvaan would know I'd cried, and it would upset him, make him feel guilty and sad, maybe even mad. He would leave his game and his buddy to comfort me. He would try to bring me solace with gentle words and lust-filled kisses. He might even succeed. He'd assure me that everything would be fine, convince me that I was stronger than this.

Maybe I was. My therapist certainly believed so. But I didn't want to be strong. I wanted to run and hide, escape my reality, banish all feeling. I wanted to smash open the translucent perfection of my snow-globe world and simply walk away.

But I couldn't do that. Not tonight. Not ever, if Nirvaan got his way and I had his baby.

So I lay in bed, stiff under the gray-and-yellow summer quilt, and wished for things I'd never had—like a normal life.

Sleep was a chameleon tonight. Sly and still, it kept changing color and time to hide from me. I counted sheep, but my mind kept drifting toward warmer shores, black-sand beaches and home.

My fifteenth birthday had dawned hot and oppressive over Surat, and it had remained so until its phantasmagorical end.

Summers were murder in Gujarat—arid, dusty and energy draining. But I hadn't complained about the weather that year. That last of May's days, my first birthday without my parents, I'd had many other concerns besides harping over a bit of sweat and grime.

Like the home I hadn't allowed myself to like.

We'd lived in a four-bedroom flat on the tenth floor of a high-rise complex erected along the Tapi River. In addition to being the diamond and textile capital of the world, Surat had just been declared the cleanest and fastest-growing metropolis in India. As a testament to my father's success, my family had, only recently, moved into the new cosmopolitan digs from a demographically Parsi neighborhood across town. We'd just begun the process of getting to know our neighbors when tragedy had struck.

With my parents gone, and both my brothers still earning their college degrees and living away from home—Surin had boarded with our father's brother in Mumbai and Sarvar had lived in a boy's hostel in Ahmedabad—my maternal aunt and uncle had imposed themselves in our home. My brothers were deemed too young and foolish to shoulder the responsibility of raising a young girl, so Uncle Farooq and Auntie Jai had thought it best to supervise my guardianship.

But that was only a pretense, we'd eventually realize. The real reason for the sudden familial love was my father's business, which Uncle Farooq wanted to usurp.

Barely twenty-two, naturally, Surin was confused. He didn't know whether to finish his studies or take over the business. He wasn't ready to be the head of the family. Relatives from all over the world advised him in various capacities, but finally, any decision that impacted the three of us was on him. For six months, he'd tried to make sense of our father's affairs, and from what I overheard him tell Sarvar late one night on the weekend before my birthday, he was afraid the business was crumbling about his ears. The factory workers, suppliers and clients who'd had implicit faith in my father's business acumen had none in a mere boy's, and orders had begun to drop like overripe fruit from trees. He'd decided not to go back to college by then.

Surin was overwhelmed by his responsibilities. Sarvar was worried about our future. So, I worried, too.

I didn't like my uncle and aunt. I'd never liked them, but I didn't tell my brothers that. I had no wish to add to their burdens. My mother had never spoken against her older sister, but I knew they hadn't gotten along, either. I didn't like how Uncle Farooq spoke to Surin, as if he were an idiot. I didn't like how nosy my aunt was about my parents' life insurance policies and our material holdings.

If Surin didn't ask them to leave soon, I planned to run away. Where? How? When? The logistics didn't matter. I felt trapped in my aunt's presence. I wanted things to go back to how they'd been. I missed my mother terribly.

I didn't want to celebrate my birthday that year. Friends from my old neighborhood offered to treat me to lunch, but I refused.

"I am in mourning," I told them.

The truth was, it pained me to see them. They reminded me of my old life, of my parents and happy days, and I couldn't bear it.

My brothers overruled my wish not to celebrate. They even brought home a birthday cake, as if we were a normal family. We went out for dinner, and I got money as presents, no other gifts. No one knew what to buy for me. It was always my mother who'd bought the gifts in our family even if the name tag on the gifts stated otherwise.

That night, Smriti invited me to a beach party. Smriti was a neighbor of similar age who I'd interacted with off and on since our arrival in the building complex. Before I could think of an excuse, Sarvar urged me to go and have fun. Surin frowned, clearly unsure of whether to allow poor hysterical me out of his sight since I'd spent the day locked in my room, weeping. But much to my disgust, he, too, nodded and smiled in encouragement. It was the one and only time I wished my aunt would butt in and barricade me in my room. But, nope, she didn't.

Unbeknownst to me, Surin had already asked my aunt and uncle to leave our home. Within a month, they'd be gone for good.

I squeezed into the back seat prison of a silver-colored Maruti, jammed from door to door with five other girls.

"Whose party?" I belatedly asked.

"Nirvaan from C building," replied Smriti, the designated driver.

Smriti and I resided in Ram Bhuvan B, and besides her and a few of her friends, I knew no one.

"He moved to California two years ago and comes down every summer to meet his grandparents. He throws the best parties. They're wild and…" Smriti paused to grin at me through the rearview mirror. "There will be lots and lots of booze. Imported."

All the girls in the car giggled at the revelation, except me.

"I know what you're thinking. Gujarat is a dry state, so no boozing. But who follows rules these days, *na*?" Smriti said when I remained silent and slightly horrified by her disclosure.

"Even government officials don't follow rules," added a pigtailed girl, riding shotgun, in a patronizing tone.

"And Nirvaan has connections. I mean, his father has connections and a green card, so he's allowed," Smriti said smugly.

Connections or not, dry state or not, fifteen-year-olds should not be boozing.

What if we got arrested? Would the American boy's father bail us out? I wondered if Smriti had thought this through.

Too late, it occurred to me, if she was my age, she wasn't old enough to drive.

Crap.

What was I doing here? Why had Sarvar pushed me out the door? Couldn't he stand my company for even one evening?

I wasn't an adventurous soul. I was wary of crowds, basically a homebody. That wasn't to say I was timid or obedient. I wasn't. But my bratty nature had been blown to bits, along with my sense of security, the night the police had called and informed us about the accident. A drunk driver had rammed his truck into my parents' car, killing them on the spot. The accident had happened on the highway near Udvada as my parents drove back from a visit to the fire temple that housed the world's oldest Atash Behram, the sacred fire Zoroastrians paid homage to. The irony of my parents coming to mortal harm while on a holy pilgrimage wasn't lost on me. I'd lost my faith in Ahura Mazda that night.

So, that was how I knew if we got into trouble, neither God nor a green-card holder would come to our aid.

I stayed quiet on the drive while the other girls laughed and yakked around me. When we hurtled down the highway past Dumas Road, I was startled out of my silence.

"*Arre! Kya jai che*, Smriti? Where are you going? You missed the turn for Dumas Beach."

"We're going to Dandi," said Riddhi, the girl squashed against me. "Dumas is overcrowded, *yaar*. No privacy at all. Dandi is our go-to place for these types of parties."

What in Khodai's name did she mean by "these types of parties"?

It struck me that I was way out of my comfort zone here, and for the rest of the hour-long drive to Dandi, I alternated between cursing my luck and crossing my fingers. I also begged my parents to watch over me as my brothers clearly were doing an awful job of it.

The car bumped along Dandi road until the concrete disintegrated into sand. We drove past a massive black granite plaque jutting out of the ground with Dandi March and a long commemoration carved on its face. This was where Mahatma Gandhi had led thousands of protesters on April 6, 1930—including my freedom-fighting grandfather, Rustum Batliwala—in the Salt Satyagraha in defiance of the British Raj and their overbearing tax laws on Indians. It was a historical landmark, but contrary to its fame, it was not very touristy.

Smriti parked the Maruti next to a jumble of cars. Remixed pop pumped out of a massive music system from the roof of a van. Bunches of girls and boys flooded around an enormous beach bonfire. Half of the girls from my group had already disappeared into the throng.

I became Smriti's shadow. I went where she went, drank what she drank and danced when she danced. I talked little and tittered a lot. When you knew no one, it was easy to lose your inhibitions. I didn't have to make an impression or accept pitiful condolences from strangers. I didn't have to listen to geriatric aunts compare my looks to my mother's or my nose to my grandfather's, the same one who'd fought for India's freedom. I was no one here, no one important. I could forget my burdens for tonight, forget that I was orphaned.

I finally got why Sarvar had pushed me out the door—not that I forgave him for it, but I understood. There was life beyond death, and it was all around me. I tried to have fun. I tried very hard.

"That's him!" yelled Smriti, waving her arm in a sort of dance move.

"Who?" I shouted back, squinting in the direction of her wave. "Nirvaan?"

"Yeah. He's so *chikna, na*?" She laughed and shimmied to the beats of a pop song.

"I see several *chikna*-looking boys there."

There were many, many cuties to wade through. Most of the guys were shirtless. Most of us girls were in cutoffs and thin T-shirts or tank tops. It was nasty hot, even with the tepid sea breeze. The bonfire aggravated the heat, but it was necessary for light and ambience.

My mother had loved dining by candlelight. *Firelight is a boon to women,* she'd told me once. *It erases age and enhances our natural beauty.*

She was right. We glowed golden brown.

Black sand sparkled beneath naked feet, mirroring the night sky. Dozens of coolers poked through the sand like half-buried treasure chests, openly displaying their glittering booty of imported beer, sodas and water bottles. The beer, naturally, depleted faster than the rest of the drinks. I'd consumed three cans so far. As most of us were quite buzzed by then, and sweaty and stinky to boot, it was no surprise when some partygoers began to cool off in the water. It was stupid and dangerous to swim in the sea in the middle of the night. But at fifteen, stupid meant cool, and dangerous was even cooler.

Dandi Beach, like many others along Gujarat's coastline, was endangered land. Due to overdevelopment and deforestation, the unstable coast had succumbed to the Arabian Sea. But I ignored everything my father had cautioned against. I dived into the water, breaking free of all restraint. I didn't panic when I lost sight of Smriti in the floating crowd. I was a worry-free bird tonight. I didn't care if Surin found out I'd been boozing. I didn't care that my father would have disapproved of my midnight swim. He wasn't there to lambast me, was he? No, he was dead. And Surin...

Surin...with his stupid threats of locking me in my bedroom, of washing his hands of me and leaving me to rot with Auntie Jai. I wished Surin were dead instead of my parents.

My gut heaved like the buoyant waves, making me vomit

and cry. I clawed my way to the shore, and after grabbing another beer, I started running down the beach.

Why did you die, Mumsy? How could you die and leave me so alone?

I wanted to curl up in a dark hole and sob my heart out. I ran farther and farther away from the party. Had I been thinking straight, had I not been upset, I would never have set off alone. I ran past cars, kids, desertlike vegetation and the hemline of dilapidated shacks, abandoned and eerie little huts, along the sand. The villagers had been forced to move inland to safer ground. The government had started projects to save the beaches, but it was a long-haul process, and most of the villages had become ghost towns. I knew all this because Daddy had been passionate about saving the environment.

Daddy...oh, my Daddy...

The beach came to an abrupt end on a jut of rocks rising out of the sand. I had found my black hole to sink into.

I began to climb. *Please, no snakes, no crabs.* I could abide anything but snakes and crabs. I stepped on something squishy—*yuckity yuck*—and then something poked my sole, and I nearly lost my balance. I was barefoot, my slippers languished in Smriti's car. I'd thought it sensible to remove them there. I'd stopped feeling sensible the minute I stepped onto the beach.

Tossing away the beer can, I clambered up the rocks on hands and feet. A great sense of accomplishment swept over me when I reached the top. It wasn't high, just a few feet above sea level, but I felt like I'd climbed a mountain.

I breathed in deep and let it out. I flung my arms out, staring at the limitless horizon. Without the music blaring, I heard the waves whoosh and slap against the rocks. Without the bonfire, the full moon dribbled silver light onto the world.

My name meant silvery light in Persian. I was born on a full-moon night, and so my parents had named me Simeen.

My parents...

I dropped my arms as guilt stabbed at my chest. *No! Khodai, please, I don't want to feel anything anymore.* If only I'd gone with my parents instead of arguing.

I have plans for the weekend that don't involve driving from temple to temple with a couple of old killjoys. I want to hang at the mall with my friends, okay? Why are you forcing me to go and not Surin or Sarvar? I'm almost fifteen. I can stay home alone. I hardly need you to babysit me.

My last words to my parents had been antagonistic, churlish.

If only I'd gone with them.

If only I hadn't been so selfish.

If only...

I remembered thinking that. I vividly remembered the feeling of sinking breath by breath into the quicksand of despair that night on Dandi Beach. I remembered screaming into the dark, raging at my parents, calling for them, begging them to come back.

Please come back. I need you. I lied. I need you, Daddy, Mumsy.

I pleaded with Ahura Mazda to take me, too, to stop punishing me. I wished the sea would swallow me. I should've died with my parents. If I were dead, I'd stop feeling, stop grieving. I didn't remember leaning over the edge, but I must have because, if only for a second, I was staring at a pile of shiny black rocks before I was yanked back hard.

Someone shouted, but I didn't know who or why or what. A pair of arms locked tight around me. A hand pressed my face into a wet, warm chest.

He smelled of the sea and tasted of it, the night Zayaan saved me. He let me go, only to push me into Nirvaan's arms. Hopping from boulder to boulder, Zayaan disappeared behind a large outcropping, only to reappear within seconds in swimming shorts.

With gentle but firm words, they calmed me. They sat me down on the sand and made me drink overly sweet Frooti from a Coke bottle. They petted me like I was a newborn kitten. And I, desperate to confess my sins, spilled my guts.

Only after they'd handed me over to Smriti and I was on my way home with the taste of cake in my mouth, did I wonder how they had known it was my birthday or why I'd sipped Frooti from a Coke bottle. Only then did I recall what my peripheral vision had first registered but hysteria had censored.

Zayaan had been naked, totally completely *naagu*, when he saved me. And there had been a girl half-hidden between the jut of rocks where he'd come from—a partially *naagu* horrified-looking girl.

I grinned in the dark, smearing the tears that had pearled in my eyes with a thumb before they leaked down my cheek. Reliving the Naked Savior incident always lifted my spirits, reminding me that life wasn't all despair and darkness but could be as sweet as a Frooti and funny, too. I thought of how much I'd laughed that night.

That first volcanic introduction had defined my relationship with the guys. That chance encounter had changed my world again, ripping me out of my shell, out of my grief, making me bold and greedy in a way I'd never been before.

I turned on my side, hugging my pillow. Exhaustion made my eyelids heavy, but I wasn't anywhere near ready to fall asleep. Stars had popped up in patches in the blue-black sky. The rain clouds had finally been lured away, letting rain fall somewhere else for a change. I breathed in the gentle breeze blowing in through the open windows, fluttering the wind chimes on the deck.

Smells could trigger memories. Carmel's salty, fishy odor would often take me home to Surat in spirit, reminding me of the beaches in Gujarat, family holidays taken at various beach resorts, and of the hundreds of happy days and nights I'd spent in Dumas and Dandi with the guys. All three of us were beach babies or beach horses or whatever people obsessed with the sun, sand and water were called. We didn't mind other vacation destinations. We'd taken plenty of holidays where not a single beach had been on the itinerary. But if you asked us where our favorite place to chill was, without a doubt, we'd say the beach.

Maybe it was, in part, because of the way we'd met. That night on Dandi Beach had been a gift none of us had expected, and everything that followed only brought us closer.

The guys had sought me out the morning after the beach party. To check on my health and state of mind, they'd claimed. After confirming I was indeed sound in both, the true reason for their visit was revealed. They'd put me through a subtle interrogation about how much I'd seen and what I'd inferred from it.

"Don't gossip about us." Zayaan's low, hoarse baritone was as potent in daylight as it had been at midnight. "If you do, we won't keep our mouths shut, either."

"Is it gossip if it's the truth?" I teased with false bravado. Not that I wanted people to think I was some kind of nutcase or suicidal. I wasn't. Or I was over it by then.

They took me to lunch—a blatant bribe. If I blabbed to anyone about the naked bits, the girl's reputation would be ruined, and the guys' wouldn't fare any better.

What I hadn't known then was that Zayaan couldn't afford a tarnished reputation. His father was the administrator, the *mukhi saheb*, of the local *jamaat khana*, which was the Khoja community center-cum-mosque. No matter what sort of mischief Zayaan got up to behind closed doors, in front of the world, he had to be the no-nonsense *mukhi saheb*'s son.

I was super-duper intrigued by the naked *naagu* bits. I was appalled, at first, but intrigued more. I'd spent the night picturing all kinds of debauchery, and I couldn't get the image of a girl sandwich out of my head. I felt breathless just thinking about it. To be completely truthful, I felt hideously jealous.

I wanted to be the sandwich filling. *I* wanted the growly-voiced guy to press my face into his chest while the American-accented guy with the quick hands massaged my back. I'd smooched a couple of boys from my old school. It'd been nothing impressive, just some suction action on the mouth accompanied by a waterfall of slobber. Totally *yuck*.

I imagined smooching Zayaan and Nirvaan and decided it wouldn't be yuck at all.

I felt naughty. And for the first time in six months, I felt alive.

I put forth a bold proposition in exchange for my silence. I offered myself up as their secret second helping. Not that Anu, the sandwich girl, was much of a secret. The guys had openly vied for her attention, like Archie and Reggie over Veronica. Other kids in our complex would bet over who'd win a date or a kiss or something much cruder from her. Most would put their money on Nirvaan. He was, after all, a homegrown boy even if he was an expat now.

Zayaan, on the other hand, had moved to Surat only a year ago from Pakistan. Plus, he made the other kids wary with his quietly clever disposition and grown-up manner. He had a job already. Zayaan helped his father run the *jamaat khana*. He was being groomed to step into his father's footsteps. He wasn't overfriendly or spontaneous like Nirvaan. Neither did he throw awesome parties. Money was an issue for him. He never seemed to have any, so Nirvaan would pick up his tab.

Zayaan was night to Nirvaan's day, yet they shared everything. It was soon apparent that no one but me—and Sandwich Anu—knew the extent of their sharing.

Nirvaan, after a stomach-clutching hooting session, took me up on my offer and allowed me to tag along wherever he went. Zayaan refused to be blackmailed. I'd set myself up as Betty, and in true *Archie Comics*–style, nothing I did thawed Zayaan.

If I'd known then how sacred a clean reputation was to him, I could've forced the issue.

My behavior should've embarrassed me. It didn't at all. I was fed up with being a good girl, and I had come to the conclusion that good things happened to wicked people, and vice versa.

I didn't seem to threaten Anu darling's space, either. Naturally not. I was plain faced, where she was gorgeous. Flat and gangly like a ten-year-old boy, where she was voluptuous and sultry. I had short boyish hair. I'd walked into a salon one day and hacked off my locks, unable to care for it without my mother's guidance. I'd cried for two whole weeks in the aftermath, and nothing my brothers said, complimentary or not, had cheered me up. I sported a *tapeli*-cut hairdo while Anu's hair cascaded down her back like a movie star's. She treated me like the guys' pesky younger brother instead of the enemy I'd set myself up as.

Pretty soon, the dynamics of our pack began to change and solidify. For every moment the guys and I spent apart, we would spend twice as many together. In keeping with my bold metamorphosis, I kept up with their boisterousness. We raced scooters on highways, played pranks on elderly heart-attack candidates and jumped off walls of our complex into the Tapi River, earning ourselves the Awesome Threesome sobriquet from our peers. We did everything naughty and some things nice.

Sandwich Anu faded into the background within a month. I never heard of her again.

It was serendipity. I believed, with every atom of my being, that my parents were behind my change in fortune. I was convinced the guys were my birthday presents from them.

The day Nirvaan flew back to California, we'd made a pact to keep our threesome awesome and shining forever. For three reckless years, we'd managed.

Then the world had intruded on our idyll.

5

"G'morning, baby."

From his perch on the lounge chair, Nirvaan watched me stare at the coffee machine as it hummed and spit out my early morning manna in a giant coffee mug. The mug was white and had a black-and-gray sketch of Eeyore wandering about the Hundred Acre Wood, wondering, "What's so good about this morning?" It was my favorite morning coffee mug, a gift from Nirvaan's niece and nephew, Nikita and Armaan, on my last birthday.

I added three drops of hazelnut creamer into the steaming liquid, stirred once and took the first eye-opening sip. The morning slowly came into focus. Hands wrapped about the hot mug, I joined my husband on the deck as he reposed like a snug bug in a rug, waiting for the sun to dazzle the world anew. It was a mandatory item on the Titanic Wish List, under "smell the roses," to witness all sunrises and sunsets from this day forward for as long as each of us lived.

I inhaled a bigger sip of my coffee, swirling it in my mouth before swallowing. Only then was I capable of reciprocating my husband's good-morning wishes without croaking.

Ruffling his hair, I bent and took his mouth in a lazy kiss, mingling the tastes of minty toothpaste and delicious java on our tongues. Unlike me, Nirvaan didn't need an adrenaline-boosting beverage to jump-start his day. He went straight for breakfast whenever it was ready, which was whenever I felt awake enough to prepare it. And I would. Soon.

The world was still dark, but the horizon had begun to pinken. Waves licked the shore like a frontline of gamboling puppies rootling in their mother's teats. I groaned and stretched sleep from my bones, eager for my in-laws to arrive and for the fun and games to begin. I smiled, wondering what new mischief my father-in-law would instigate this weekend.

From the corner of my eye, I noticed Zayaan sitting on a lounger he'd dragged several feet away to where the porch turned around the house. It wasn't as if I hadn't known he was there from the get-go. My sense of him had always been strong—I couldn't ignore him if I tried—but I liked to pretend we didn't have that connection anymore.

His eyes were closed, his lips restless in a soft-spoken ritual as ingrained in him as the making and drinking of coffee was in me. His face and chest hailed the Kaba from six thousand miles away, which one would assume was directly eastward. It wasn't.

Years ago, on Zayaan's very first visit with us in San Jose, I'd heard him explain to Nirvaan the intricacies of the *qi'bla*, the direction one faces while praying or giving *dua*—as the Khojas called it—and why he'd chosen northeast and not simply east or even southeast, which would be the direction a bird would take to fly between here and Mecca. It had to do with latitudes, longitudes, true north and the roundness of the Earth. I'd rolled my eyes at the ridiculousness of facing any worldly structure or direction instead of directly into space, if one was inclined to communicate with God at all.

I, of course, had stopped bothering with ritualistic trivialities. I didn't believe in any form of organized religion. While I might believe in a Supreme Being of some sort, His refusal to actively eradicate the evils in this world made Him a largely suspect entity in my mind—not to stress on the extremely unjust and personal grudge He had against me.

Disinclined to start another day fighting with Ahura Mazda, I sat down on the lounger by Nirvaan's feet and, out of habit, I began to massage his blanketed foot while savoring my coffee. I wasn't completely sure, but I didn't think my husband had come to bed last night.

"Did you guys get any sleep?" I asked in a low tone so that I wouldn't disturb Zayaan, who'd bent his head in respectful *sajdah* to Allah for the next segment of prayers. I might have lost my own faith, but it didn't mean I'd disrespect another's.

Nirvaan gave me a lazy smile and flopped his head from left to right in a no. Even with little to no sleep, he didn't look tired or rumpled. He seemed pleasantly torporish. Zayaan would be, too, I imagined. He'd probably showered already, prepping for *sajdah*. At the very least, he had splashed his face, hands and feet with fresh water while I looked like the massacred thing the neighbor's cat had left on our front porch last week.

I wasn't exaggerating. I'd seen myself in the bathroom mirror not five minutes ago. My eyes were glassy and felt as if I'd rubbed sand in them, thanks to crying myself to sleep. My hair was a nest of knots, and my complexion was sapped of color because I'd tossed and turned fretfully all night, warring with a phalanx of subliminal dreams.

If that wasn't proof that Khodai had it in for me, I didn't know what was.

Nirvaan wiggled his foot under my hand. He winked when I looked up, as if he could see inside my brain. I scowled because he probably could.

His smile expanded, and he sat up to rumble in my ear, "Guess what we were up to all night long?"

"Nothing good, I suppose?" The fine hairs on my body stood to attention when he brushed his lips across my cheek and took a gentle bite of my jaw.

Nirvaan was such a tease.

He gave a sinister chuckle. "Depends on who you ask."

I leaned back a fraction and stared into the twinkling depths of his eyes. "You did not take the Jet Skis out without me!" I exclaimed, forgetting to whisper. I would've heard the commotion of the motors, surely?

Nirvaan tried to look guilty. The failed antic gave up his game because I knew him well, too. I buffed his shoulder with a fist and rolled my eyes, sure now that they hadn't ridden anywhere in the dark. Nirvaan rocked back against the lounger, his shoulders shaking with quiet mirth. He, too, was mindful of keeping mum during Zayaan's prayers.

"The photos have been scanned and uploaded, Simi." He took my hand and brought it to his lips, gloating with accomplishment.

"What? All of them?"

I was impressed. On Nirvaan's request, a few months ago, his parents had brought back a suitcase full of old photos from India. They were pictures of Nirvaan mostly, from his birth onward, but about a thousand of the three of us were bundled in the lot. I'd been sorting them out in chronological order for the past many weeks and getting damn frustrated by the sheer volume of the task. Plus, critical and unimpressed by my younger tomboy self, I'd threatened to burn the ones with me in them. I'd been joking, but Nirvaan wasn't taking any chances, so ever since, he'd housed the suitcase in Zayaan's room. I wasn't aware he'd been doing something with them.

"Is that what you've been doing on the nights you don't come to bed?" The borderline accusation in my question gave me pause. I sounded jealous, like a shrew-wife pissed off at her husband for spending more time with his mistress than herself.

It had been my job to sort out the photos, and I hadn't done it. It was my job to make my husband happy and comfortable, and I wasn't managing that, either. Couldn't I do anything right?

Nirvaan gave me a sharp glance but chose not to answer. He groped for the tablet hidden beneath the blanket and switched it on before handing it to me. The pictures hadn't only been uploaded but sorted, dated and organized into albums, too. He'd even made movies from some.

A funny, fluttery thing awoke inside me when I tapped an album titled *Jab We Met*. The title was stolen from a blockbuster Bollywood rom-com. The album, not the movie, was about the summer the three of us had met. I'd fallen asleep thinking of that summer. It sometimes spooked me how in sync Nirvaan and I were, how in sync all three of us were.

The first picture was of us blowing candles on a giant chocolate cake. I looked dazed, which accounted for my total memory loss about this part of the night. I couldn't remember cutting the cake even though the picture was irrefutable proof that I had, and from the looks of the subsequent photos, I'd enjoyed smashing some of it on the guys' faces.

"My Frooti was spiked. It had to be," I declared, yet again in defense of my actions.

Nirvaan pleaded the fifth, as usual.

I frowned into my empty mug. "I need more coffee if we're going to rehash our lives, one picture at a time."

Rehashing the past was on The List, too. Nirvaan wished to recount and relive every moment of his life. He was creating a slide show to play at our birthday bash and wanted to make sure he didn't forget a single person or event he was grateful for. I found the whole idea unnecessarily Hallmark-ish and morbid. Plus, you couldn't really sieve the good moments out without stirring up the bad.

But it wasn't my biopic, was it? I snorted, thinking if I ever got sentimental enough to create one, mine would play out in five pictures flat. Okay, maybe six.

"Wait. It's almost light, baby." Nirvaan tipped me onto his lap when I half rose from the lounger to get more coffee.

I usually had two mugs before breakfast.

I waited, shifting to get comfortable against my husband's chest. His arms came around me along with the blanket, and I felt warm even though I hadn't been cold in my thick flannel robe and woolen socks. My husband warmed me from the inside out. He always had.

I raised the tablet high and took a picture of us.

"Dawn of the Dead," said Nirvaan, critiquing my handiwork when I showed it to him.

I ignored the fact that he was right. "Shut up. You're ruining the mood." I clicked another one. It was an improvement, and with a bit of photo editing, we wouldn't appear so insipid. *There.*

Not to be outdone, the sun rose majestically, and in a never-ending flash, it brought the sea, the beach and the gulls in front of us into the light.

For all its ugliness, the world was a beautiful place.

I didn't think I'd ever tire of watching a sunrise. I knew I'd never forget the feel of my husband's arms around me. And though I wanted a second cup of coffee quite badly, I stayed put until Nirvaan's stomach gurgled against my back.

We started another day on a laugh.

Pleased and heart-happy, I stood up and made my way back into the kitchen where the coffee machine diligently refilled my mug. I propped the tablet on the counter and set it to display a slide show, grinning fondly at a picture of the three of us in our youthful folly, piled one behind the other on a bright yellow Vespa, blasting hapless pedestrians with cold masala milk from cheap plastic pistols. I had been the instigator and the driver of the Masala Milk Adventure. It'd been my scooter, after all.

Just as I began to prep for a batch of semolina veggie waffles, the house phone rang. We'd installed a landline, as cell phone reception was a bit wonky in some parts of the house. My cell worked only near the front door and in the kitchen.

"Hello?" I chirped into the cordless instrument, sandwiching the phone's receiver between my ear and shoulder. I pulled out peppers, carrots, peas and some other stuff from the fridge, keeping one eye on the slide show. I wondered suddenly if Nirvaan had included Sandwich Anu's pictures in the album. I was not going to be a happy beach bunny if he'd dared.

"Hello?" I repeated with impatience into the static silence of the phone. It was too early for telemarketers, so I checked the caller ID. London codes. *Crap.* It was too much to hope that it would be one of Zayaan's sisters or colleagues and not his mother.

"Simeen, I'm trying to reach Zayaan. He's not answering his mobile. Is Nirvaan okay?"

The softly anxious voice had the same hair-raising effect on my nerves as a live telecast of a terrorist beheading. Forget Sandwich Anu. Gulzar Begum Mohammed Ali Khan was the true bane of my existence. And there was no way Nirvaan hadn't uploaded her photograph into the tablet as part of a nice Khan family portrait. Khodai! Did that mean Zayaan's bastard brother was in there, too?

I closed my eyes and counted to ten. I would not let evil thoughts poison my day.

"He's peachy, Gulzar Auntie. Zayaan *dua bole che*, so his phone might be off."

I didn't add that she should've checked the time difference between England and California before calling us at the crack of dawn. It wouldn't have gone down well if I had. Zayaan's mother did not like me and was civil to me only because her son would stand for nothing less. I reciprocated in kind for the same reason and because my mother had taught me to be polite to my elders—even bigoted, rude ones who'd raised a monster and let him loose in the world.

It was Zayaan's father who'd adored me, approved of me—inasmuch as a pillar of the Khoja community could approve of a non-Muslim girl his son had brought home one day. I didn't know if I would've converted to Islam had things worked out the way we'd planned. I knew Zayaan had expected me to when we talked of marriage. Aga Khani Muslims were a liberal lot, and for the most part, they followed very different customs and weren't considered *real* Muslims. But Zayaan's mother belonged to a staunch branch of Sunni Khojas, and to please her, her family had strictly practiced certain Islamic customs.

I'd sometimes imagine myself married to Zayaan because that would mean that night had not happened. I'd sometimes imagine my parents were alive. They would've approved of Zayaan but not of a religious conversion. They would've adored Nirvaan. My parents, devoted Parsis though they were, had been broad-minded people. Bottom line, they would've wanted me to be happy.

A sigh shuddered out of my mouth. It was pointless to think about the past, but I couldn't seem to escape it. Maybe Nirvaan was right with this slide-show business. Maybe we were the sum total of our memories...and fantasies.

"Have him call me when he's finished praying." Zayaan's mother's exasperated voice broke through my musings.

She'd been talking, but I'd tuned her out.

I peered through the patio doors. Zayaan's eyes were open, his head turned to one shoulder. He was almost done, but I held my tongue.

"Of course," I said, preparing to hang up.

"How are you, *beta*?" she asked before I could.

Compassion rang in her voice, and her use of the endearment *beta*, or "child," rendered me speechless.

I wanted to smack her down with a flippant, *Oh, I'm peachy, too. So looking forward to widowhood. Any tips on how to get on?*

But I forced the bitchiness back into my intestines. "I'm fine. Thank you," I answered instead.

How dare she. How dare she offer sympathy now when she never had before. How dare she call me *beta* in that sickly sweet tone.

Zayaan's mother had a knack for making me feel like shit, but I'd strive to be polite for my own mother's sake.

"How are Sofia and Sana?" I asked in return.

Zayaan's sisters were several years younger than me, and I got along just fine with them. They were open-minded, honest women, more like Zayaan than their mother.

"Are they around?" *Say yes, so we can quit this absurd attempt at a conversation*, I mentally urged her. Why didn't she hang up? *Why didn't I?*

On the dawn-tinged deck, Nirvaan performed a series of twisty torso stretches. He had on a full-sleeved orange swim shirt and black wetsuit-style shorts and was obviously champing at the bit to try out the Jet Skis.

I flapped my hand to catch his attention. *Save me, my hero.*

"No, *beta*. Sofia went out with friends straight from work, and Sana is getting ready. We're having dinner at Waseem's house."

Zayaan's youngest sister, Sana, was engaged to Waseem

Thakur, the prescreened, fully approved—by Gulzar Begum—Khoja from East London.

"That's nice," I muttered.

She began a familiar lament about her remaining two children who refused to bring her similar solace. She'd blamed me for Zayaan's single status for a long time, even after I'd married Nirvaan. She'd blamed me for a whole lot worse twelve years ago. I'd believed her then. I'd been too young, too frightened and too confused not to succumb to the authority of an adult, and she'd taken advantage of it.

I wasn't that naive anymore. If I chose to blame myself now, it was in full cognizance of my own actions.

Nirvaan came into the kitchen, grinning like a shark, as if he enjoyed seeing me tortured.

Dog.

On cue, Zayaan's mother brought up Marjaneh, the perfect bride for her perfect son, and I pounced. A dog was so much shark fodder.

"Oh. Here's Nirvaan, Auntie. He's dying to talk to you." Grinning, I shoved the phone into his hands but not before I heard the gasp.

Narrow-minded, judgmental creature that she was, I'd shocked her by my word choice. Too bad, but I'd quit dancing around the word *death* and its variations a long time ago. When cancer lived in your home, inside your husband's body, there was no avoiding the word or state.

"What the hell, Simi?" Nirvaan whispered as he pinched my butt. He was a trooper, though. He pressed the receiver to his ear, and with innate flair, he began to charm the devil out of Zayaan's mother.

My husband could sell fur to a bear for a profit without much effort. I left him to it and resumed the breakfast preparations.

"You're coming for the party, Auntie. No excuses," he said after a whole lot of rubbish conversation.

Hearing him, I wilted like a week-old rose. Much as I'd hate Gulzar Begum raining on my parade, I'd have to suck it up. After all was said and done and forgiven or not, she was Zayaan's only living parent. Sure, guilt was the forerunner in that relationship, and she took immense advantage of her son's feelings. Zayaan's father and brother were dead. Zayaan was the only male left in his family. His mother knew just where to drive in the screws. But I also knew Zayaan loved his mother and thought the world of her. He'd want her at his thirtieth birthday bash—and Marjaneh, too.

I wilted some more.

Zayaan came into the house, a prayer book pressed between his arm and torso. He went into his room, and within seconds he came out empty-handed. He gave me the evil eye, letting me know that, deep in conversation with Allah or not, he'd heard every word I'd said to his mother, and he was aware of every negative vibe flowing between here and London.

I wasn't sorry for any of it or for the way things were between us—they couldn't be any other way—yet an apology jumped to my lips. I bit it off and poured yellowy batter onto the heated waffle plate instead.

Fifteen minutes later, the mama's boy hung up the phone and joined us on the deck to consume three ice-cold waffles. He ate them without complaint.

Nirvaan wouldn't have been so obliging. He would've fed the floppy waffles to the seagulls and demanded a reorder from the house chef. And because Zayaan hadn't complained and he always defended me to his mother, I brewed him a consolation cup of double espresso. As apologies went, it was unremarkable, but it made him smile.

A long time ago, my whole existence had revolved around Zayaan's smile.

I took a deep breath and, on a ten-count exhalation, I let the past fade from my mind. I leaned over to kiss my husband. He was my life now.

Next order of the day, the guys dared me to a Jet Ski race, and lots more pixels were added to the *Jaws* album.

6

Kamlesh Desai was a one-man riot with a deep-chested guffaw he was unafraid to overuse.

It was easy to see where Nirvaan had gotten his energy and charm even though the father-son duo looked nothing alike. My father-in-law was a small, spare man with a big mustache and a full head of hair. Even as he pushed toward sixty, it was a natural jet-black. He swore that the daily application of a hibiscus-infused coconut oil was the secret to his hair's health. He kept it parted to the left and combed it several times a day in an offhand unconscious manner with a small maroon comb he carried in his wallet at all times.

I loved my father-in-law's little quirks. I could watch him for hours and never get bored. For such a petite man, he had a king-size personality and an even bigger heart.

Compared to her husband, my mother-in-law was a mouse. She was quiet and serious but in no way timid. My in-laws were equal partners in life and in business. You picked up on it immediately from the moment you met them. They reminded me so much of my own parents that I sometimes found it impossible to be around them without getting emotional. But the same also made it easy for me to love them.

I used to tease Nirvaan that the only reason I'd married him was because I was madly in love with his father. And since I couldn't have my main man, I'd settled for his gene pool.

"Your uncle just can't sit still," my mother-in-law muttered, shaking her head at her husband who was expelling his inexhaustible energy rather loudly into a karaoke mic.

Smiling at my gyrating father-in-law, I winced when the surround sound suddenly blared off-key and filled the house with shrill maniacal bleats. Besides enthusiasm, he had zero aptitude for singing.

It also amused me that my mother-in-law never addressed her husband by name, not directly, not even when she spoke of him in context. It was always "your uncle" or "your daddy" or "Mr. Desai" or "my husband" or "that man," if she was angry with him, but never simply "Kamlesh." It was an old Indian custom—I supposed, a sexist one in the guise of respect—which forbade a wife to call her husband by his given name. I had no idea why my mother-in-law still practiced it.

She was a modern woman. She wore Western clothes, even shorts on occasion, though never for community or religious functions or in India. She was a workingwoman, had been for most of her life. My in-laws had come to America, leaving their six-year-old daughter and two-year-old son with their parents, to build a better life for their family than the one they'd had in India. They'd come in search of the American Dream and found it.

Kamlesh Desai had worked at gas stations and grocery stores while Kiran Desai had cleaned houses and cooked for people until, between them, they'd saved enough money to invest in a California highway motel. Still, they'd worked three jobs each, pouring their savings into their first motel and then another and another. Eventually, they'd quit the other jobs and focused their energies on expanding their motel business. Once their green cards had come through, they'd brought their teenage children to LA and settled down there.

My in-laws were self-made, hardworking people, even now.

So it baffled me that my mother-in-law still held on to an antiquated custom in a country she, too, refused to call home. My own parents had addressed each other by name and a whole slew of endearments, including *bawaji* and *bawiji*, which most simplistically translated to "Parsi man" and "Parsi woman."

My in-laws were different from my parents in so many ways, but in the ways it counted most, they were exactly the same. Family meant everything to them.

"Simi," Nirvaan bellowed from six paces away, "you're up."

"Khodai save me," I groaned under my breath. But I set the knife down on the cutting board and washed my hands in the kitchen sink before dragging my feet into the living room.

I was not a nightingale. I was more like a crow when it came to singing, but the whole family had to participate in the stupid karaoke competition, and no one was exempt. If the lot of them wanted to listen to me caw, who was I to deny them the pleasure?

I plucked the mic from Nirvaan's hands, stuck my chin in the air and belted out a not-too-passé Bollywood hit song, "You Are My Sonia." Luckily, one could not hear one's self sing.

Torture complete, I mock-bowed and marched back into the kitchen as consolation applause rang behind me.

Dinner wasn't for another hour even though my mother-in-law and I had been toiling by the stove for some time. The guys had come in from their evening rides exhilarated and not the least bit tired. After showering and settling in front of the TV to watch the news, snacking on some fried munchies and nonalcoholic beers before dinner, my father-in-law had had the brilliant karaoke idea. His vivacity truly knew no bounds.

If you knew Indians at all, then you'd know of their obsession with their music, especially catchy songs or item numbers. If India as a nation had a passion, it was singing. Dancing, too, but I believed singing more. Indians could break into a song at the drop of a hat. You didn't have to ask twice. We were a loud, hectic people, and our music reflected our passions.

When it was my mother-in-law's turn to be center stage, I took over watching the stove sizzling with pots of mixed vegetables, *kadhi*—the sweetened curry version native to Surat—and boiling rice. We were having a full Gujarati *bhonu* this evening, and the kitchen was puffing out spicy steam like smoke signals for the hungry.

The guys kept flitting in and out of the kitchen to taste and steal samples. Zayaan hovered by a plate of steamed fenugreek *muthias*—dumplings—awaiting a final garnish of oil and spices. I raised my rolling pin, daring the *muthia* thief to try his luck under my watch. He did and didn't even flinch when I smacked his hand. He shoved a huge dumpling into his mouth, grinned roguishly and turned about to praise the current singing sensation.

"*Wah! Wah!* Mummy, you're amazing." Whether he was praising her singing or cooking was anyone's guess.

Either way, my mother-in-law was the star of the night. She sang not well but in tune and with the right amount of emotion. She'd chosen to sing a *ghazal*—a melodious poem—from the movie *Umrao Jaan*. The lyrics spoke of a couple falling in love and learning to trust one another.

We clapped for her long and hard, as she deserved. Zayaan whistled, and my father-in-law hooted and gyrated his hips again. Nirvaan lifted his mother off her feet and spun her around, making her giggle like a toddler on a merry-go-round. My mother-in-law wasn't prone to laughter like her husband and son, so when she did let loose, it was like the sound of rain pattering over the Thar Desert.

I loved watching my husband with his parents. There was so much love within their family. They all had such big hearts, as big as their laughs. They were passionate, joyful people and...

Khodai, are You watching them? Are You really going to destroy this gorgeous family? Snuff out their joy, their laughter?

My heart rolled with the pain that was now a part of me. I took a deep, deep breath and released it at the count of ten. I stared at the *kadhi* as it rose and bubbled in a slow boil, stirring it around and around so that the spiced yogurt and chickpea gravy wouldn't burn and stick to the bottom of the saucepan.

My mother-in-law gently nudged me aside, an accomplished smile on her lips. I stepped to the side. I didn't know what she saw on my face, but her smile faltered and then faded.

"Simeen...*beta*..." She said my name as if it hurt her throat to say it. She touched my back with her aging yet strong hand.

That was all she did. She touched me, and I wanted to wrap my arms around her and cry forever.

"Come. Come now. It will be all right. It's all in God's hands."

We lingered over dinner, enjoying the food, the conversation and holiday island ambience, while savoring each other, as God knew there wasn't much else we could do.

The only time my father-in-law sat still was during meals. He ate as he lived—with gusto. His eyes brightened with interest when I served him the first sample of my mother-in-law's latest gourmet experiment—chocolate *rasgullas*. My father-in-law was partial to Indian sweetmeats while the guys had requested a chocolate dessert to go with dinner. She'd combined both requests and—*voilà*, as the French said it. She'd made the *rasgullas*—which were sweet milk-based balls soaked in sugar syrup and were traditionally from the Eastern shores of India—from scratch, using organic milk, cocoa powder and brown sugar. We tried to limit our use of processed foods in this house and strove for chemical-free freshness in all things. Every little bit helped Nirvaan, we liked to believe.

"Is it good?" I asked my father-in-law.

"It has an...interesting flavor...earthy," he replied, but requested I serve him one more. Which meant he liked it.

Both Nirvaan and Zayaan had served themselves three chocolate *rasgullas* each and had consumed them in seconds. I liked all manner of sweetmeats and helped myself to two *rasgullas*, too, whereas my mother-in-law took none. She wasn't diabetic. She just didn't have a sweet tooth like the rest of us.

Later, after a few hands of rummy, I planned to sizzle the brownies I'd whipped up from scratch and serve them with ice cream, honey and nuts.

I'd brought my mood under control by the time the table was set and the food was laid out. Even so, I was quiet through dinner, contributing little or nothing to the free-flowing conversation. My introversion wasn't an anomaly, but more than once, I felt Nirvaan's gaze on me.

Zayaan and my father-in-law were in deep discussion about his thesis.

Aside from Nisha, none of the Desais had finished college. My in-laws hadn't gone to college at all. And Nirvaan had attended the University of Southern California for two years before he'd dropped out to join the family business and travel the world. By the time we'd gotten married, Nirvaan had shouldered the lion's share of the motel business responsibilities. He'd shown no signs of slacking, even after the cancer. He'd wheeled and dealed in properties and stocks right from the hospital bed, sometimes even scant hours after a treatment.

Nirvaan's street smarts had been—were—something to behold; he just wasn't academic.

I was. I wasn't as versatile as Zayaan, but I'd liked school. And college had been a refuge during some bad times. Besides, I liked to learn. And what I'd learned in college was that I liked to manage stuff. I had a degree in business management, which I'd put to use right after college. I'd worked at Batliwala Plastics in Surat and then in the San Jose motels with Nirvaan.

Maybe I should start working again. I could manage the running of a motel. I could keep the books or...

I squeezed and squeezed the sugar water out of the *rasgulla* onto my plate. It was no use, making plans. I couldn't imagine a future without Nirvaan, bereft of the shelter of his arms or his laughing presence in my life. Could I live in LA with my in-laws, or would it be too painful to see each other after he was gone?

I couldn't contemplate moving in with Sarvar even if he offered his spare room in exchange for my housekeeping skills. And I knew he would ask—when the time came. I balked at the idea of moving back to Surat. I'd been the mistress of my own house for far too long to suddenly be a guest in someone else's, no matter how welcoming either of my brothers were.

"You're squeezing the life out of the *rasgulla*, baby." Nirvaan took the crumbling chocolate milk ball from my hand and fed it to me before I mangled it into paste.

I ate it, making the appropriate delighted sounds that my mother-in-law expected.

I supposed I didn't need to decide my future as my husband had decided it for me.

Nirvaan's parents didn't know about the IVF. We didn't want them to know in case it didn't work. I'd actually been relieved when Nirvaan had asked me not to mention the fertility treatments to them, not until we had positive results. With any luck, we'd never have to tell.

"Coffee anyone?" asked Zayaan, covering a soft burp with his fist.

I drew my eyes over the table spread. Most of the food was gone. When we all declined, Zayaan excused himself from the table, taking his plate and glass and several other platters with him. I felt too heavy in mind and body to clear the table just yet, and I was grateful for his agency.

"Kiran, did you talk to Nirvaan about Kutch?" my father-in-law suddenly asked as he flicked his nails against his water glass, making musical pings.

"What about Kutch?" Nirvaan divided a stare between his parents.

Kutch was a large state district in northwest Gujarat, mostly desert land. Were my in-laws thinking of investing in land there?

The Desais owned a lot of real estate in Gujarat—farmland, villages, a couple of city blocks in Surat and Baroda. They owned a lot of land in the US, too.

My mother-in-law didn't look especially pleased with her husband for serving business at the table and even less so when he didn't wait for her response and plunged on.

"There's an Ayurvedic health center in Kutch, renowned for its cancer cures. Radha personally checked it out and has reserved a room for you there. A family room, so Simi can stay with you. We can all go. Okay? You have to stay for at least two months—let's say June and July—for the full benefits of the treatment," he said.

Oh, wow. No wonder my mother-in-law hadn't brought up Kutch.

I bit my lip and slanted a peek at my husband. His eyes were narrowed into slits.

Nirvaan didn't have much faith in alternative treatments. He'd lost faith in all cancer treatments, in fact. He'd refused to go in for the stereotactic radiosurgery until I'd made the baby bargain. He didn't want to prolong the inevitable; he'd told us so when the tumor had made itself known.

My mother-in-law respected Nirvaan's decisions. My father-in-law had no qualms about calling his son a bloody fool.

"I'm not going to *Kutch*," Nirvaan said, as if Kutch were hell itself. "Tomorrow, I'll thank Radha *fui* for her concern and have her cancel the reservation." His jaw snapped closed so tight that his molars made an awful clicking sound.

Radha *fui* was my father-in-law's younger sister. She lived in Surat and was a bit provincial in attitude. Even so, most people believed they meant well when imparting free medical advice.

"You'll do no such thing. They've cured hundreds of patients. They walk out of there completely cancer-free."

"That's a patent lie. If such a miracle cure actually existed, the entire medical universe would know of it. Come on, Dad, stop fooling yourself."

Nirvaan's father pounded his fist on the table. "Is it fooling myself for wanting the best for you? For wanting you to get well?"

For the next few minutes, strong words and opinions flew across the table. My mother-in-law sat huddled and quiet, like me.

Every few months, a relative or family friend would tell us about some miracle cure they'd heard of from some random person they'd bumped into. Again, people mostly meant well, and maybe those other patients really did get cured—miracles did happen—but it wasn't going to happen for Nirvaan.

It wasn't only the cancer for him. Non-Hodgkin's lymphoma demanded an aggressive treatment. Nirvaan had been bombarded by high doses of chemotherapy and radiation and surgery for eighteen months, and for two years after, he'd been cancer-free.

Then, about a year ago, the headaches had started, and we'd found the tumor. It was small but deep-seated. And it was growing. They couldn't cut it out without damaging healthy cells. They could shrink it, but it would keep growing. His headaches would get worse. He'd get seizures. He'd already had one a few months ago. His eyesight would eventually fail.

But the worst was, he was losing brain function because of where the tumor was situated. We had to watch for slurred words and missed steps and a whole lot of things his doctors had listed. Over the next few months, the tiny tumor would slowly eat into Nirvaan's brain, and all any of us could do was watch it happen.

The strong smell of coffee mingled with the ocean air, and I inhaled greedily as the argument zinged around me. Zayaan came to stand by the table, but he didn't sit down. I regretted declining his offer to make me an espresso. It was going to be a rough night.

Zayaan had never once offered medical advice to Nirvaan—not in my presence, at least. I saw him reach out and rub the back of his hand on my mother-in-law's cheek in comfort—once, twice—and then he dropped it back to his side. Another piece of my heart broke and floated away.

"You are going, Nirvaan. *Bas*—that's that. What's the harm in it?"

"Are you joking? I'm not going to India for two months. What if I fall sick there? What if I get worse? I'm not checking into an Indian hospital, much less some quack ashram in Kutch. I don't want to die there, Dad."

My father-in-law stiffened at the harsh reminder of what was to come, but he didn't back down. "I'm looking into a medical jet facility in case…in case we need to fly you back overnight."

Nirvaan gave an incredulous laugh. "If this place is supposed to work miracles, why in the heck would I need an emergency evac? Shouldn't I waltz out of there on my feet?" He frowned at his father, and after a few seconds of fraught silence, he gave a long sigh. He didn't look so pissed anymore. "Daddy, please, I don't want to spend the rest of my days in futile treatments and hospitals. I want to live strong. God, I want to *live*. Then I won't mind dying so much."

My in-laws wept then—not badly, but pain glittered in their eyes, as sharp as diamonds. I had to avert my gaze to the star-studded darkness till I got my emotions under control once again. I knew the quality of strength required to discuss the business of death with your beloved. I knew intimately the devastation of being utterly helpless in a bad situation.

I'd once wished upon a shooting star and gotten the shoes I'd wanted—red Mary Janes with silver buckles. What would I wish for should I see a star tonight? That Nirvaan would find relief soon, so all of us could be free of this constant heartache? Or that he would linger and suffer so that we might have more time with him?

I was glad I didn't spot a falling star tonight. I was very glad I didn't pray anymore.

7

I pulled Nirvaan aside that night and made him promise not to fight with his father for the rest of his parents' visit. I guessed my mother-in-law must've extracted the same promise from her husband, as my father-in-law did not bring up Kutch again. Hopefully, we'd banked all altercations for the weekend.

I tried to give Nirvaan plenty of time alone with his parents. After all, I had him all to myself daily while they had to make do with weekends. If we still lived in LA, it would've been different, not to mention so much easier. But we didn't, and I wanted to give them time to make more memories.

In light of that, I would take off every chance I got. I ran errands, got the car cleaned, held my brothers and sister-in-law hostage on the phone for hours, cleaned the house without getting in anyone's way, finished reading two books on Saturday afternoon by the beach, and so on.

Zayaan made himself scarce the whole of Saturday, too. He left the house after breakfast with a briefcase full of papers and books and his laptop, informing us of his intention to spend the day at the library for research.

So when I received a text from him, asking me to meet him at The Caramel Bookery near the town's center, I couldn't help my reply.

Aren't you sick of books by now?

He texted back promptly.

No. Come quick. They're about to close.

No matter how much I loved books, I wasn't this obsessed with them. But I went, as he wouldn't have asked if it wasn't important. It didn't take me ten minutes to get there by car. I found a parking spot right in front of the store.

The Caramel Bookery was a quaint little indie book and coffee shop hidden behind three pretty weeping willows on a small curving street in the middle of the seaside town. It had a narrow entrance, made smaller by sleek tables stacked high with books and toys on each side.

I took a nostalgic breath as I entered. I loved the smell of dust and books, stale food and spilled coffee. It reminded me of my childhood home—the old cramped flat in the old crowded neighborhood where nothing bad had touched my family. Surin had sold the flat to save the factory.

I wove my way inside, carefully holding on to my beach tote so that I wouldn't jostle anything over as the store was stocked cheek by jowl with stuff.

Zayaan waited in one corner of the store. He hadn't seen me yet. His head was bent, reading from the open book in his hands. Silky black hair flopped over his forehead, and a five o'clock shadow darkened the lower half of his face.

Zayaan shaved every day, sometimes twice a day, to keep his jawline clean. He'd started shaving way before I'd met him. I used to love his face rough with stubble. Loved the feel of the soft, soft bristles on my skin, against my lips, beneath my fingers.

Perhaps I still did. Or perhaps I would shudder in revulsion.

My heart dropped to my stomach, afraid it would be the latter. My stomach clenched tight, even more afraid it would be the former.

Berating myself for constantly thinking nonsense, I continued forward. Zayaan looked up as I neared. A slow half smile bowed his lips. Ruthlessly, I ignored my jumping insides.

"I'm here. What's the deal?" I asked, pressing the tote against my heart like a shield.

He closed the book and slid it into its slot on the shelf.

Rumi, I read off the spine. Zayaan's favorite Persian poet. He used to quote Rumi all the time when we were kids. I hadn't seen him read poetry, much less quote a couplet, for a long time. No one who knew him now would've guessed that staid and to-the-point Zayaan possessed the soul of a romantic.

That night had taken many things from us.

I had taken Rumi from Zayaan, and for that, I couldn't be sorrier.

He led me to the cashier's desk cluttered with an insane number of items and asked for the things he'd set aside. Turning toward me, he held up a book on Lord Krishna in one hand and a box containing a silver-plated Om in the other for inspection.

"What do you think?" he asked.

"They're...cool." I blinked at him. "Going back to your Hindu roots, are you?"

Some sects of Khojas were converted Hindus, which was why their language, customs and even their food were more Gujarati and Kathiawari in style than Islamic.

Zayaan did a double take before he burst out laughing. "Your punch lines always had perfect timing, Sims. Good one."

"Hmm. Great. Though I'm not joking." I peered at the objects closely.

"For Mummy. Mother's Day." He gave a shy little shrug. "Can't decide what to get her."

My heart became a puddle of chocolate goo at my feet. It couldn't be helped. I went up on tiptoes and kissed his stubbly cheek. But I quickly stepped back when he leaned in just as unconsciously, exactly as I had in reflex. He stiffened as I moved away.

Khodai. We'd become so awkward around each other, never knowing which lines to cross and which ones to leave alone.

"You're sweet, Zai. Let me see. She'll definitely love the book," I said, roving a critical eye over both objects.

Lord Krishna was the patron God of Nirvaan's family, and the book was an intricately illustrated romp through Krishna's early life as a cowherd. The pictures were augmented by well-known hymns and poems.

Krishna was known as the Complete Man in Hindu philosophy. He was a prankster, a flirt, a diplomat, a musician and a great orator. If ever there were classic examples of God's influence on His believer, Lord Krishna and Nirvaan were them.

"Well," I said, flipping through the glossy-paged book, "the artwork is beautiful."

It was. The artist had done a brilliant job of creating the village of Mathura and the forest of Vrindavan where the Lord and His flock of female devotees danced and flirted through the night.

I gave the Om-shaped incense stand a cursory glance. True, my mother-in-law would light incense sticks every morning in their home temple as part of her daily prayer ritual, but...

"Give her the book. You chose it because the renderings of Krishna look like Nirvaan, didn't you? Apart from the skin tones," I guessed shrewdly.

Lord Krishna was always depicted as a blue-skinned deity.

"That's why I wanted a second opinion," said Zayaan, giving me an adorable squinty-eyed grin. "I thought I was being fanciful. Like you."

Fanciful. Yep, that was me.

I shook my head, letting him know he wasn't. The book would please my mother-in-law. In truth, I fancied it would bring her immense succor to see her son's face in her Lord.

They said faith in God could relieve us of pain. It was a good thing I had no faith, then, because I didn't deserve to be free of my pain. Ever.

I spent Sunday morning doing laundry.

It being Mother's Day, we women had been banished from the kitchen for the day. The guys were making breakfast—and creating a holy hell of a mess they'd better not expect me to clean up—and had plans in place for a late barbecue lunch, after which my in-laws would pack up and leave for LA. I'd brought up the fact that I wasn't a mother and should pitch in for my mother-in-law's day of honor, but the guys wouldn't hear of it.

"May as well start practicing," Nirvaan had murmured for my ears only.

I kept an ear to my bedroom curtain, surreptitiously checking on the show going on in the kitchen, as I folded a stack of T-shirts on the bed. Occasionally, a breeze would lift and flap the curtain up to reveal the unfolding chaos.

My father-in-law stood in his pajamas by the kitchen island, directing the show without getting his hands dirty. He was disheveled from neck to feet, but not a hair was out of place on his head. I grinned as he bossed about, eliciting major grumbles from the younger men.

It went on like that for a while until the good-natured rumblings suddenly suffused with tension.

Were they arguing about Kutch again?

No.

I sat up, straining my ears to catch the words. It wasn't Nirvaan and my father-in-law, but Nirvaan and Zayaan at it this time.

"Have you forgotten I live in London? How much help do you think I'll be? I think you should…" The words blew in with the breeze.

"Doesn't matter where… I want you…" Nirvaan said a lot more, but that was all I caught.

What were they discussing in front of my father-in-law? They couldn't be arguing over the guardianship of the baby, could they?

Before another question chirped inside my head, Nirvaan shouted for me to come out.

Crap. He'd told them, hadn't he?

I mouse-crept out of the bedroom and stopped by the sofa where my in-laws sat, a sheaf of documents spread out on the coffee table in front of them. Zayaan stood by the fireplace, his shoulders tense, his eyes stormy, while Nirvaan flipped cheese sandwiches on the kitchen grill, looking just as unyielding.

"Simeen, come sit by me. You need to go over some papers," said my mother-in-law.

That was nothing new. I'd been signing papers and checks since I joined the Desai clan. When your husband's business was transaction-based and vast, there were always papers to sign. I signed above my printed name without reading the document. I didn't need to read it. I trusted Nirvaan and his family.

But I got nervous when they asked Zayaan to go over the same documents. He did so while shooting evil looks at Nirvaan. He read through the papers as if he meant to memorize them for an exam. Only then did he sign them.

It belatedly occurred to me that maybe I should've read them, too.

What did I just sign? My hands and feet went cold. Had Nirvaan drawn up a contract appointing Zayaan as our baby's godfather?

Personally, I had many reservations about it and obviously, Zayaan had them, too. I understood Nirvaan wanted his child—*if* there were a child—to have a father figure to count on. I also got that there was no one in this world he trusted more than Zayaan, but...

If we had a baby—and that was a big bloody *if*—I didn't think it would lack for father figures. My two brothers, Nirvaan's father and his brother-in-law would gladly step into those shoes. Our baby didn't need some distant, absentee and reluctant guardian.

I certainly didn't want to be tied to Zayaan in such a way. I'd told Nirvaan it would be awkward and difficult, and not only because the man lived an ocean away. Zayaan had his own life. He shouldered enough responsibilities between his mother and two sisters, and Marjaneh would soon join the pot. We couldn't impose on him like this.

Nirvaan, of course, had scoffed at my reservations. He didn't think of it as an imposition. *I'd do the same for him,* he'd pointed out.

My mother-in-law patted my knee. "It's to safeguard your future, *beta.* Nirvaan's stocks, life insurance policies and property have been put in a trust for you. Your uncle and Zayaan will be the trustees. They'll make sure you never have to worry about a thing."

I stared at my hands, my cheeks burning. I didn't think I'd ever been more embarrassed by my husband's wealth before. I didn't deserve it. I didn't deserve him. He'd taken care of everything. He was even preparing to care for me from his grave and I...

How could I live here after he was gone? How could I take and take from his family without giving back in return?

I stiffened as it occurred to me that I could give them something back. Something that would be far more precious to them than a trust fund.

Much later, once my in-laws were gone and it was just the three of us again, we took the Jet Skis out as the sun sank into the horizon. The guys ganged up on me, repeatedly spraying me, as they zigzagged figure eights around me. The ocean was choppy, and I was unsettled. I got knocked into the water a lot. Every time I pulled myself back on the bike, I tried not to resent how cleverly Nirvaan had trapped me in his baby-making scheme.

But it was my body, my decision to have a baby or not, and I would not be bullied.

8

The next morning, Nirvaan and I started the day and week off with a relaxing *vinyasa* session conducted by our yoga instructor via video chat from LA since we hadn't found a center or teacher that appealed to us in Carmel. I had several recommendations for both—group classes and private gurus—from reliable sources but had been too busy settling in to call and ask for rates, trials or schedules.

I approved of the standard, familiar way of countrywide establishments. It made me feel less like a fish out of water when we moved, and we'd moved way too many times for comfort in my life. Surin called us vagabonds with no small amount of envy in his voice, but I didn't care for the label. I would gladly stay put in one place if I had a choice. Sadly, our LA yoga center did not have a branch or affiliation with any chain gyms in Carmel, hence the need to find one. I also needed to find a mixed martial arts center and enroll in their self-defense program. I'd generally take self-defense classes twice a year to keep my reflexes sharp. I might look frail, but my body was strong. I would never be powerless again. Never.

Then, just as I'd psyched my mind and body into feeling empowered, Nirvaan sprang his coup d'état. I realized that, no matter how well I honed my physical strength, emotionally, I was a vulnerable kitten.

"We need to have an early lunch, baby. Your appointment with Archer is at one o'clock."

I'd been about to pour myself a glass of orange juice, post-yoga, when my hand froze in midair. My head snapped toward my husband and I was greeted by his gym-shorts-clad backside as he rummaged in the fridge, pulling out leftover food containers and piling them on the counter.

Zayaan, who'd been working at the breakfast bar with several tomes and photocopied scrolls and sheets of scribbled pages spread in front of him like the sands of time, stood up to reorganize his makeshift desk to make room for our meal. He shrugged when I glared at him, indicating that he was as puzzled by this turn of events as I was.

"I don't have an appointment. I didn't make one yet," I confessed, my hands suddenly twitchy. I set the jar down, flexed my hand a couple of times, and then picked it up again.

I'd meant to make the appointment. And I would next week. Or, sometime next month. I'd thought and thought about it since Thursday, and I was nearly convinced...

Damn it. Why can't I just tell him how I feel about having his trust fund baby?

Nirvaan popped the lids on the containers and dumped the food into pans and skillets for heating. He turned around and smirked. "I made it."

Three succinct words, spoken softly, but they hit me like a ton of bricks.

Like a robot, I finished pouring juice, set the table and served lunch. I ate little, for I'd lost my appetite.

My husband didn't trust me to handle this. My stomach hollowed with guilt. He was right to mistrust me. But did he have to be so high-handed all the time? Sudden anger churned my blood.

Lunch was over quickly, and the guys helped me clean up after.

As we were pressed for time, Nirvaan and I shared the shower. My dream of wallowing in a warm tub of water, followed by a siesta, evaporated along with my yogic calm. Neither one of us spoke or so much as smiled when our hips bumped or when our slippery, soapy skin made contact. It was telling in itself, because Nirvaan never passed up an opportunity to tease me about how *love was best served naked*.

Nirvaan knew he'd twisted my arm. He knew he was being irrational about the baby. Maybe we both were. Our silence was our stand and our apology. But neither one of us was willing to relent.

It took me longer than my husband to get ready. When I walked out of our bedroom, head high and haughty like a martyr's, I found the guys in deep discussion by the door. I sat on the sofa to slip on my heels. It didn't strike me to ask why Zayaan looked angry now or why my husband was still barefoot until it was too late.

Nirvaan claimed he was tuckered out and wanted a nap. "Was a long weekend, baby. And my head's starting to hurt."

He was lying about the headache. By now, I could tell with some certainty when my husband was tired or felt under the weather and how severe or mild those ailments were. I'd seen him in various stages of sickness for five years—more, if you counted the periodic coughs and colds and fevers we'd nursed each other through since our engagement.

"If you're not well, Zayaan should stay home with you." I touched his cheek. Nothing. It didn't feel hot or cold or clammy. I was right. I could've called him out on it but didn't think it was worth the aggravation.

I wondered what Nirvaan was up to. I didn't think I could

bear any more surprises that he seemed to enjoy springing on me these days.

He kissed my forehead, my nose, and gave me a brief peck on my lips. "No way. Blood and doctors freak you out. Someone needs to hold your hand for the tests and drive you back and forth. And I'll be fine...once I sleep. I'm going to knock myself out with some NyQuil."

I didn't tell him it was *his* blood, *his* pain and suffering, that freaked me out and not my own. Nor did I point out that no one but a husband should hold his wife's hand when her uterus was being examined—especially when the checkup was solely due to *his* whims and wishes.

Zayaan seemed to have developed a fascination with the car's key fob, refusing to look at either one of us during this dialogue. His ears had turned red, though. I knew if I touched his lobes, they'd be hot. They always grew hot and red when he was angry or embarrassed.

Without further ado, Zayaan and I got going, leaving Nirvaan to his NyQuil daze. I pulled up the clinic's address on the GPS and turned the satellite radio to a top-hits station, raising the volume high to deter conversation. I didn't want to talk about this. I was too busy fostering my anger and martyrdom into hurricane category 5.

Zayaan gave me a good ten minutes to cool off before he turned the volume down. "If you're this against having a child, why don't you tell him to piss off?" He sounded well and truly aggravated.

Not a pleasant sensation, was it, to have your arm twisted behind your back?

"Why haven't *you*?" I asked calmly, staring out the window.

It was a lovely sunny day, crisp with light and a mild breeze and a potential for joie de vivre.

"Nirvaan didn't want you to drive back alone. You'll be light-headed…maybe have cramps?" Now he sounded doubtful.

The question also confirmed that Nirvaan had discussed some things with him. Private things. And I did not like it.

I hoped my expression was as serious as a heart attack when I looked at Zayaan. "I meant, why didn't you say no when he asked you to drop everything and come live with us? Why didn't you refuse to raise his child for him? How do you propose to do that? You live in London. And what makes you think I'll allow it or even want it? We have nothing in common. Not anymore. Why make this more difficult than it already is?"

Why don't you just say no, so I don't have to?

Throughout my little speech, Zayaan kept shooting me brief glances, as he couldn't fully look at me while driving. He didn't say a word, though. Not during, not after. He was mulling things over. Probably selecting the right words from the gigantic multilingual lexicon in his head to offer a dozen different solutions to the issues I'd listed.

But he still hadn't spoken when the GPS announced we'd arrived at our destination.

"Please drop me at the front," I instructed when he would've turned into the parking lot. *"Merci beaucoup."* I tried to soften my words with horrible-sounding French. I'd been reading a lot of books on Napoleon and had now progressed—in my reading but regressed in time—to the reign of Marie Antoinette and Louis XVI, the dauphine and dauphin of France. Today, my head, aside from all the other rubbish, was swimming in an eighteenth-century French court.

I couldn't help but compare Nirvaan to Napoleon, both tenacious little plotters.

Zayaan pulled the Jeep up near a set of wide automatic

doors. Of course he replied in blemish-free French. *"Pas de problème.* I'll park and come find you."

I shook my head. "Nirvaan isn't here. We don't need to pretend, Zai. You and I both know that neither one of us wants to be here." I got out of the car and held the door open. "I'll be a couple of hours at least. Go away. Do something... somewhere else. I'll call you once I'm done."

"Simi." He sounded confused and frustrated, en garde to argue.

I forced myself to meet his eyes. "Zai, please. I'm embarrassed enough for both of us. And I have to do this alone." Without waiting for a reply, I shut the door and turned on my heel, walking through the automatic doors and into a waiting elevator.

Sooner or later, I would be alone, so why not start acclimating now?

After jumping through the familiar hoops of medical formalities at the front desk of Monterey Bay Fertility Clinic, Martha, a pudgy nurse in blue hospital dregs, guided me into an examination room with a pit stop to the restroom where I peed in a cup.

She weighed me, took my blood pressure and asked if there'd been any changes in my health or medications since the last time she'd seen me three days ago.

"Have to ask, honey. That's just the way it is," said Martha with a naughty eye twinkle. She handed me a green paper gown and requested I change into it. "Take off everything."

"That's Just the Way It Is" was the title of a '90s song by Phil Collins. I had a sudden vision of my mother singing it— or rather, humming it. I couldn't have been more than six or seven, but I remembered her singing so clearly with her soft, wavy hair, her pretty smile, and peaches-and-cream skin that smelled like rose water. If genetics was to be believed, I had the DNA to be a good mother even if I didn't have much luck with life.

When Dr. Archer came in—a smile teasing his countenance, as usual—and asked how I was doing and if I was ready to roll, I asked him if he knew the song. He did, fondly. After those pleasantries, he told me what was on the menu today. He really said "menu," as if we were ordering a box of à la carte goodies from Godiva instead of a bunch of tests to determine the best way to get me pregnant.

We started with the ultrasound. I had the image of my mother in my head as I lay down, but it vanished when chilled gel was squeezed across my stomach to the pelvic bone. I sucked in a breath. My abdomen quivered, and so did the glob of jelly on top of it.

"Sorry," Dr. Archer mumbled automatically. "Try to relax."

Why was he sorry when he'd do it over and over until he got the right images? And why should he be sorry for doing his job? If anyone should apologize to me, it was Nirvaan. Had he really expected Zayaan to hold my hand in here? God, how embarrassing.

I winced as the probe pressed against my empty bladder.

"Does this hurt?"

I sucked in a breath. "No. Just some pressure."

"Mmm-hmm," the doctor hummed and continued with the probe.

I craned my neck toward the monitor. My insides looked like a nebula of exploding stars in black and white and sounded like it, too, with the accompanying erratic beeps.

"You said your cycle is irregular?"

"That's right." I tensed up, but more from what had flashed through my mind than the probe pushing at my ovaries.

I hadn't always been irregular. For the first two years after my menarche, I'd bled every month like clockwork. Then, after the night of my eighteenth birthday, I'd had to go on the pill. I'd begun to lose weight I couldn't afford to lose. I'd become emaciated and depressed. The birth control pills had exacerbated my hormonal imbalance and mental state, messing up my system for good.

I gave Dr. Archer the gist of my medical history.

He gave me a breather after the ultrasound and left the room with a brief commiserating squeeze of my arm.

Dr. Archer was a good, gracious man.

A nurse came in with a toolbox dotted with blood-drawing paraphernalia. She stabbed me twice—without compassion—before hitting the right vein and drew several tubes of blood samples from my arm to check hormone levels, thyroid and pituitary gland functions, and infections. They needed to make sure I was in peak medical health and that nothing would hamper the fecundity of my reproductive organs.

Martha came in and plied me with water, some ibuprofen and a fresh paper gown.

Then the nurses left me alone for so long that, at one point, I cracked the door open to check if they'd forgotten I was in there. They hadn't. They were waiting for the painkiller to take proper effect. I'd thought they'd given it to me to relax my muscles after the ultrasound, but Martha explained it was to prepare me for the HSG, the hysterosalpingogram.

I closed the door, took a deep breath and blew it out in ten counts. To deny I was anxious would be fruitless. I hated medical processes. I especially hated procedures that couldn't be done without me lying on my back with my legs spread wide and exposed. It wasn't the pain I minded. In fact, I welcomed the pain. It kept me grounded in the here and now and not on past traumas.

My shrink had shown me how to take control of my mind

when all it wanted to do was flash to the past and panic. It didn't always work.

You're never going to forget what happened, Simeen. Just about anything will trigger a déjà vu or a panic attack. The way you take control is to remember it here—in this room, with me. Break it down, piece by piece. Then rebuild the memory and face it square. Control it. Understand that it was not your fault.

I hadn't consciously brought up that night in a long time. I hadn't needed to. I'd removed myself from all the things that reminded me of the rape—accidentally or on purpose. I didn't live in Surat anymore. I didn't draw attention to myself in public, not by dress or words or actions. I'd distanced myself from Zayaan and his family. I'd married Nirvaan, so all those things would be possible. I'd married Nirvaan, so I could safely bask in his glory, and no one would notice I lived in the shadows. No one would realize I'd stopped being brave.

With care and precision, I'd placed those dominoes around me.

But, now, they were falling.

What we did for love.
Wasn't that a song, too?
Dr. Archer began the hysteroscopy. To say it was painful was an understatement, even with the painkiller swimming in my bloodstream. I was used to the speculum, but then he injected a fluid inside me, a saline solution, and heaven help me, I began to cramp within moments. The slow stabs of pain were worse than the worst menstrual cramps I'd ever experienced. I wanted to curl up in a fetal position and cry like a baby.

I closed my eyes tight, my thighs trembling, and concentrated on puffing out breaths.

Dr. Archer was a constant stream of information, but I

tuned him out. I didn't care what, where, why or how the procedure was going. I just wanted it to be over.

After what felt like a horrendously long eternity, Dr. Archer patted my leg and stood up. Martha—I didn't realize she'd come into the room—gently arranged the gown about me, helped me roll on my side and started rubbing my lower back in soothing circles.

Dr. Archer repeated some of the instructions and told me what to expect and what to look out for. I'd bleed, but if the bleeding were like a period, I should call him immediately. He didn't foresee any changes or see any problems in my latest blood tests or any other tests, but they'd wait for the results. Once I was cleared, we'd dive into the IVF process.

I was awarded with a personalized cocktail of fertility drugs, which I'd begin administering on the third day of my coming period at the end of the month. My egg retrieval would be about ten days after.

The cramps were fading but not Dr. Archer, who prattled on about stimulating my ovaries and fallopian tubes and how we'd maximize the ovulation cycle.

"Lastly…"

Thank Khodai. He was almost done.

Blinking, I tried to focus on his face. He smiled at me like a benevolent Santa Claus but without a white beard and potbelly. Dr. Archer was a very handsome man, sexy even, with beautiful eyes, grayer today than the usual light blue. And so sweetly compassionate. Dr. Archer was a prime package, wasn't he?

Lucky Mrs. Archer, I thought inanely.

"You might find intimacy with your husband uncomfortable and unappealing for a few days. It's normal after an HSG."

I nodded, like he'd expected me to. But, inside, I became a hot, hot mass of shame.

He didn't know about my issues with intimacy. How unpleasant I found sex sometimes. How frightening. I'd been assured that it was normal for a rape victim to feel so.

Nirvaan didn't know about the rape. By the time we'd reconnected with each other again, after three years of not meeting and rarely speaking, I'd come to terms with a lot of things. I didn't cringe when a man touched me anymore. I didn't collapse in a panic attack. I didn't shut myself in my room and pace until exhaustion claimed me. I'd stopped blaming myself for what had happened that night—mostly.

And for all his hooliganisms, Nirvaan was a patient man and so very gentle.

I'd tried hard not to let the rape affect our marriage bed, but there were times, especially when we'd begun dating, when I'd flinch if he held me too tight. Of course, Nirvaan wasn't dumb. Short of full nudity and intercourse, I'd fooled around with both the guys all through the years of our friendship. He'd wondered why I was suddenly averse to—forget kinkiness—simple intimacy. I'd told him I'd been Eve teased in Mumbai, touched inappropriately in buses and on the streets, and that it had scarred me. He'd believed the lies I'd fed him.

Why wouldn't he? I was his wife.

Nirvaan had been so careful with me, so giving and undemanding, the first time we'd made love and every time after.

I'm ashamed to say that I took it all for granted—Nirvaan, how he kept me safe and spoilt me, how easy it was to forget everything around him. I, a person who expected the devil at every turn in the road, had started to feel happy again.

It'd been two years since I'd made love to my husband. His patience had finally run out. Nirvaan had begun needing a chemical aid to get erect and maintain the erection while I couldn't get past being skittish in bed. He had also become weak and couldn't frolic endlessly until I gathered the courage to gratify us both in some manner.

The crossed wires had led to huge amounts of frustration and instructions and, eventually, tears and accusations of who'd done what wrong. It was easier not to bother with sex at all. We'd convinced ourselves that our love didn't need sex to thrive.

We remained convinced—for the most part.

9

Again, I was left alone to recoup inside the examination room until I could sit up without wanting to vomit my insides out. The cramps didn't disappear, but they became bearable, and I got dressed. I checked in with Martha at the nurses' station just outside the exam room and asked if I was done for the day.

I wasn't.

Martha handed me a personalized fertility folder complete with a thumb drive containing videos on how to prepare and administer injections.

"Here, honey, so you don't need to come back for this. It's information on what the doc already told you and some he'll go over now. How are the cramps? Better? Good. Remember, nothing strenuous for the rest of the day."

I smiled and nodded. Then I shuffled into Dr. Archer's office, which was beginning to feel like a second home. He wasn't in the room, and I sat down to wait for him. I dug my phone out of my handbag and checked for messages. I'd missed several calls and two texts.

Nirvaan had texted an hour ago.

What's going on, baby?

I rolled my eyes. *What do you think? Ugh.*

Zayaan was less vague.

Are you okay? I'm waiting in the parking lot.

No, I was not okay. I was anything but okay. Right this minute, I wished both of them to hell...or to a prostate exam. Then we'd see how okay they felt. I considered not replying to either one of the concerned parties, but in the end, I couldn't be such a bitch.

I sent them both the same message.

Waiting for the doctor. I'm fine. Not long now.

Dr. Archer bustled in ten minutes later. "Feeling okay, Mrs. Desai? How are the cramps?"

"Better," I mumbled, giving him a small smile.

"Good, good." He handed me several more sheets of print-outs and a small brochure. "It's some literature on IVF. Did Martha give you a dossier?"

"Yes." I touched the folder in question.

"Good. It contains instructions on how to order and administer the injections. You can also come in for a live demonstration sometime next week." After more general intructions, Dr. Archer outlined the coming month and a half and the costs involved.

I was aware of what an IVF cycle cost, yet the numbers following the dollar signs in my packet shocked me. There were drugs listed costing five thousand dollars a shot—to be paid out of pocket because none of it was covered by health insurance. This was money we should be spending on treatments in Kutch, not Monterey.

I waited for the panic to set in as we discussed my future

baby, but for some reason, it didn't. My abdominal pain had used up all my adrenaline.

"Any questions, Mrs. Desai?"

"You know our situation, Dr. Archer," I began, grabbing on to the last thread of practicality trying to break free of my hopelessly tangled life. "Do you think… I mean, I'm obviously stressed about everything. It can't be good, right—to be stressed while trying to get pregnant? What I mean is, will it affect the outcome of the IVF?" I wasn't about to waste good money on a doomed thing. "And don't advise me to take up meditation and calm down because it's not going to happen."

Dr. Archer gave an astonished bark of laughter at my abrupt show of temper. I supposed I had surprised him. I'd never been so chatty with him before.

"IVF is stressful for most people, regardless of their circumstances, yet lots of couples get pregnant through it. Life is stressful, Mrs. Desai, on the best of days. Getting pregnant, even naturally, is taxing for your mind and body. Therefore, no, your emotional levels won't have any effect on the IVF. It's a simple matter of an optimal incubatory environment—and some luck," he said.

Then he looked at me with his penetrating eyes, and I wanted to fidget like a schoolgirl who'd forgotten to do her homework.

"Mrs. Desai, I encourage you to see our in-house counselor." He opened a drawer in his massive desk, took out a card and slid it toward me.

I picked it up. Dr. Eva Green, Family Counseling. "I…I already have a therapist," I told him, my cheeks heating up.

I hadn't spoken to Dr. Asha Ambani in a while, not since Nirvaan's remission, but she was still my therapist. And I kept her updated about my well-being with sporadic emails.

"Good," he said again.

Was *good* his word of the day?

"Talk to her or him. I want you to be one hundred percent sure before we start."

And that marked the end of the consultation. I guessed the good, kindly doctor had no patience for my wavering mind.

I walked out of his office, mired in doubt again. In the reception area, lots of pregnant women sat or waddled up and down the room, waiting to see their doctors. I slid gingerly between them, trying to avoid bumping into the bellies, as if pregnancy were contagious.

Do I want a child or not? And if I didn't, if I absolutely did not, I needed to grow a spine and tell my husband.

I shook my head. What was I thinking? The minute I reneged on the baby bargain, Nirvaan would cry foul and stop his treatments. No, I couldn't tell him.

I pushed open the door of the clinic. I had to do this…at least until the last of his treatments was done. And with any luck, the IVF wouldn't…

I stopped short once I exited the fertility clinic. Zayaan was standing by the door with a little brown-haired girl, no more than two or three, in his arms. My heart squeezed painfully to see him holding a toddler, even as laughter threatened to set my belly cramping again.

"Wow. Is this clinic prolific or what?" I joked.

Against my will, I thought of the day we'd drawn our family tree in the sand on Dumas Beach. Zayaan had wanted two girls with my hair, my smile and, yes, even my nose. I'd wanted a miniature Zayaan or two or three, keeping me busy until my old age. We'd agreed two boys and two girls would make an ideal family—the Khan dynasty tradition. We'd been so young. Just under seventeen. Pathetically young to be so much in love.

"Another good one." Zayaan chuckled and patted the girl's

back when she whimpered against his shoulder. He glanced at the frosted glass doors of the clinic. "Scary in there. I've never come across so many pregnant women in one room before. It's like an overdose of estrogen or something."

I didn't want to be amused. "And who's this?" I moved close to whiff the sweet, powdery stink of baby and run a finger down the tot's chubby cheek.

She was fast asleep in his arms, a pacifier in her rosebud mouth.

"Thanks, man. You're a lifesaver." The gruff words came from behind me.

I turned to see a tall man in a suit holding his arms out for his little girl. Somehow, the men transferred the sleeping toddler without waking her.

The man smiled at us. "And good luck to you and your wife. Those doctors are miracle workers, and I know it."

"No trouble, mate," said Zayaan, shaking the man's hand. "She's an angel."

I'd frozen at the words *you and your wife*. I couldn't, for the life of me, return the man's smile before he went into the clinic to be with his family.

Zayaan tugged my heavy tote from my shoulder and onto his. "Nice guy. We got talking over coffee. They have twins. His wife is inside with the other child. She couldn't handle two sleeping toddlers alone, and she's pregnant with twins again. Anyway, I offered to carry this one while he went to the loo."

I stared at Zayaan all through his explanation as we waited for the elevator. Wasn't he the least bit mortified that the man had presumed we were married? Why hadn't he corrected the assumption? *Why hadn't I?* And if we had, wouldn't it have raised more eyebrows than ironing things out?

Was this a glimpse into my future? If I had this baby and

Zayaan fulfilled his promise to watch over us, was this what we'd go through every time we stepped out?

I moaned softly, and it had nothing to do with cramps.

"Simi?"

"I'm fine," I said, walking straight into the elevator as it swished open. I leaned against its flaky side wall in support.

The elevator lurched one floor down, and people crowded in, shifting to and fro for standing space. Zayaan's arm came about my shoulders, and he pulled me close to him to make room.

I could've easily laid my head on his shoulder. Barefoot, my ear fit perfectly over his heart, just like with Nirvaan. I used to say it was the reason we were so in tune with each other—because I had direct listening access into their souls.

Zayaan called Nirvaan from the car to tell him I was done and that we were heading home. I closed my eyes when Nirvaan called out my name over the car speaker. I didn't want to get into explanations and arguments now. Before I could make up an excuse to hang up, Zayaan told him I was asleep and disconnected the phone, surprising me.

"Relax. You need it," he said gruffly.

I could've kissed him then.

The cramps wouldn't let me relax, though, and the parish exit came up faster than I'd expected. Once Zayaan took it, he didn't take the road home, and I was deprived of seeing the pastor's quote of the day. He turned the Jeep left instead, toward the town center. I decided he must have errands to run.

Great. The longer I could postpone throttling my husband into an early grave, the better.

Zayaan parked in front of the local supermarket. "Let's go, Sims."

I blinked owlishly at the customers walking in and out of the market. "Huh? Where? Why? We don't need groceries this week." There were more than enough leftovers and fresh veggies in the fridge at home.

"Trust me. You need this." He came over on my side and opened the door, flashing his non–killer smile at me. It was the sweet, shy one.

I got out, intrigued despite myself.

We walked half a block to a local ice cream parlor, and Zayaan bought me a big, gooey sundae with all my favorite ice creams and toppings. I was in brain-freeze heaven with the first bite.

The town square was littered with pretty benches and potted gardens. We sat on one such bench right by the Jeep, devouring the sundae between us. Over our heads, a grand cherry blossom dappled us in light and shadow as its leaves flirted with the sunbeams.

"'The wound is the place where the Light enters you.'"

I hadn't heard Rumi's beautiful words in a long time, but I recognized them. I looked at Zayaan without my usual reticence. His eyes weren't on my face, though. He was staring at the sunlit bandage hiding the puncture site of my blood test on my bare arm. A breeze riffled the wispy ends of his poker-straight hair, and my fingers itched to push them back into place, to gauge if the texture had coarsened over time or if it was as silky soft as before.

"Talk to me, Simi," he demanded, as if our friendship hadn't suffered a dozen years of exile.

And, suddenly, I was desperate to. I wanted to tell him everything. To share my troubles like I used to before his brother had destroyed us. I wanted to lean on him. To let him be the Light and the World, as he'd once been to me. To let him bear my burdens so that I could be free.

I pulled back from him, even as I thought those things. I could never do that. If I hadn't told him the truth then, there was no reason to tell him now. Rizvaan was dead. He'd been shot down by Ahura Mazda's justice the very night he raped me. The creep was dead and shamed for eternity even though his mother persisted in endorsing him as a martyr.

And I was married to Nirvaan now. Nirvaan, who didn't have a sliver of evil in his bones but was dying young all the same. Such was also God's justice.

"There's nothing to talk about, Zai," I said as I bent my head to the ice cream before forcing a spoonful into my mouth.

By nightfall, the cramps, with their constant ebb and flow of pain, had made me restless. I huddled and rocked myself, and when it didn't help, I paced. I tried cat stretches and fetal positions and even soaking in the tub, but nothing helped for long.

Currently, I was sprawled on a lounger on the deck, hugging a hot-water bottle between my stomach and raised thighs. I rocked back and forth, trying to jiggle the pain away. I'd taken a dose of painkillers again, as per the doctor's instructions, and I was waiting for it to kick in.

I'd also encouraged the guys to take the Jet Skis out. They hadn't ridden them all day, for my sake, and to combat boredom, they'd been video-gaming the silence out of the night. My head had boomed with the sounds of bombs until I'd ordered them to be gone. I'd craved wallowable peace more than their constant concern.

Unlike Nirvaan, I was a terrible patient. I didn't know how to be sick or accept help gracefully. It was because I had a high threshold for pain—physical pain. I'd been like that, even as a child, and I had the scar to prove it.

I'd gotten the scar during a two-day camping trip from school. Twelve or thirteen, I'd been in the eighth class of an all-girls school. Being a puny girl, I'd often overcompensated my lack of stature with false swagger. On the first day of camp itself, I'd slipped a dozen feet down a brush-strewn slope because I'd taken a steeper path to overtake a bunch of sporty girls in my class. My jeans had torn, and a thorned branch had gouged a five-inch slit into my thigh. Mortified, I hadn't called for help. I'd ignored the burn and the pain and finished the trek. Then I'd washed the wound and tied a handkerchief around it for the rest of the trip. I'd needed a tetanus shot by the time I got home and a heavy dose of antibiotics, as it had become infected. It was the first and only time I'd thought my mother might smack me.

Nirvaan thought it foolish to suffer in silence. Not that he was a cumbersome patient, but he didn't underplay his health or his mental state. Of course, he'd learned not to.

Zayaan was like me. He could bear pain quietly and would seek help only as a last resort.

His brother had beaten him with a belt, with a cricket bat, with his fists all through his childhood—a big brother's due for babysitting his younger sibling. Zayaan hadn't called it abuse, but Nirvaan had had no such reservations.

I'd stumbled across the truth only because I caught Zayaan in a weak moment and asked about the scars. The beatings had long stopped by the time I got to know him, but I wouldn't ever forget the little white worms that marred his back and upper arms. Once Zayaan had grown as big and strong as his brother, he'd fought back. But by then, Rizvaan had found his calling in terror.

Life was a strange beast, wasn't it?

Zayaan's family had left Pakistan to remove Rizvaan from the influence of bad company. It was always the other who was bad and never your own. But like attracted like, and Rizvaan had quickly gathered a band of nasty men around him in Surat, too. They were destructive, disgusting creatures who'd wreaked havoc wherever they went. I'd known he was vile, but my mistake had been in thinking of him as Zayaan's brother. They looked alike, so much so that people would ask if they were twins. But that facade of good looks was the only thing they'd had in common.

I'd been warned to keep out of Rizvaan's way. Zayaan had kept me under his family's radar for a long time. But we'd been too close and too joined at the hip not to have at least some interaction with our respective families. I'd wanted to meet his parents right from the first, even before our relationship had progressed to the serious level. I'd hated feeling like an orphan, and so I'd sought whole new families to belong to. Nirvaan's family was wonderful, and they'd sort of adopted Zayaan and me into their clan. I'd naively believed Zayaan's parents would be the same. At first, Zayaan's father had been wary, but I'd won him over. Gulzar Auntie's overt disapproval was another story. And Rizvaan, it seemed, had always hated me and Nirvaan. He'd hated Zai, most of all.

Yes, life was strange.

After everything that had happened since the night Zayaan had rescued me at Dandi Beach, I still couldn't regret knowing him. And that scared me because I didn't want to forget. And I didn't wish to forgive.

The *chug-a-chug-chug*s of the Jet Skis announced the guys' return. Our patch of the beach was semiprivate, but we had no pier to dock the bikes. After each use, the Jet Skis would have to be dragged over sand, and either left by the deck, weather permitting, or stored in the carriage house.

I got to my feet and went into the house to grab a couple of thick towels. I'd usually leave a stack on the deck, but I'd forgotten today.

Nirvaan bounded up the stairs, talking a mile a minute. "Baby, you missed the dolphins versus humans race."

"Down!" I yelled, leaping back from him. I pointed at the outdoor shower. "Shower off the sand, hose down the wetsuit, hang it to dry. Then you may join me on the deck."

"You're feeling better," he said, beaming at me.

Completely ignoring my orders, he jumped me. I screamed like I was being murdered. My nightgown got soaked, as it was plastered against his dripping wetsuit. As I opened my mouth to scream again, his mouth came down on mine, slick with salt and sand and delicious cold.

"If the neighbors call the police to report a homicide, I'm skipping town," said Zayaan.

Nirvaan released me and stripped out of his suit as I grumbled and spit the ocean from my mouth. He threw the suit at Zayaan, who'd stripped off his and was hosing it down. Nirvaan made a lewd comment about inviting the cops to join our striptease party, before stepping into the shower. Zayaan said something equally crude in return.

The perfect comeback bloomed in my head. I would've said it, too, had my tongue not glued itself to the roof of my mouth. *Dear Almighty God.* Every day, I'd see the guys in various stages of dress and undress, but tonight, in the sparse light of the moon, combined with the beam of yellow light from the deck, they both looked beyond lickable.

Dr. Archer had said my hormones and libido would go nuts while on fertility meds. Apparently, I didn't need to be drugged to go nuts.

Water rippled down slick muscles and pooled inside their swimming trunks. Zayaan wore a knee-length pair, riding low on his hips. And Nirvaan—I grinned in delight—wore my favorite pair of cobalt-blue designer swimwear. Any skimpier, and he'd be wearing a thong. His bum muscles flexed and relaxed as he moved, and I admired them with impunity.

I hadn't made love to my husband in two years, but I wanted to tonight. I needed to tonight.

I didn't want to remember the past. I didn't want to forget it, either. And I would not forgive. Most of all, I wanted to place the dominoes back around my heart.

Dr. Archer had said that sex might hurt after the HSG, but I couldn't wait. And I wasn't hurting now. The cramps had subsided. The medicine had worked.

"Boys, there are towels by the stairs. You've soaked me to the bone, Nirvaan. I'm going to change," I said over my shoulder.

Excited by the plan and more than a bit aroused by the swimwear models, I walked into the bedroom and drew the curtain all the way across for privacy. In the bathroom, I stripped off the wet nightgown along with my underwear and wrapped a towel around my body.

I looked in the mirror. My face, my shoulders, the tops of my breasts were flushed with excitement. I smiled and bit my lip. I could do this. There was no need to be shy or afraid. My reflection shivered even though I wasn't cold.

Suddenly, my smile dimmed.

Shit. Nirvaan would need a stimulant, and I couldn't remember where I'd stashed the pills. So much for spontaneity.

I opened the medicine cabinet. Not there. I rushed into the bedroom and checked in both nightstands and the dresser and—*yes, yes, yes!* I found them in a box buried under my birth control pills.

"Nirvaan," I called out as I pressed a tablet out of its packet. "Honey, I need you."

"Yeah, baby? Whatchu need?" He came in, flinging the curtain aside.

I yanked it closed again and faced him.

"*Ooh.* What do we have here?" He gave a lecherous chuckle

and hooked a finger between my breasts, tugging on my towel. He could've easily stripped me naked. He didn't. He joked and teased and leered, but he never stripped me naked anymore.

I showed him the pill. If I hadn't been staring at my husband's face, I would've missed the flare of panic in his eyes. His wolf-smile slipped for half a second and bounced back full force.

"What's that? I've taken all my medication," he said carefully.

He knew bloody well what was on my palm, and it bothered me that he was pretending otherwise.

"I want to make love to you," I said clear and loud so that there was no misunderstanding.

I didn't know of any husband who'd hear his wife say those words and take a step back from her. Mine did. He kept smiling, though, as if I'd made a great joke.

But I wasn't going to back down. Not tonight. I was bold tonight.

I stepped closer.

His eyes grew round and huge. "What about the cramps?"

"I'm fine." I put a hand over his heart. It was racing as wantonly as mine.

Nirvaan used to have whorls of hair all over his chest. Now the mat was sparse and patchy, his skin almost translucent in spots, through which his ribs showed. He had scars from the surgeries and PICC line, but there was strength in him still. His skin was almost always cold to the touch now, but I was about to warm him up.

I smiled, thinking I should just tug his towel off and get started on my knees. He used to love that opening.

He darted a glance to the curtain separating us from the rest of the house. "Baby, we can't. What'll Zai think?"

"I'm sure it won't come as a shock to him that married couples have sex."

Nirvaan's chest expanded, and he shuddered out a breath in lieu of a laugh at my cheekiness. He stared at me then, a riot of emotions flying across his face. I knew the idea of Zayaan knowing...maybe even listening in...appealed to him. My husband was into kinky sex—or had been before we'd gotten married. And I was guilty of taking that freedom away from him.

"What? It's not like he hasn't heard us or seen us do stuff before. Have you forgotten what the three of us got up to during those summers in Surat?" I pressed my thumb to his nipple.

He pressed his hand on top of mine to stop my thumb from worrying his nipple. "We were kids, Simi. We didn't know whether we were coming or going back then." Nirvaan ran a hand through his hair. A line of sweat had beaded up along his upper lip.

"What about these last few weeks when you've constantly talked of those days, reliving our glory days and wild nights? More than once, you've thrown Zayaan and me together in awkward situations. What has it been about, then?" I curled my hand under his. I wanted to rake it down his chest for making me crazy.

"It's not been about a threesome, Simi." He looked... unhappy.

With me?

"I know that. Khodai. But I thought, maybe, you were feeling better...that you wanted me."

God, I'd misread the signals on purpose. He really didn't want to make love...*because of Zayaan?*

I yanked my hand free from his grip, my cheeks burning— from anger this time.

I recalled Zayaan's expression from this morning as he'd

stood by the door. I'd thought he was angry at whatever Nirvaan had said, assumed it'd been something about my uterus.
What if it hadn't been anger but embarrassment making his
ears red?

"What have you told him?" I asked my husband. "Did you
tell him about our bedroom problems? Does he know you
haven't touched me in two years?"

When he didn't answer, all my insecurities, my guilt, my
regrets came flooding back. My husband didn't want me as
a lover. Even worse, Zayaan, the man I'd rejected, knew it.
It didn't matter that they talked about everything under the
sun. This was one thing Nirvaan should've kept between us,
kept sacred.

I'd never felt more betrayed in my life.

10

I didn't know what to think or how to feel, so I locked myself in the bathroom and counted to fifty. I ignored Nirvaan's knocks and apologies.

"Don't be upset, baby. We can do it if you want to. Just come out."

Wow. Just wow.

I blew out a breath and counted backward to zero while Nirvaan offered up a dozen different ways we could *do it* to try to make up for his obvious rebuff.

I stripped off my towel and hung it on the rail to dry. Then I yanked open the bathroom door. Nirvaan stood there, mouth open, fist raised, ready to knock again. I brushed past him into the walk-in closet and pulled on underwear, a sports bra and my cropped yoga pants.

He came up behind me, slipped his arms around me, hugging me tight. "Simi, *please.*"

I didn't know what he was begging for.

Please, Simi, let's make love, or *Please, Simi, try to understand why I can't.*

Can't or don't wish to, I added, savagely yanking on a sweatshirt.

I turned in his arms and wrapped my own arms about him, hugging him back equally hard. "It's okay. We don't have to.

You certainly don't have to make me feel good like that. You make me happy in so many other ways."

I squeezed him once more, ducked out of his embrace and walked out of the closet. I picked up my phone and earphones.

"I'm not upset. Truly," I said, glancing at him, as he stood in the closet, frowning fiercely. "I'm going for a walk."

"Simi."

I hardened my expression just like he'd done when he rejected me. "I'm going for a walk on the beach. I'll be back in half an hour."

Then I ran out of the house before my anger ran down my cheeks.

Nirvaan knew me well enough to leave me alone until I'd gotten my mad under control. He didn't follow me, but as I marched away from the house, I heard him shout from the deck that if I wasn't back in half an hour, I'd regret it.

Ha. Regret it. You bet I regret...something. I just wasn't sure what.

I couldn't believe I was turning myself inside out trying to have his baby, and he couldn't do this one thing...one thing for me. I didn't care that he couldn't physically do what I wanted without aid. We had the aid. But we'd had performance issues even with the aid before...and maybe that was what worried him?

"*Argh.* Stop making excuses for him!" I shouted into the night.

I came to a stop by the edge of the water and tried to calm down. After ten breaths, I continued onward at a more sedate pace. I didn't want the cramps to come back.

The wind whispered against my face and hair, cooling my anger-hot cheeks. It was late at night, but the beach wasn't dark and scary—not like Dandi. The scattered houses along the turf were mostly occupied, and if not fully lit from inside, they had at least a couple of lights switched on to give me direction. I walked along the shallow, cold water.

Thick clouds of thoughts whirled in my mind. Nirvaan's unhappy face floated to the forefront like a gathering storm. I couldn't believe he'd refused to make love to me. Usually, it was the other way around. And I couldn't believe he thought I wanted Zayaan in our bed.

Ha. Like I'd ever now.

But I'd wanted it once. Chosen it over love and friendship, once.

I slowed the pace, letting my toes dig into the sand for purchase. We'd never had a proper threesome. We'd come close to it, though, because of me, my choices, my *greed*. Our trifecta existed because of me. It had begun with me and ended with me, never mind that it was Nirvaan who'd suggested the idea of it first.

He'd flown down for his cousin's wedding during his senior year Christmas break. He'd been feeling randy and hungover, possibly jet-lagged, after the bachelor party. I remembered him bringing up The Threesome Pact the very next afternoon at our favorite daytime hangout place—Nanubhai's Pizza Parlor.

"We're going to be eighteen freaking years old in less than six months. College awaits us. Fucking adult life awaits us. We have to do something spectacular this year," he said, pulling me into his armpit for a boisterous hug. "Let's have that threesome."

We stared at him, speechless—me in growing excitement, Zayaan in insufferable irritation. We'd been putting off The Threesome Pact for years because of Zayaan. For once, the smell of fresh oven-baked pizzas didn't rule our stomachs like the conversation had.

"Let's not," Zayaan barked out, from which ensued a prolonged three-way debate.

Zayaan was dead set against a threesome involving me.

"It might cause problems between us to have sex together," he warned.

He loved me and was disinclined to share me anymore. The declaration didn't shock Nirvaan. We'd discussed love and commitment in front of him before—sometimes in jest, and sometimes not. But Zayaan wasn't joking that day.

"Look, Sims, I'm serious about marrying you. I'm in love with you. This isn't a joke."

"You bet it's not a joke. Did you seriously, *seriously*, just propose to me in a pizza joint?" I asked, delighted and terrified and intrigued all at the same time.

I'd been drowning in my love for him, deeper every day with every breath. But I'd wanted the threesome for so long. I wanted to eat my cake and have it, too. I wanted them both that day.

Nirvaan laughed and slapped Zayaan on his shoulder. "Yeah, man. Have some clue as to what a girl wants."

Zayaan flicked a violent glare at Nirvaan before his eyes snared me in their thrall. "What do you want, Simeen? Tell me what you want, and it's yours."

He wanted me to choose monogamy. He wanted me to choose him. I saw the dark hope sparking his eyes. I felt unspeakably powerful then and so vastly naughty.

"I want you so much," I said honestly, groping for his hand under the plastic red-and-white table.

He could've thrown a smug victor's smile in Nirvaan's direction, but Zayaan had always been too smart for his own good.

"But?" he asked, somehow knowing I wasn't done choosing.

"I want you. I want marriage with you, a whole life with

you. But I want Nirvaan, too. I want this threesome even if it's just one time. I've dreamed of this, Zai, for three years. You made me wait. You made Nirvaan wait. You owe us this."

He didn't get upset with me.

I understood now that he'd had every right to be offended. I'd chosen him, yet I'd not. He hadn't berated me or tried to change my mind. He'd nodded, frowning, maybe even in relief because, in his heart of hearts, he'd wanted it, too.

I turned to Nirvaan then and laughed at his somber expression. "I don't think I've ever seen you serious. Having second thoughts, Mr. Big Talk?"

"No." He took my other hand in his, lacing our fingers together before bringing it to his lips. "But you be very sure, babe. And if you decide not to go through with it, no hard feelings, okay? Or if you decide to marry me instead... problem solved," he said, ending the discussion on a deliberately light note.

All hunky-dory assurances aside, I made it clear to Nirvaan that I wished for Zayaan to be my first.

As it'd turned out, neither of them had been my first.

My phone rang just then, arresting my mind from vaulting into Karmic consequences for wickedness and divine justice.

It was my brother Sarvar. "*Su garbar karee?* What did you do? Your husband called, said you'd run off in a huff. Everything okay?"

"My husband is driving me nuts," I said.

I was not especially surprised Nirvaan had called my brother. He had known I'd need to talk to someone.

Sarvar was the only person in the world who knew every single thing about me. Surin knew the important bits, but Sarvar knew my deepest, darkest secrets because I didn't hide anything from him. Zayaan used to be that person. Nirvaan might've been that person had life been gentler with us.

"So, what's new?" Sarvar asked, midyawn.

"Apparently, we mustn't have sex because Zayaan…bloody Zayaan…might *hear*. I don't care if he hears. I don't care if the whole neighborhood thinks we're porn stars. I want to make love to my husband."

Sarvar cleared his throat. "*Riiight*. Understandable."

He already knew about the two-year hiatus because Nirvaan wasn't exactly discreet about his condition, joking about it like he joked about everything else. People put two and two together. Sometimes, I didn't understand why my husband said or did the things he said and did. I wasn't really being indiscreet here, not like Nirvaan had been about us with Zai and Sarvar and Khodai knew who else. At least when I discussed such things with my brother, I was talking to my own conscience, not stirring up mischief.

"Isn't it? But, no, my husband doesn't seem to think so. He had the gall to offer me a pity fuck through the bathroom door," I said, getting riled up again. *Not to mention a side order of oral sex*. But I didn't say that aloud. I couldn't be that crude.

"Whoa. *O-kay*, Simeen, darling…do I need to hear this?"

"Who else can I talk to, Savvy? Tell me." I pressed a hand to my forehead, afraid my head was going to explode. "And don't say 'your therapist' because I don't want my head examined. I want to vent." And scream. And kick something. Or someone.

Nirvaan was going out of his way to point out all the deficiencies in our marriage, and I did not like it.

After a moment of silence, a great, sonorous sigh came through the phone. "*Riiight*," my brother said again. "Go on."

I vented for a while.

"I keep thinking of that night because of Zai. I mean, Zai doesn't scare me. Of course he doesn't scare me."

Not in the way his brother had. But he made me feel… things I shouldn't be feeling.

"There's this chaos inside of me, Savvy, and I'm afraid to let it loose. I don't know if Zai is the trigger or Nirvaan, but I keep thinking of Surat and…and the rest," I said. The photos… the guys and I living together…the reminiscing…the IVF… Khodai—my life was pure torture these days.

"Of course you're thinking of the past, darling. It's perfectly understandable."

I looked into the night sky, feeling utterly lost. I couldn't help wondering whether I'd handle life better if my mother were alive. "I miss Mumsy. So much."

"I know, honey. I miss her, too," Sarvar said softly. "I wish you'd call Dr. Asha. I don't know what to say to you or how to help you. You're going through a lot, sweetie."

"Really? I hadn't guessed." Immediately, I felt bad for taking my upset out on Sarvar with sarcasm. "I'm sorry, Savvy. I didn't mean to sound like a brat or put you on the spot."

"Forget it." Then he said the same thing Zayaan had. "Talk to Nirvaan. Tell him what's in your heart. He'll understand, you know."

Of course he'll understand, I thought, yo-yoing between guilt, despair and anger. But how did that make me any less of a leech? Always taking from him, never giving back.

It struck me how crazy I sounded. Just a short while ago, I'd accused Nirvaan of not doing nearly enough while expecting the world from me. It was my turn to burble out a sigh.

"I can't tell him, Savvy. I can't disappoint him. Anyway, I have to go, or Nirvaan will worry."

"Tell him, darling," repeated Sarvar. "And, Simi? Call Dr. Asha. You can always talk to me…but I want you to speak to her, as well."

"I will," I promised. Wouldn't hurt to get my head examined, after all.

Before hanging up, Sarvar brought up our upcoming hiking weekend. He and a few of his buddies were going into the mountains and had invited us along. Nirvaan had already agreed, but I told Sarvar it would depend on how the radiation went.

After saying good-night, I clicked the phone off and slid it into my pocket, wishing I could spend the night on the beach and not go home.

Home was supposed to be your shelter, a place to hang your heart and your hat. But when your own home was the cause of your problems, where did that leave you?

My mind a mess, it was no great surprise that sleep eluded me. Cozy as I was while spooned against Nirvaan on our bed, I still couldn't relax.

Yes, we'd made up. He'd even forgone a chance to win some epic seven-day-long game for a night of cards, wine and chocolates with me, in bed, without our chronic shadow.

I awoke for the third time at about 2 a.m. to answer a bladder call. By the time I finished my business and went back into the room, I was wide-awake. I got in bed, careful not to disturb Nirvaan, and switched on my e-reader.

I'd read exactly one page when Nirvaan began to mumble something about losing his body pillow. It took me a few seconds to realize he meant me. He rolled onto his back, crosswise on the queen-size bed, and started snoring. Grimacing, I slipped out of bed and stole out of the room. There was no way I'd fall asleep with that racket even if I managed to nudge him back to his side of the bed.

The house was dark, except for a wobbly sliver of light escaping through the drapes of the den. As I went deeper into the living room, I heard Zayaan's throaty murmur. He worked best at night. Plus, his colleagues and friends lived in a different time zone. It was ten in the morning across the pond. Perhaps he was talking to his mother.

I should make use of my wakefulness, too, and email Dr. Asha. But the thought of explaining my conflicting thoughts in an email daunted me. It'd be better to call and speak to her like Sarvar had suggested. I'd have to wait till morning, though—when it was her night—to avoid catching her in a session with a patient.

I poured myself a glass of water, and with a defiance bordering on masochism, I poked my head into the den.

Zayaan had a pair of fancy headphones on with a mic curving across his mouth. He paced as he spoke. His surprise upon seeing me was so minor that I wondered if he'd expected me. Of course, he hadn't.

He lifted his chin and mouthed, *What's up? Nirvaan?*

I flapped my hand in a carry-on gesture, letting him know it was nothing serious or important. "Can't sleep," I whispered.

He held up both his hands, flashed his fingers twice, indicating he'd be done in ten minutes, without breaking the flow in conversation.

I nodded, looking about the space while I tried to dissuade my eyes from staring at him. They wouldn't listen and kept swinging back like boomerangs. He wore striped pajama bottoms and nothing else, so my eyes had a lot of swoonworthy maleness to cover.

The windows were open a few inches, enough to give vent to a cool breeze that had the drapes over the door and windows rippling. Yet I felt hot in my sleep shorts and flannel robe. I should've let Nirvaan take my edge off, as he'd offered. And I would have to start masturbating again. I hadn't since we moved to Carmel, so it was no wonder I felt snappish.

For some insane reason, I was embarrassed to take care of my needs with Zayaan in the house, as if he'd sense what I'd done. I couldn't get over the ridiculous juxtaposition of living in a ménage with two of the hottest guys on the planet, ones who could ring my bell with only a look, with no bells ringing anywhere.

The den was small, and with me standing in a corner, pondering the criteria of a cosmic joke, Zayaan had a lot less room to pace. I walked to the desk and set down the glass of water and, since the office chair was free, I took it.

I peeked at the papers strewed over the desk. There were papers stacked all over the den, in fact. I sifted through some, passing a cursory glance over headings, highlighted words, passages he'd marked with different colored pens and Post-its. He'd said his thesis had to do with the psychology of the Islamic culture. I shot a glance at him, wondering exactly what his work was about. I hadn't bothered to ask.

He was talking in Farsi, I decided. I always got confused between Arabic and Farsi accents because, to an untrained ear like mine, both languages sounded the same—foreign. But there were differences, if you knew where to look. Also, once you heard both for a decent stretch of time, you'd realize that Farsi sentences tended to lilt softly as opposed to lilting harshly like in Arabic. And one spoke it fast and not lazily.

Zayaan frowned in the middle of his next downward march and stopped short in the middle of the room. He laced his hands behind his head, raised his head to the ceiling and closed his eyes, arching his spine. I smiled, instantly recognizing the man-thinking-hard pose. Perversely and without permission, my eyes swept down the line of finely trimmed hair from his navel to his abdomen where they darted across the twin blades of his hips jutting out of the elastic of his pajamas. Goodness gracious, but he was an exquisite specimen of humanity.

Zayaan had an innate sensuality that he wasn't unaware of but tried to downplay. Nirvaan was handsome and knew it, and he worked hard at being sexy—with superb results, I'd admit. In Zayaan, it was effortless. While both men grabbed attention and appreciation wherever they went, it was on Zayaan most eyes would linger even though he came off as aloof and unapproachable because he was shy, if you could believe it. In contrast, Nirvaan took admiration as his due. He'd wink at his admirer, say something flirty or nice, and put the person at ease in two seconds flat.

Okay, enough comparing and contrasting. This wasn't a competition for Prime Man, and I wasn't the judge.

I turned back to the desk and picked up the first folder I could reach. A quote from Rumi jumped out at me in Zayaan's flawless handwriting.

Out beyond ideas of wrongdoing and right doing, there is a field.
I'll meet you there.

The seductive scrawl flowed from margin to end, words evenly spaced with dips of mystery and curves I couldn't take my eyes off of. Just like the man. He'd always had beautiful handwriting, due to learning to write in the calligraphic *Nasta'liq* script used in Urdu.

I turned the page. There was an index of sorts and tabs sticking out from all directions—History, Arabic Mythology, Tales from Pre-Islamic Arabia, the Old Testament, the Crusades, the Moghuls. A whole list of Persian and Arabic literati with their specialties were noted on a spreadsheet, dated for original and translated works.

Zayaan had always been organized in the extreme about his work, maybe even his life.

On the next page, under Psychology, there were several subheadings—Locus of Control, Submission, Indoctrination, Consanguineous Marriages, *Mein Kampf* (*My Struggle*), and *My Jihad*.

I snapped the folder shut. My heart banged against my rib cage. Not only certain men, even specific words could strike terror in my soul.

What did Hitler's manifesto have to do with jihad? And where was Zayaan going with this?

He wasn't talking so much as listening now. He nodded, said something and nodded again. He chuckled into the mic, the sound low and husky. Intimate. Secretive. It excluded me from the conversation, from his other life. And I didn't like it.

He stopped at the desk to type in his laptop the name, email and phone number for a doctor. Not a medical doctor, I surmised quickly. As he stood above me, his natural scent caught my nose, warm and musky, layered under the crisp soap and ocean spray. It was…nice and so different from how he used to smell. I was grateful for that small mercy.

Finally, Zayaan said goodbye. He removed the headpiece and threw it on the desk.

"Fuck, I'm tired," he groaned as he stretched his back and neck. His eyes roved over my face. "What's wrong?"

Were you talking to Marjaneh? I wanted to blurt out. "What's this?" I pointed to the folder, which now officially gave me the creeps.

"Notes, articles, outlines…" He chuckled again. It was not a low, husky, I've-just-rolled-out-of-bed chuckle. "My life currently." He rested half a hip against the desk and opened the folder I'd just closed.

I kept my eyes on his. "Hmm, interesting choice of words because I think all of this—" I paused and pointed at the folder "—might just cost you your life. Oh, my God, Zai, are you going to publish that? Like, for people to read? *My Jihad*?" I squeaked.

"It just means 'my struggle,' and I'm struggling with it, believe me." He looked half amused, half irritated by my reaction. "*Mein Kampf* is one of the few books translated into Arabic in the last many decades and is widely read as *My Jihad* in and around the Middle East. It's just data, Simi." He shrugged.

I curled my lips downward. "Where are you going with this? What psychology? What possible reason, other than utter depravity, could there be for these people to behave as they do? You're not like them. You've never been like any of these men you're writing about." *You are not like your brother.*

"The only difference between *these* men and me is that I recognize the fact that I have free will." He huffed through his nose. "No, you're right. I'm not like them. Neither are the vast majority of Muslims. But, for some reason, the world has chosen only to see and hear *those* men and render the rest of us invisible."

My eyes widened in surprise. He was...right.

"I'm not saying there isn't something insidiously wrong with modern Muslim culture. But Islam wasn't like this. It used to be tolerant." He patted a book, *Islam: A History*. "Islam might be a product of the Dark Ages, but there's evidence of cultural assimilation and reform, and not all of it is bloody. If people are reminded of those times, made aware of their options and that they can choose to exercise them, things will change. They have to change."

"Options? Such as?" Despite the topic of discussion, I was charmed by how little Zayaan had changed.

He'd always been impassioned about his beliefs and showing me the positive side of such things.

"How much time do you have?" he countered with a jaw-breaking yawn.

"Oh, sorry. You're tired." I got up at once, but he forestalled me with a hand on my shoulder.

"Sit, Sims."

He exerted pressure until I sat. Even through the cloth, I felt heat where he touched me, and I flinched. I couldn't stop my reaction. He snatched his hand back and muttered an apology. I scooted back in the chair and tucked my legs beneath me. I didn't dwell on the sensation of Zayaan's hand on my shoulder. I didn't wonder what he was sorry for and why I'd recoiled.

"So, tell me, Zai. In that field between wrong- and right-doing, how do you propose to start a revolution?"

Of course, he didn't want to start any sort of revolution, Zayaan clarified, first and foremost. He only wanted to earn his doctorate, write some papers and boost his platform in academic circles. Maybe he'd write a couple of books in the next few years. He had the outline ready for a nonfiction piece he'd loosely titled *The Muslim and the Infidel*. He planned to continue attending and lecturing at world cross-cultural conferences on behalf of the Share Khan Foundation. He also wanted to teach Islamic philosophy at a prestigious university and other places and impress on young minds that the locus of responsibility for their actions lay solely on them. If he were a finalist in the Miss Universe Pageant, he'd end this lofty list by hoping for world peace.

But he did not want to start a revolution.

I didn't know whether to be impressed by his ambition or alarmed. I decided to be impressed, as I'd given up my right to be alarmed.

We stayed up all night. He entertained me with stories and panegyrical epics from times long past. I was introduced to Omar, the champion of Damascus, and his Christian damsel; to Shayk Nūr al-Dīn and Miriam, the girdle girl; to a prior who'd become an imam and an imam who had wished to be baptized. My favorite one was about a Turkish princess who'd ridden off into the sunset with a Knight Templar. I loved the romanticism of history.

"When I am with you, we stay up all night. When you're not here, I can't go to sleep. Praise God for those two insomnias and the difference between them," I paraphrased the lines Zayaan had whispered to me a thousand times.

How could a poet who'd lived more than seven hundred years ago know our hearts so well? I'd asked Zai a long time ago.

We'd never come up with an answer.

Rumi's words transported us back in time. We became entranced with each other, as we'd been countless times before. I lost my will over my senses, and I couldn't shake my eyes off him. Neither could he off me. His face was shadowed with thick, bristly hair, and it made his lips look white as they pressed together. He swallowed hard. His Adam's apple moved. I looked at it for a brief second. It was enough to break the spell.

A fire started in my cheeks and rippled down to my soles.

Nirvaan, Marjaneh and all the things that haunted me took their sentry positions around my heart once more.

I had no wish to start a revolution, either.

11

For the next two nights, I resorted to sleep aids, deterring any more nocturnal chats. But while my nights were deep and dreamless, my days turned into pure chaos.

We began practicing the dance numbers for the party scheduled for the end of the month. Nirvaan and I would dance to "Nagada," a bass-heavy song from the movie, *Ram-Leela*. The guys had several dances to memorize—solos, duos and group ones. So did I. The guest participants were spread all over the world. All of this was being choreographed and symphonized by dance guru, Hari "Disco" Patel, via video chat.

Bollywood-esque party stoppers, personalized by family members and close friends, were the lifeblood of any *desi* celebration. Strategically placed between the hour of cocktails and dinner, the shows were annoying, to say the least, if you weren't into that sort of loud thing, and boring in the extreme for the guests not close enough to the family to be participants.

No one was allowed to be annoyed or bored at this party. Nirvaan had sent out a mass email to all three hundred guests, inviting them to participate in the dance bonanza in whatever capacity they wished. I'd been horrified to learn that more than a third had emailed back with enthusiasm, some with costume options.

I wasn't at all sure I could hop and shimmy all over the

stage while wrapped in a sari without falling flat on my face. But it wasn't an immediate concern of mine.

The sleeping aid got me relaxed enough to face the day-time Bollywood drama with aplomb. Two torturous days flew by, and before I could cry uncle, it was Radiation Thursday.

Stereotactic radiosurgery was a noninvasive procedure and targeted specifically for brain tumors with little to no associated complications for the patient. It was a piece of cake, as offerings of cancer treatments went.

Nirvaan would check into the hospital the morning of the procedure. His head would be locally anesthetized and fitted with a head brace. He'd go in for an MRI, to facilitate the team of doctors to confirm tumor size and positioning as of the morning, and then wait around until the radiation oncologists figured out the best dosages and angles for the gamma rays to cut or shrink the metastatic tumor significantly. The radiation itself wouldn't take longer than an hour. After which, they'd wait for the anesthesia to wear off before sticking bandages on Nirvaan's head where the brace had been screwed in. All in all, Nirvaan would be home by noon, barring traffic situations.

Still, it upset me when Nirvaan insisted he had this under control, and I should go back to bed. It upset me, yes, but in one cowardly corner of my soul, I was relieved.

At least he'd offered a better excuse than the one he'd given on Monday. He didn't want me anywhere near radiation since we were trying to get pregnant, he'd reasoned.

It was impossible that I'd go back to sleep after the guys left. I had been up since sunrise, had three cups of coffee, shared a huge breakfast with Nirvaan and showered in preparation for the day. And now I had nothing to do but wait in tension till they came back home. Zayaan had promised to text me every fifteen minutes, but...

What did Nirvaan mean by banning me from the radiation, and on Monday, by not coming with me for my IVF appointment? What did he mean by substituting our presence in each other's lives with Zayaan's?

I needed to make sense of what was happening.

It had been impossible to separate from the pack over the last two days and call my shrink, as I'd meant to. And it wasn't as if Nirvaan didn't know about her. When he'd come looking for me eight-odd years ago, I'd told him that a therapist was helping me come to terms with the deaths of my parents. It wasn't a lie. But it had not been the truth, not the whole of it.

After pouring myself a fourth cup of coffee, I called the formidable woman who'd reestablished my faith in myself one heart-to-heart at a time.

She picked up on the first ring. "Hello? Dr. Asha Ambani here."

The calm, melodious voice was a balm to my nerves. "Asha Auntie, it's Simeen." I didn't know why she'd asked me to call her Asha Auntie instead of Dr. Asha or Dr. Ambani on our first meeting. I only knew I'd never addressed her as anything else.

"Simeen, I was expecting your call."

I pictured her face—bespectacled and oval with rounded cheeks that jiggled when she talked, perfect white teeth and fleshy lips that were never without gloss. She was a large woman with an ample bosom that I'd used as my crying pillow during many a therapy session.

"Really?" I said, blinking. "Sarvar called you?"

"He emailed. So, tell me, *bachcha*, how are you doing?"

One of the reasons Dr. Asha Ambani was so successful at her job was because she was the mother most of her clients had never had. She worked exclusively with troubled young women, and somehow, through sheer force of will, she would make us believe she was on our side.

"Physically, I'm fantastic. Emotionally and mentally, I'm floundering," I said, hitting the issue head-on. "I'm angry the cancer is back. I can't bear to think about what's going to happen. I hate seeing Nirvaan like this. I want to make him happy. But I'm afraid I've promised him the moon, and now I don't know how to get it for him. I'm not sure I even want to."

I stopped being vague and poetic. I told her about the IVF and the trust fund...about Zayaan. "He can't want us to be together. He can't. He knows all the reasons why I can't be with Zayaan. He was the one to point out most of them."

From the beginning, or when we'd begun dreaming of marriage, Nirvaan had cautioned me against Zayaan's family and our cultural differences. But I'd put it off as jealousy and bias then.

"He doesn't know the real reason, Simeen. He can't read your mind," she said, a not-so-gentle reminder that I hadn't told Nirvaan about the rape. Even so, she didn't ask me to tell him.

Back then, when it had just happened, she'd told me to do what I thought was best for me. File charges or no. Tell Zayaan about his despicable brother or no. Only once had she counseled me to reconsider keeping a secret from my fiancé, and that was also because she'd known I still abhorred a man's touch. But that had been then, and this was now.

"No. I can't do that to him...to them. I won't allow them to blame themselves for not protecting me that night." Tears crept down my face, but I wasn't crying yet. I got up from the sofa and snatched a few tissues from the coffee table before walking out on the deck.

From inside the house, it looked like another beautiful day in May with picture-perfect blue skies and a jostling of clouds tumbling toward the sun. But chilly air hit me like a bulldozer as soon as I opened the patio doors.

Life was just such a farce. It came in a warm, fuzzy package, but once you opened it, it smacked you hard like Pandora's box.

"He sent Zayaan with me for the IVF consult. And, today, he took Zayaan with him for the radiation. Why is he doing this? What's his game?" I'd been haunted by these questions for the past two days. "Why won't he touch me? What did I do wrong?"

"Do you think he's punishing you for something?" asked Asha Auntie.

"Doh," I said through my nose because I was crying now. I paused to blow it. "No, he's not punishing me. I think he... loves me too much."

I was a bad person. I took and took and took. Then I stole into another man's room in the middle of the night and looked at him with lust.

What's one more Romeo between your thighs, hmm?

My head began to pound. I'd kept the nightmares at bay at night, but I couldn't do anything about them with my eyes open.

"Don't you deserve his love?" Shrinks had a brilliant way with rhetoric. "Do you not love him just as much in return? Haven't you made him happy all these years?"

Cock-teasing bitch. Is this how you keep those motherfuckers sniffing around you?

"Yes. No. I don't know." I wanted to vomit.

Early in our marriage, Nirvaan and I had fought like cats and dogs—mostly about Zayaan, but not in the way most people might expect.

After my rape, I'd broken contact with the guys. I'd made Surin bar them from contacting me, to stop circling me like dogs around a bitch in heat, as people had begun to talk. I was

a young woman now. I wasn't a child running around playing pranks anymore.

Do you want her reputation in shreds? he'd thundered at them.
It had worked. They'd backed off.

On the pretext of a better college education, I'd moved to
Mumbai to live with a cousin, distancing myself even further.
It had been easy to break away from Zayaan, as his family had
been going through their own hell and had moved to London
soon after. Nirvaan hadn't been so easily rebuffed. He'd kept
in touch even though I never returned his calls or replied to
his emails. He kept coming to Mumbai to see me even when
I always stood him up.

Only when I'd moved back to Surat three years later had
he forced the issue by barging into my house. We'd fought
that day. Nirvaan had wanted me to speak to Zayaan. He'd
wanted us to make up and be friends again. He'd wanted to
know why we'd stopped. I'd thrown his latest gold cell phone
to the ground, smashed the screen and walked away. He'd accused me of hiding from life, of being a coward and giving in
to society's demands. I'd retaliated with apathy. But no matter how cold I'd been or how viciously we'd fought, he didn't
leave my side. He hadn't since.

Right after Nirvaan had gotten sick, he'd tried to divorce
me, using our infamous fights as an excuse to shove me away.
When the tactic hadn't worked, he'd tried to convince his
family that I was too young to be stuck with a dying man, that
I'd be better off as a twenty-five-year-old divorcée.

I'd stopped going out. I hadn't wanted to do anything without him. I'd been content to sit by his bed and read. He'd
resented me for that more than anything else. Hated me for
choosing to stay home when he would've sold his soul to go
out and live.

I wasn't as bad now, but Nirvaan was afraid I was heading

down that path again—the lack of desire, feeling, connection. He wanted to make sure I'd have something or someone to live for once he was gone, and that was why he was doing all of this. He fancied himself as Jack, and I was his Rose.

"I know what he's doing, Asha Auntie. But it won't work. He's not some lightbulb I'll replace with a baby when he winks out." And I definitely wasn't going to replace him with Zayaan.

How could I love him still? How could I burn for him right under my husband's nose?

The fact was, no matter how vile Rizvaan's actions had been, his assessment of my character hadn't been wrong.

I was a slut. I was faithless. What was inside of me wasn't normal.

For three years, we'd built up to the night of our eighteenth birthdays.

Of the three of us, Nirvaan was the most adventurous, and most of our shenanigans were his brainstorms. That didn't imply Zayaan and I were content to stand by and twiddle our thumbs. Oh, no. We'd hear out Nirvaan's suggestions and spice them up to the next level.

"Flicked the keys to my aunt's bungalow," Nirvaan said, dangling the bunch in front of our faces. "It's at Ambawadi, not too far, and completely empty for the summer. Better than a hotel room, yeah?" He waggled his eyebrows, looking entirely too pleased with himself.

A thrill shot through me. We'd been in discussions about tonight since Christmas—Zayaan and me, Nirvaan and Zayaan, all three of us on conference calls—but seeing the keys to the bungalow gave it a ring of truth. It was really going to happen, and I was beyond excited. I was electrified. I'd forgotten how to be afraid.

"I'm not sure we should do this. What if you get pregnant?" asked Zayaan, ever the doomsayer.

Nirvaan and I turned to give him the you're-joking-right look.

We'd planned it all out, down to the last condom, and he was still unsure. I'd even gone to a gynecologist a few weeks before to get myself checked and to get a prescription for birth control pills. I'd found the doctor through the recommendation of a recently married classmate. It turned out that pills weren't magic wands and didn't work instantly. I needed to be on them for a month at least, two would be safer.

To be safest, we decided to use more than one prophylactic aid.

Randy and audacious we might be, but we weren't stupid.

"I brought half a dozen boxes of condoms from California, *chodu*. Wear two, one on top of the other, if you think that'll help," said Nirvaan.

I started giggling, and Zayaan cursed Nirvaan for being so flippant all the time.

"And in case something does go wrong—which I highly doubt—you planned to marry anyway. So, it'll be a few years early." Nirvaan shrugged, as if a shotgun marriage at eighteen was no biggie.

No biggie for him maybe. His parents were cool, and he was loaded. But Zayaan and I had a long road to travel before we could commit like that—education and job security, getting a nest egg started, convincing his Medusa of a mother that I was way better than any imam's daughter.

"Are you game? Or are you having second thoughts, too?" Nirvaan asked, quirking an eyebrow at me. He got into his cousin's Opel Astra that he'd borrowed for the night and started the car.

This night was my birthday present, and I wasn't going to

let Zayaan's latent possessiveness or practicality get in my way. He'd already delayed our sexcapade for too long. He hadn't allowed more than smooches and touches until I turned eighteen. To be honest, I was grateful for his sense and restraint, but I didn't want to restrain myself a second longer.

"No second thoughts. We're coming," I said as I pulled Zayaan's arm.

He allowed me to push him into the back seat. I took the front seat, and we were on our way. I turned around, grinning at my sweetie pie. He looked cute and slightly tense. I loved that he worried about me, but he really didn't need to. And I was positive he wanted this as much as Nirvaan and me.

"Hey. It's us, the three of us, like we always planned. And I bought special clothes for tonight. I'm not letting them go to waste."

"Oh, baby, what have you got on...or not got on?" Nirvaan tried to snake his hand under my skirt, but I slapped it away.

The car swerved, and we were blasted with a lot of car horns and shouts from other drivers on the road.

"Drive. Don't kill us before we get there," I said, laughing.

I'd put a lot of thought into my attire and decided on a fairly new print silk shirt, a black thigh-length flared skirt, and brand-new black cotton undergarments. The only thing I wasn't sure about with this whole affair was my body. I couldn't seem to shake off my stick figure. I was hesitant about getting naked. It would get awkward enough without full exposure.

They'd dressed up, too. Nirvaan was in a crisp new Polo shirt and jeans while Zayaan wore a starched white shirt and stonewashed jeans. They smelled identical. Nirvaan always bought them the same cologne on their birthdays. I'd dubbed the scent Nirvana.

Ten minutes into the drive, Nirvaan's mobile began to ring. "Shit. Can you fish it out of my pocket?"

"You're just trying to get me to feel you up first," I said, with an eye roll. But I did as he asked while he made fake orgasmic sounds. I flipped the phone open and put it to his ear.

"Yo! What? Yes. Yes, he is." He jerked his head away from the phone and darted a quick look at Zayaan through the rearview mirror. "It's your *ummi*, man."

Wow. Gulzar Auntie's radar had struck again. How she managed to interrupt our dates every single time, I had no idea. Talk about possessive mothers. As Zayaan didn't have a cell phone, she treated Nirvaan's and mine as if they were Zayaan's.

I made a face but handed the phone over, thinking how surprised Zayaan would be at midnight when we handed him his birthday present—the latest Nokia in lacquer black.

My internal glee faded as Zayaan's expression changed from puzzlement to screaming horror. His face went white, and his ears flashed fuchsia. Most alarming was, he wouldn't meet my eyes.

"Turn the car around. Abu had a heart attack." Zayaan's voice wobbled, but he sucked in a breath and went on, "Rizvaan is in trouble. The police are looking for him. They have an arrest warrant out for him. Abu collapsed after the police left, and my uncles rushed him to the hospital. Ummi's waiting... I need to go. My sisters... I need to... I need..." He looked scared out of his wits. "Fuck. What do I do? What the fuck has Rizvaan done?"

My heart had begun to beat wildly as Zayaan spoke, and now it was lodged in my throat. Nirvaan asked for the phone back and dialed furiously with one hand while whipping the car around in an illegal U-turn. The car swerved madly again, and we just missed hitting a van. Horns blared and drivers shouted at us, but Nirvaan didn't slow down.

Don't think of the accident. Don't fall apart. I shoved my parents' car accident out of my head and held on to the dashboard with both hands.

"Dad, something's happened. Can you meet us at Zai's house in ten minutes? Yeah. It's fucking urgent. Great. And get money." He shut the phone and floored the accelerator. "Don't worry, *yaar*. Dad will take care of everything. You take care of your dad, okay? Okay?"

I swallowed, feeling Zayaan's horror and pain as my own. *Khodai, please let Zai's* abu *be all right. He's a good man.*

Rizvaan was a punk, always getting into trouble, always creating trouble for his family. But I didn't wish bad on him, either.

The guys debated on whether to drop me home first, but I wouldn't hear of it. Zayaan needed me.

We parked the car on the street outside his house. The *jamaat khana* rose behind his house on a parallel street. The two matching buildings were connected by a narrow well-kept garden. The building complex Nirvaan and I lived in was just down the street.

We rushed into the house. There were so many people there. The *mukhi saheb* was a popular man in the community, always there for people in need. It seemed the community was returning the favor. We waded through relatives, neighbors and friends to get to Zayaan's mother.

She sat on a sofa, stiff and unyielding, her sobbing daughters on either side, but when she saw Zayaan, she broke apart. He fell to his knees before her and gathered her up tight in his arms. He kissed her forehead, murmuring assurances over and over.

I stopped short, watching them. It was the first time I'd seen

Gulzar Auntie's head covered. Her face was unveiled, but the way she'd wrapped the long, dark scarf around her head, neck and shoulders made my stomach lurch. It occurred to me that I'd have to cover my head, too, once Zayaan and I married.

Then Kamlesh Desai walked in, and within half an hour the house emptied of people. Zayaan's mother was dispatched to the hospital with a relative and a chunk of money, and Zayaan, Nirvaan and his dad set off for the police station to find out how best they could help Rizvaan. It didn't look good. The police had accused him of planning extremist activities. And he'd absconded.

I took charge of Zayaan's sisters and the house phone, which rang ceaselessly. People kept dropping in with news or to ask for news, and it got exhausting, explaining the same things over and over.

By midnight, the bustle began to taper down, and a couple of matronly neighbors offered to man the fort, coaxing Sofia, Sana, and me to have dinner and go to bed. Relieved, I sat with Zayaan's sisters until they cried themselves to sleep, the poor girls. I left their room door ajar and went down the hall into Zayaan's room to lie down myself.

I'd been in his room only a handful of times. Mostly, it was Zayaan who'd come over to my house, or we'd hang out in different places or at Nirvaan's when he was around. So I looked about in shy curiosity.

I tried to picture myself living here once we were married. The room was big and a bit worn-down. It had two of every-thing—beds, desks, cupboards, windows. I knew he shared the room with his brother, but one side didn't look lived in at all. Rizvaan was rarely home these days, Zayaan had men-tioned. Rizvaan wouldn't even come home at night, and it'd worried their father—justifiably, it would seem.

There was an old picture of Zayaan and his siblings on his

desk hutch—two brothers, standing strong, shoulder to shoulder, their hands resting on the shoulders of their younger sisters. The brothers, only sixteen months apart, seemed like mirror images. These days, Rizvaan looked much older than his nineteen years with his full beard and mustache and hateful eyes—nothing whatsoever like his handsome, scholarly brother.

Zayaan had been awarded scholarships to several universities in India, the UK and the US. Nirvaan wanted him to accept the Stanford scholarship. But I wanted him not to leave me behind. I wasn't clever enough to be offered scholarships, and my brothers couldn't afford to send me abroad to study. And no matter how much I was tempted to race after the guys to the US, I wasn't going to let Nirvaan's dad fund my education.

I was jealous. I admitted it. I was green with envy that the guys would live it up dorm-style for the next four years. Would they even remember my name after those drunken college adventures Nirvaan had vowed they'd have? Would Zayaan fall in love with a smarter, bustier college girl in Stanford? Would he keep his promise to come back and marry me, or would California snare him in her shiny web forever?

I laughed at myself for having such silly doubts. Of course he would come back for me, for his parents, for his sisters. Maybe even his brother. Zayaan understood responsibility and was a man of his word. Nirvaan, I wasn't so sure of.

I picked up another photo frame from the desk. It was from a picnic last year. The guys carried me like a hammock between them. They were laughing as I was screaming. Moments after it'd been taken, they'd flung me into the Tapi River and dived in after me.

I yawned, blinking at the alarm clock on Zayaan's desk. My birthday was way past over. And from what I could tell, the guys' birthdays would be spent shuttling between the police station, hospital and search parties. So, we'd unwrap our presents a few days late this year. No biggie. Family came first.

Yawning again, I got under the blanket on Zayaan's bed with the photo. One way or another, I was sleeping with my guys tonight, I decided with a smile.

I didn't think I'd fall asleep. And I couldn't have slept for long. When I woke, I was still clutching the frame to my chest. The ceiling lights were bright in my eyes. Even so, Rizvaan looked positively menacing as he loomed over me. He was such a creep.

I sat up and swung my legs off the bed, arranging my skirt beneath the blanket. I looked at the wide-open doors of the room and his cupboard with relief. There was a half-filled duffel bag open on his bed.

Is he running away or surrendering?

He smirked, like he knew I was uncomfortable with him in the room, but he turned his back on me without saying a word and resumed stuffing his clothes in the bag. He didn't even zing me with some jaundiced comment about sleeping in Zayaan's bed, and for a moment, I was nonplussed.

I stood up, thinking he must be too stressed about jail or whatever to be nasty to me. "It's good you came home," I said, setting the picture back on the desk. "Everyone is so worried. Abu is in the hospital and—"

"Abu?" He cut me off, his mockery making my back stiffen. "Ah, yes, my dear *abu*, who has blessed the union of my little brother and his little slut." He chuckled, as if greatly amused. "You've fooled everyone, haven't you, with your good-girl act?"

A door clicked shut, and I prayed it was the cupboard I'd heard.

Before I even turned from the desk, I knew how much trouble I was in. Blood began to pound through me. The veins in my wrists, my temple, my neck throbbed. My heart started hammering against my chest, and I wondered if it would break my rib cage and leap out.

I wanted to run and pound on the door till someone opened it. I should've screamed the house down.

But I couldn't move. I'd frozen at the sight of the gun in his hand.

"Let me out of the room, Rizvaan. You're in enough trouble as it is." I hoped I sounded bolder than I felt.

He nodded, many times. "Yes, I am."

The solid sincerity in his words jarred me. In that moment, I realized there was nothing I could do or say to stop what was going to happen next. Rizvaan knew he was doomed. Tonight, he'd either be locked away or be ostracized forever. He wasn't going to go down alone. That, too, was clear on his face.

He wanted someone to blame, and he'd found me.

Yet I pleaded with him. I begged him to care about his father, his mother and his sisters, who were sleeping just down the hall. I begged him to think of his brother, of his family's reputation. I warned him of the women in the living room who'd hear the gun go off.

Please, Khodai, let him shoot me fast.

He laughed.

"Those aunties were snoring like whales," he said, "when I walked past them."

He was entertained by the idea of them startling awake and screaming at the gunshot. He estimated by the time they labored their fat bodies up the stairs and succeeded in breaking down the door, he'd be long gone out the window. The only hitch in the scenario was he didn't want to shoot me. It was too easy a sentence for the countless times I'd snubbed him.

When he told me point-blank what he intended, I threw up.

"*Tcha, tcha, tcha.* None of that now. Think of it as a bargain—your life in exchange for your virtue. As for your reputation, it'll be our secret. You're good at keeping secrets, aren't you? You and your Romeos…you think you've been so clever, fooling everyone. But I know. I've always known about you. What's one more Romeo between those beautiful thighs, hmm?"

It happened fast. One second, he was debating on how to exact my pound of flesh, and the next, he was on me. I didn't know how he'd come close enough to press the gun to my forehead.

"Lie down."

I was numb. I felt such terror and disbelief and revulsion that I couldn't breathe. My throat closed, and I didn't think I could've screamed even if I'd tried.

I didn't try. I could only beg.

He pushed me down on Zayaan's bed. I believe he did that on purpose. He straddled me when I struggled, caught my jaw in a bruising grip when I tried to bite him. He reminded me that if I didn't care to be a good girl, there would be hell to pay—and not just for me.

He tore my flimsy panties off with one hand. The hand pressing the gun to my cheek didn't even tremble. He fumbled with his jeans and pulled his cock out. I didn't know why I was watching.

I cried when he penetrated me—not because it hurt, though it did. I cried because he was surprised I was a virgin. He called it a bonus. He didn't smirk. He wasn't cruel. He looked so much like Zayaan that my heart shattered.

I closed my eyes. I couldn't bear to look at him then.

But I snapped them open when I smelled him. He'd sprayed Zayaan's cologne on himself. I dry heaved, sobbing uncontrollably. When he finished, he thanked me for my cooperation and spit on my face.

I'd always known evil existed in the world. That night, I realized it lived inside me.

12

My talk with Asha Auntie lasted for over an hour and afterward I sat on the deck for a long time, staring at the horizon. Thoughts danced in my head like tumbleweed on a windy day. None of them made sense. Yet, all of them did.

I wondered at which point the ocean blended into the sky, or night started masquerading as day, or what happened when life bled into death.

Zayaan theorized such questions were the constructs of an active imagination, of man's inability to remain undefined. Because some things had no definition, we made them precious and beautiful, abstract and blurred.

It's the horizon. It's twilight. This is a soul, and that's heaven.

My mother had disliked whiskey, and my father would drink nothing else.

One man's Ohrmazd is another man's Ahriman, had been Daddy's way of explaining the inexplicable.

The same was true of sex. The same act of penetration but without consent and love became rape.

Eventually, my thoughts stopped bouncing from horizon to sky, from the past to the present, and went quiet. It was so quiet that I once again became aware that I lived at the edge of an ocean and far, far away from Surat. The neighbor's dogs were chasing the seagulls out for their morning meal. The few people strolling along the beach were in jackets. The sun was out, and the air was blue.

I was dressed for hospital cold. I wore a long-sleeved T-shirt and a mohair sweater with my jeans. My hair was brushed, and my face was creamed with tinted sunblock. I was dressed with nowhere to go—just like that night twelve years ago.

I shuddered out a sigh. *Let it all go.*

A crisp breeze shook the clump of Monterey cypress demarcating our property from the neighbors' on our left. Below, hardy ice plants grew out of sand and rocks. They weren't in bloom yet, not like the Japanese camellias. Hither and thither were bursts of purple flowers and waxy green foliage. It was a pretty house we lived in with a pretty view.

And I was a slut.

I'd known better than to say that over the phone. Asha Auntie would've taken the words as a personal failure, not to mention been disappointed in me for regressing to victim blaming. My head knew how stupid the thought was, but that broken, shriveled up thing hiding inside me refused to agree.

If only I hadn't teased Rizvaan or flaunted my convent-school Queen's English in his face.

If only I hadn't worn strapless dresses or paraded about in shorts.

If only I hadn't fallen asleep in Zayaan's room.

If only I'd stayed asleep or kept my mouth shut.

If only I hadn't loved two boys...

I stood up. I wouldn't let my idle mind become the devil Ahriman's workshop. I needed to do something physical, exhausting.

It was too cold and windy to walk on the beach. I thought about setting the house to rights, but I'd cleaned and mopped and dusted and wiped only yesterday.

As promised, Zayaan texted me with an update. This one

was accompanied with a video clip of Nirvaan getting fitted with the head brace. Anticipating the removal of tiny patches of hair on his head where he'd be injected with local anesthesia before the pins were screwed in, Nirvaan had buzzed off most of his hair in a short military cut. We'd also been warned that his hair would probably fall from those sections in the next two weeks and might not grow back at all.

Nirvaan blew me a kiss and said he was trying on his Halloween outfit. "Call me Gamma Ray Hornet. *Muahahaha.*" He pestered the radiologist who was intently screwing a pin into his left temple to blow me a kiss, too.

That decided it.

I went into the house, my spine uncurling with determination. I got ready for a long, brisk walk, locked up the house and set off toward the hospital. It was barely five minutes away in a car. It took me a good twenty to walk there.

I would not allow Nirvaan to shut me out of his life. He could protect me all he wanted. He could take care of my future, even force me to abide by his nonsensical Titanic Wish List, but he had no right to shelter me from the wicked. He couldn't anyway, as fate had proven over and over.

I never used to be weak. And, frankly, I was tired of feeling helpless. It was time this turtle broke out of her shell.

Once I reached the hospital, slightly sweaty but not out of breath, I checked in at the front desk and slapped a visitor's sticker over my heart. I didn't look at Nirvaan or Zayaan as I stalked into Radiology and plunked myself down on a seat next to my husband in the waiting area. He wore a hospital gown with his arm connected to an IV drip and earphones plugged into his ears beneath the head brace. He was watching *The Godfather* on the tablet.

I imagined he was surprised. Though, when I finally met his eyes, he looked more thoughtful than curious. Zayaan, on the other hand, had his lower lip caught between his teeth, as if he was trying hard not to smile. His nostrils flared, and his eyes fairly danced with humor.

"Everything we do, we do together," I repeated the Awesome Threesome's mantra. I felt as if a tremendous burden had lifted off my chest. I shot them both a narrow-eyed look. "Within reason, okay?"

Then I laced my fingers with my husband's and settled in to wait for the MRI results.

The ringmaster of Nirvaan's team of doctors gave him a two thumbs-up approval to go hiking on the weekend.

After the Gamma Knife procedure, Nirvaan slept for a total of twenty-eight hours, getting up only to eat and use the loo.

By Friday evening, he was his usual intractable self although he admitted to feeling tender and itchy in the spots the pins had been poked into his head. That was normal—one of the few normal happenings in this house. And by then, the bandages the nurse had dressed his head in had to be taken off anyway. He complained of a headache but nothing he couldn't stand, he assured the oncologist and me. The headache being the only reason he was home on a Friday night, he added, affecting a martyr's moue worthy of Bhagat Singh, India's illustrious freedom fighter.

So, late Saturday morning, we loaded the Jeep with camping equipment and drove south to the Los Padres National Forest in the Big Sur Valley. We met up with Sarvar and his party of five at the campground's designated parking lot, and from there, we set off on an easy five-mile hike to our reserved campsite.

The nature trail meandered through the forest, jumping over a stream, bridging a gorge, leading to a clearing at the edge of a cliff that dropped fifty feet down to a rocky cove.

The campsite had a single cabin with a kitchenette, a bathroom and a separate toilet—the only reason I'd agreed to go camping. I wasn't about to let Nirvaan sleep in a tent where insects and Khodai knew what else could bite him. Even though his nervous system had been pumped full of intravenous antibiotics just days before, I worried. I'd disinfected the puncture sites and sealed them with fresh waterproof bandages and a knit cap, making him swear on his mother that he wouldn't take it off for the whole trip.

Hour after hour passed in the midst of nature without any mishaps, and I began to relax, even enjoy myself. Name one girl who wouldn't bask in the attentions of seven clever, cute and courteous guys.

Sarvar had brought his best bud, Zeus, an American-born Parsi whom I knew very well. Zeus was a great grizzly bear of a man with a voice to match. He was an intellectual property lawyer in the IT industry and was doing pretty well for himself. I loved him like a brother. I especially loved his quirky *bawaji* ways that he held on to for dear life even though he'd never stepped foot in India.

Physically, my brother couldn't have been more different from his best friend. Sarvar was soft-spoken and almost dainty in appearance. He was short, like me. I guessed my family had patented the petite gene, as even Surin wasn't a big man.

But where it counted most, Sarvar and Zeus were like two peas in a pod. They both loved Parsi food, especially *dhansak*. They both were passionate about work and old black-and-white films—an acquired taste, to be sure. And they both were self-professed bachelors. They wouldn't marry unless and until lightning struck them stupid.

And here I was, a woman whom lightning had struck twice, doubling my stupid quotient. Stupid and confused—that was what I felt around Zayaan and around Nirvaan, too, sometimes.

I groaned, stopping to take a sip of water, and then clipped the steel bottle back on my pack. My thighs, my back, my arms hurt.

Rick, one of the hikers from the group, came up behind me on the trail. "You okay?" he asked.

The others bounded ahead of us.

I nodded, refusing to give up, and trudged on.

It was the first time I'd met Rick, Manoj and Jason—gym buddies of my brother and Zeus. The five had recently started training for a marathon together. Rick and Manoj were family men, and Jason, the oldest of the group at forty-two, was as yet unattached but hopeful. He was gay. He hadn't told me that, but I'd guessed.

As the day wore on and I got comfortable with them, I began to appreciate being the only girl in the group. Except for Zayaan, none of them threatened my peace of mind, and I let my guard down enough to flirt back.

After setting up two triple-occupancy tents in front of the cabin I'd reserved for Nirvaan and me, we took another nature trail down to the cove. The rocky inlet seemed to be a perfect place for cannonballing, and the guys began discussing a variety of height and ledge options to try out. When I heard mention of diving off the top of a cliff, I put my foot down about Nirvaan jumping from anywhere. I literally sat on his lap, so he'd sit this one out.

The sun hit the huge boulder we were sitting on, cozily warming us, as we watched the group roughhouse around us. I closed my eyes, relaxing in my husband's arms, with the sun's rays on my skin and the echoes of masculine banter in my ears. I might've dozed off, but I awoke instantly when Nirvaan adjusted the cap I'd pulled over my face and kissed my earlobe.

"Don't make any sudden moves," he murmured when I would've squirmed. His arm tightened around me, keeping me still, and I fought off my instinct to break free. "Easy, baby. Look down, on the right."

I looked and swallowed a gasp. A baby seal was poised on the edge of our boulder where it dipped into the ocean. It stared at us, eyes round and unblinking, its tail swishing in the water. Suddenly, it heaved up and settled on its flappers in a mermaid pose. Its skin was patchy, not the smooth dark gray pelt one saw on mature elephant seals. I wondered about its gender. I knew mature males had an ugly proboscis-like snout protruding from their faces. This one didn't have it. It was cute, in truth, with a large button nose and silvery whiskers that twitched as it sniffed.

The lagoon had gone silent, I realized. One by one, the others began to join us on the boulder as quietly as they could manage.

"Is he sick?" Zayaan's question rumbled close to my right shoulder, soft and gravelly.

My skin erupted in goose bumps, but I pretended it was the sight of the baby seal and not his voice affecting me.

"No. He's shedding," Jason whispered.

He slowly reached for his discarded jeans, pulled out a slim camera and began clicking. The guys had, of course, stripped down to their underwear before diving, their clothes piled in a minimountain on one side of the boulder.

The seal heaved forward and stopped inches in front of me. We were totally face-to-face. This time, I couldn't hold in my gasp.

"Um, guys? Why is it looking at me like I'm his next meal?" I muttered through the corner of my mouth. I wondered if seals had sharp teeth.

"I think he's fallen in love, baby," said Nirvaan, his chest vibrating with mirth.

"Shut up," I whispered, even though I preferred his interpretation of the staring match to mine.

"He's right, Sims," Zeus said in distinct amusement.

But his thick not-quite-a-whisper distracted my new suitor. The seal turned to him in much the same way—all agog and in love.

We burst into laughter, all of us, except for Zeus. It was a crazy, wonderful moment, and my heart overflowed with joy. The seal hitched another foot forward, looking highly amused, too. It began sniffing the air, splitting its attention between Zeus and me.

"Holy wow," I said when the seal pushed forward on its stomach and put its nose against my booted foot.

It nudged me, hard. An electric current passed through my leg and up my body, and I valiantly tried not to wiggle or scream.

"Someone please tell me that seals are vegetarians," I squeaked when it nudged my boot again. "Will it bite me? Should I move? What does it want me to do?"

"Don't make any sudden moves, and you'll be fine," said Jason, though he didn't sound convinced of his own advice. He sat down next to me, taking picture after picture. "He's just curious, like we are about him. Good thing he isn't fully grown, huh?"

Oh, wonderful thing.

I wasn't afraid of animals. Nirvaan and I had swum with dolphins in the Bahamas and gone deep-sea diving among sharks on the Gold Coast. I'd even wrapped a yellow-skinned python around my neck in Bali. But those had been controlled experiences with expert staff ready to jump in at the first sign of trouble. I'd had confidence that I was safe to some extent.

In comparison, this experience was wild and scary and oh so Hogwarts.

We were all mutually enraptured by the friendly baby seal. I named him Tickles, as Jason was sure the pup was male. And Tickles got so comfortable with us that, at one point, he heaved himself onto my lap. Imagine, I had a three-foot-long, two-foot-wide, seventy-pound wild animal in my lap.

As I was sitting in Nirvaan's lap, his "Holy fuck" adequately described my sentiments, too.

The other guys were in splits by this time, cracking jokes about lap seals.

Then, the seal belched, setting everyone off again. He'd smelled fishy to begin with, but when he opened his mouth—*ugh*. You did not want to be near a seal when it opened its mouth, trust me.

Sarvar said, "*Ka-pow*. He's a male, all right. That was a five-star belch."

"He's probably lost. Some species of seals come ashore in spring to molt for a month or two. This one seems to have broken from his herd, or maybe he's just a rebel, looking for his own turf to flop in the sun now that he's been weaned off mama." Jason was a fount of marine life information.

His commentary made me bold enough to pat Tickles on his back. He was surprisingly warm to touch. His fur was silky smooth where it was still there, and his skin was mottled where he'd already begun to shed in patches. Just like Nirvaan. I felt absurdly maternal toward the baby seal—and my husband—at this moment. I wondered if he'd let me hug him.

But the minute I placed my hand on Tickles's head, he slid off my lap and wiggled toward Zeus, who yelped in fright.

"No, no. Not here, buddy. Fuck. What the hell is it doing? Get away from my nuts!"

Tickles buried its nose between Zeus's legs, grunting and

sniffing. It was such a comedic sight that I wondered if we'd ever stop laughing. The guys, of course, were making extremely crude jokes to the utter horror of Zeus.

The enchanting episode lasted for a good half hour. At the end, Tickles slid back into the water and swam away without so much as a backward glance. We watched his head bob up and down in the water, moving farther and farther away from us.

I felt blessed to have experienced this at all, yet I felt horrible because I'd never see Tickles again. I started crying. "He was just a baby...just a lost, sweet little baby..."

Nirvaan rocked me in his arms, murmuring inane words of comfort, telling me over and over what a great mother I was going to be. He was having a hard time holding his own tears in.

The enormity of the experience hit us all. We sat there for a long time, not talking, not laughing, staring out into the ocean where Tickles had disappeared. I hoped with all my heart that he would find his way home. When I finally stopped crying, we rose and lumbered back to camp.

Nirvaan fell asleep right after a dinner of sandwiches that Sarvar had bought from his favorite bakery, and hot canned soup.

My sandwich was pesto, ham and cheese on focaccia. It was delicious, definitely gourmet, filling and prepackaged for longevity. My stomach was a happy camper, not so much my head, though.

I wasn't sleepy at all. With Nirvaan settled in bed, I took a quick shower and changed into pajamas. I sprayed insect repellent all over me and went out of the cabin.

Forest regulations didn't allow campfires, so electric lanterns and the cabin's porch light lit pockets of our camp.

The guys were playing poker on one of the picnic tables. Music wafted out of someone's phone—Sarvar's, if I guessed correctly, as the playlist was the hits of the '80s.

I avoided looking at Zayaan. I'd tried to avoid him all day. I'd kept a minimum of six feet and a slew of other men between us, but it hadn't worked. It was like he was the sun, and my senses were orbiting planets.

I declined the guys' invitation to join the game. Instead, I fished a beer out of the cooler and made my way to the cliff's lookout point. I sat, dangling my legs over the edge, and watched the water rippling in the breeze while slowly enjoying the beer.

When branches snapped beneath someone's boots behind me, I wished with all my heart that it were Zayaan coming to me. I wanted to talk to him. About Tickles. About Nirvaan. About us. About a baby. *Am I really suited for motherhood?*

I wanted to kiss him. I wanted him to kiss me.

My brother tugged my braid. It hurt just enough to bring me back to my senses.

"What a day, huh, Sissy?" Sarvar plopped down beside me.

It was an old nickname my brothers had for me—Sissy. It meant sister when they were full of love for me. But if I'd annoyed them, it meant pain in the ass.

He put his arm around me and stole a sip of my beer.

"A magical day, Savvy. One of the best days of my life," I whispered, resting my head on his shoulder.

But like all days, even good ones had to come to an end.

13

All too soon, it was our birthday weekend.

We drove into LA on Thursday, three days early, to help with the last-minute frenzy of the party. We hadn't even stepped out of the Jeep, and we were accosted by the event planner, Neelu Patel, regarding last-minute details, changes and glitches. Then there were people to greet, caterers to meet and guests to receive. Dozens of rooms had been blocked off for the out-of-towners at the Desai motel closest to the house.

Hari Patel had set up camp in the sunroom, summoning specific groups in a never-ending parade to perfect the dance moves they'd learned via videos. The final practice had been scheduled for the morning of the party for the whole ensemble. All of that was above and beyond the daily minutiae occurring at my in-laws' house.

But first, we dropped in to see Ba.

Nirvaan's grandmother was a robust ninety-eight-year-old woman who still walked without aid, was in full custody of her faculties and could out-bet the fiercest gambler under the table in rummy. Wrinkled and jolly, she'd only ever worn the widow's white since her husband's passing.

I touched her feet.

She caressed my head, and as she had hundreds of times

before, she blessed me for posterity, "May Lord Krishna grant you a fertile life."

I'd often wondered at the pros and cons of the blessing, but today, I focused on the pros.

Nirvaan and Zayaan touched her feet, too, but they got a combined, tepid "*Jai Shree* Krishna," instead.

"Sexy, you're looking hot as usual," said Nirvaan, bending to noisily kiss both of Ba's weathered cheeks. "The ole geezers at the temple still giving you the eye? Anyone I need to beat up?"

I'd said this before, and I'd say it forever. My husband was an adorable, charming nut.

And he came by the craziness honestly because his grandmother gave him a haughty look and replied, "What makes you think I can't handle those dementia patients myself?"

Zayaan boomed out a laugh and enveloped Ba in his arms, kissing her forehead, as I'd seen him kiss his mother's on numerous occasions. "A woman after my own heart. Since I'm not an old geezer and probably stand a better chance at keeping up with you, let's get married, sexy," he teased, getting a pert smack on his head for his trouble.

"One marriage was enough, thank you very much. But since you think you're such a hotshot, you can be my date for the party," she slickly countered.

With such a promising start to our stay, the guys excused themselves to deal with the guests and left us girls to gossip.

Ba lay down for her afternoon nap, drawing a thick *godra*-style paisley-printed quilt over her narrow body. I took a seat on the bed by her hip and updated her on Nirvaan's health and asked about hers.

"I'm fine. *He* looks well. Happier than the last time," she said, patting my hand.

The last time we'd seen Ba was when we still lived here, in

this house. We'd just found out about the metastasized tumor, and Nirvaan had smashed the TV in our room in his rage. He'd ripped the flat screen from the wall and flung it to the floor. It had missed my feet by mere inches. Nirvaan had apologized profusely. He'd not meant to fling it at me—he'd told me so—but I wasn't convinced of his intentions, even now.

"It's Zayaan's doing. His company has made all the difference," I answered, gently pulling her gnarled, achy fingers the way she liked it.

Ba snorted, a shrewd glimmer in her eyes. "And the trouble you went to in convincing that rascal husband of yours to continue his treatments is not the reason? Waiting on him hand and foot, following him about the globe in his mad race against time, is not the reason? Don't sell yourself short, girl."

"I'm not doing anything a wife wouldn't do. And his anger isn't—wasn't unjustified, was it?"

Ba snorted again, and I had to smile.

"All right, I won't sell myself short," I said.

"Good. Now go. I need a rest before my date with that other rascal."

I left Nirvaan's pistol of a grandmother to nap and went in search of his mother with the scent of sandalwood incense clinging to my clothes and laughter curving my lips.

The Desai household became the communal hub for the weekend.

Besides the twenty immediate family members actually staying in the house—Nirvaan's parents, Ba, Nisha's family, the three of us, my father-in-law's sister's family who'd flown in from Surat, not to discount the housekeeper and her husband and extra hired staff for the party—a good chunk of the invitees kept dropping in and out for various reasons. Good thing my in-laws' sprawling fifteen-thousand-square-foot mansion had been built with large families in mind.

The township of Irvine was located several miles south of Los Angeles, and though independently run, it was considered part of LA's greater metropolitan area. Nirvaan's family lived in the Northwood village of Irvine on roughly two acres of flat land with the Santa Ana Mountains at our back. Right now, the back garden was stockpiled with tables and chairs and deflated tents.

Nirvaan and I had our own suite of rooms in a secluded wing with a private entrance in and out of the house. Even so, my in-laws had warned the guests to keep away, and though the rest of the house was treated like a tourist attraction, no one barged in on us all through the weekend—except for Nikita and Armaan, Nirvaan's niece and nephew. Not that Nirvaan or I would've minded the invasion of our privacy during the festivities, but he had before when he was sick. Well-meaning visitors had dropped in at any odd hour to ask after his health. It was how close-knit large communities functioned, and Nirvaan had loved the unsolicited attention, even while hating the prattle that had gone with it.

It was one of the reasons we'd moved to Carmel after our year of globe-trotting. The American-Gujarati community hadn't yet sunk its talons into the Monterey Bay area—at least, not residentially. No one could just drop in for tea and *maal-mishtan*. They'd have to make a special trip to come see us.

On Friday afternoon, after a grueling group *garba* dance practice, I wasn't quick enough to slip out with the guys, and I found myself caught in the net of some gossipy young women.

"Simeen, come sit with us. It's been ages since we spoke to you, *yaar*," said Dipti, one of Nirvaan's cousins.

I could've pointed out that she had my cell number, but I didn't. I hadn't bothered to keep in touch, either.

"*Arre ya*, tell us what's going on," said Meera, the wife of one of Nirvaan's friends. She patted the plastic chair next to her. "What's the prognosis? Any change? Is the tumor really incurable?"

I sat and simply looked at her, willing her not to go where I knew she would. She didn't get the message.

"Can't the doctor just cut it out? He was doing so well two years ago."

Another friend's wife, whose name escaped me at the moment, gave her two cents' worth of advice, too. "You should've stayed put instead of traveling. All that eating out and running about must not have been good for him. You should've made him stay home and recuperate."

I resisted the urge to roll my eyes at the twenty-odd women drinking masala chai, snacking on *bhel puri* and *samosa chaat*, and nitpicking about the way I took care of my husband.

Most were around my age. Nirvaan had grown up with some of them or their husbands. At the outset of our marriage, they'd been a part of our intimate circle of friends. We'd done everything together as couples and individually—holidayed, shopped and socialized.

After Nirvaan had fallen ill, we'd been dropped from the group. We hadn't been able to keep up with their schedules of entertainment, and one fine day, we'd stopped receiving invitations. I'd tried to keep in touch with the women, but it hadn't been the same. I'd realized fast that they were not my friends. They were Nirvaan's, and I'd been accepted into their circle only for his sake.

Yet I sat there and let them ask me impertinent questions. They were guests of my in-laws, after all. I answered as plainly as possible, but cancer was a subject that made most people curl their lips in discomfort or distaste.

The talk quickly turned toward children, then fashion, then movie stars and, finally, community gossip.

Who was getting divorced? Who was having an affair and with whom? Whose child was in trouble? Whose mother-in-law was a tyrant?

Apparently, most of theirs were.

"You're so lucky to have Kiran Auntie for a mother-in-law, Simeen. She's so noninterfering. She lets you do whatever you want, live however you want. My mother-in-law? She drives me nuts with her crassness and demands."

Oh, these women didn't have a clue, did they? I didn't mock them or belittle their troubles. For every person, their own problems were huge.

But I did comment that I truly wouldn't mind exchanging Nirvaan's cancer for a mother-in-law who was a tyrant. Then I left them to enjoy their tea and talk behind my back.

I walked as fast as my legs could carry me. I'd surely have snapped had I sat there any longer. As it was, I was having a hard time blinking back my tears. This was why we'd left LA—this *nosiness.*

I cursed my fate. It was PMS. My period was five pills away, which meant my IVF cycle was scheduled to start in three days.

Bloody, bloody hell, Nirvaan.

I sailed into my bedroom—well, not exactly the bedroom but the sitting room leading into the bedroom—and ran smack into Zayaan, who came out from the bathroom.

"Hey. Easy, easy," he said, holding my elbows and steadying me.

He'd showered. His hair was wet, slickly combed off his face, and he looked all crisp and spiffy in dark jeans and a black shirt. And I was all gross and stinky from the *garba* dance.

He frowned as I blinked and blinked at him. "What's the matter?"

To hell with stinky grossness, clueless women and bloody, bloody Nirvaan.

I wrapped my arms about him, pressed my face into his chest and let the tears fall. He went stiff, but his arms came around me and squeezed me hard. I didn't say anything. I didn't have to. Zayaan knew me. He was my friend as much as he was Nirvaan's.

At last, the tears stopped falling, but I didn't step away. I couldn't, not yet. Neither did he.

"Better?" He stroked my hair down my back again and again.

I wanted to purr like a cat.

"I might be allergic to the female bonding ritual." I tilted my head back to look up at him.

He'd stopped frowning. He now looked completely flummoxed.

I giggled and sniffed at the same time. "You and Nirvaan have spoiled me with your up-front, no-nonsense bullshit. I suppose it could've started with Surin and Sarvar. They made sure I played with tin soldiers and not Barbie dolls, but now, I don't know how to deal with women…friends." I hoped I was making sense.

I must have been, for Zayaan's face cleared of confusion, and he smiled. "You don't need to, if you don't want to. You have us."

"I know," I agreed. *I have you for now.* I had them both for now. With a harsh sigh of regret, I let go of Zayaan.

But nothing was ever simple. Nirvaan's sister, Nisha, stood in the doorway to my room, her face unsmiling and accusatory, and all I could think was, *Crap. Not her again. Anyone but her.*

★ ★ ★

Nisha didn't ask me why I'd been crying in Zayaan's arms. She drew her conclusions and warned me not to be stupid.

"Don't be stupid, Simeen," she said exactly that once Zayaan left the room.

She'd brought jewelry I'd wear to the party. I took the box from her, and without looking at it, I locked it away in my cupboard.

I didn't wonder at the cryptic bit of advice or pretend outrage at her innuendo. The world had never understood the bond the three of us shared, and it never would. Our so-called friends were already fascinated by our living arrangement, making lewd jokes in passing—which, if taken seriously, wouldn't have been funny at all.

Nirvaan chose to ignore the comments or joined in, depending on his mood. Last night, when some of his LA friends had come over for coffee after dinner, he'd gone on and on about the Tickles episode. Apart from its magic, it'd also disclosed that I'd gone camping with seven men. Never mind that, of the seven, one was my husband, another was my brother, a third was brother-like, one was gay and two were happily married. No, his friends had looked from me to Zayaan and pinned our names to the top of the Summer Scandals list.

For that reason alone, I decided to heed Nisha's advice. From then on, I was extra careful about how I behaved around Zayaan. As Zayaan had said, Nirvaan didn't have to deal with the aftermath of his actions or wishes. We did.

Another reason for circumspection was Gulzar Auntie and Marjaneh. Zayaan had been on his way to the airport to pick up his mother, his girlfriend and his youngest sister, Sana, when I'd accosted him with my hug. With his mother around now, it became easy to maintain my distance from him, especially since he'd moved into the hotel with them. Though, they spent most of the day at the house.

I went so far as to befriend Marjaneh and make her feel welcome and part of the group. I knew what it felt like to know only one person in a sea of strangers and the panic you felt when he left you alone time and again. Though I noticed Zayaan didn't leave Marjaneh's side as much as Nirvaan had left mine when we first married. But Nirvaan was a social butterfly, the life of any party, flitting around and holding court, while Zayaan was content to linger in the background, like me.

Whatever monster I'd conjured Marjaneh as, she actually turned out to be quite the charmer, much like Nirvaan. She was heart-stoppingly beautiful, I acknowledged with a pang. Strict about the sharia dress laws, she kept herself covered in a headscarf and full-sleeved tops and pants.

Though she wasn't averse to shedding her conservative attire for modest swimwear, I noticed, when a bunch of us spent a few hours at Laguna Beach on Friday evening. It was too gorgeous a day—upper seventies and bright—to pass up building castles in the sand.

"He's making a big mistake," said Nirvaan.

I looked up from excavating the main door of my potential sand castle and noticed my husband scowling at Zayaan and Marjaneh. She was chattering. He was laughing. They were waist-deep in the water, standing about three feet apart.

Apparently, Marjaneh's offense was that she made Zayaan laugh.

"Sure. He looks perfectly miserable around her," I said, returning my attention to my painstaking excavations. My finger dug a bit too hard, and the mound split in half. I took a deep breath, counted to ten and pressed it closed again. Then, with a gentler touch, I restarted my castle building.

I wasn't jealous. I wouldn't allow myself to be jealous. We'd established long ago that I couldn't have both my guys. I'd have to be content with one or none. And I'd chosen my one.

Not the type to give up easily, Nirvaan muttered, "She'll stifle him. She's too rigid in her ways, and she'll make him just like her."

I was incredulous. "Rigid? She's wearing a swimsuit. And she's smart and beautiful, in case you haven't noticed," I pointed out. A breeze whipped my hair into my face, and I shook my head, as my hands were full of sand.

My husband tucked locks of my hair behind my ears. "You're smart and beautiful, baby," he said very seriously. "He might be laughing, but his body language is restrained. He's too well-behaved around her."

"Honey, explain to me how that's bad."

But Nirvaan had me observing Zayaan, too.

"You know the darkness in him. He gets too serious. He constantly faces opposition and negativity in his work. It will suck him in. If I…if we don't show him the lighter side of life, he won't be our Zayaan for long."

I got what Nirvaan was saying. More than once, we'd pulled Zayaan out of a funk during our glory days when he'd been torn between the stricter dictates of his religion and what he felt in his heart. I also recalled the topics Zayaan was research-ing for his thesis. But if my husband expected me to take up responsibility for Zayaan's soul, he was out of luck.

I shrugged. "He's made his choice. He's not stupid. And we have no right to interfere in his life. Even if you think we do."

"I'm just saying, he'll be miserable," Nirvaan said stub-bornly.

But he left it at that.

Strangely, I had the feeling that my husband was jealous. But Nirvaan didn't have a jealous bone in his body. He was openhearted and giving and magnanimous and wonderful. Wasn't he? And what did it mean that he wasn't jealous about sharing me, but was about sharing Zayaan?

"Sana thinks so, too," he said after he'd fashioned a moat around our castle.

"You spoke to Zai's baby sister about this?" I'd been sitting on my haunches, and I plunked down on my butt in shock. *Ugh.* Now I had sand inside my bikini. "He'll kill you if he finds out."

"Why would he? I spoke to him, too." He dropped another bomb, shrugging.

This was too much. "Nirvaan, stop. Look at me. Explain this now."

"I asked him why he hadn't proposed to Marjaneh already, what was holding him up. They've known each other for a long time. Have been dating for a long time." He paused, his eyes narrowing on my face. If he wanted me to react to this information, again, he was out of luck. Nirvaan went on. "He gave excuses. His work. Her work. His sisters. He wants Sofia and Sana to be settled first." He snorted in clear skepticism.

"Why are those excuses? You know he worries about them."

"I didn't ask why he hadn't married her. I asked why he hadn't officially or even unofficially committed to her."

I glanced away from my husband's knowing gaze. I'd wondered the same thing for some time. "So? It doesn't mean anything."

"Doesn't it? I asked Sana. She agrees. Marriage is something their *ummi* wants rather than what Zai or Marjaneh want. And if we don't show him a way out, he'll let himself get trapped in his mother's schemes."

I laughed bitterly. "You think he'll feel any less trapped by your games? You think he wants us? Wants me instead? Give it up, Nirvaan, whatever it is you've planned to safeguard my future, because I won't have it." I didn't want it. I wanted peace. I wanted to be free. With Zayaan, I'd never be free.

"I haven't planned anything. I'm not a dictator," said Nirvaan, his words sharp as a blade. "I'm merely pointing out options."

I raised an eyebrow in disbelief.

"That's all, baby. Possibilities." Then he took my hand and brought it to his lips, sand and all. "It's such a lovely day. Let's not spoil it by arguing."

I had no problem following that dictate at all.

I'd never underestimate my husband's desire to secure his legacy. But I hadn't expected him to go about it in quite such a drastic fashion.

We had no time after the beach to discuss what exactly Nirvaan meant to do about Zayaan and Marjaneh. Almost all of our out-of-town guests had arrived by Friday night, and things got beyond hectic from then on until the party, and even after.

The only respite I got was when I went to the salon on Saturday afternoon. We'd booked the whole place, as close to fifty women needed to get their hair, nails, and makeup done and their outfits pinned. It was like my wedding all over again, albeit on a smaller scale.

Did I say respite? I erred.

Somehow, Marjaneh and I got stuck in neighboring salon chairs, and for a good fifteen minutes, we faced each other through the mirrored walls. Of course, we couldn't simply leave it at a staring match. As polite, functioning members of society, we had to hold a conversation when our lips were free to do so.

We compared the weather in LA and London and Carmel. I invited her for a visit.

"You should extend your trip. Come to Carmel since you're

here," I said without meaning it. "Zayaan must've asked already, but I'm extending an invitation, too. It's beautiful there. Very recuperative." My eyes watered as the makeup woman curled my eyelashes.

Marjaneh had requested a minimum of makeup, like me—just eyes, a light blush, and lips to match her outfit. "I'll have to see. Zayaan's taking us to LA proper tomorrow for a sightseeing holiday for a couple of days. And we fly back to London on Wednesday."

"Oh, right," I said, feeling totally stupid.

Of course Zayaan's family hadn't come only for the party. Of course he'd spend his birthday with them. He didn't celebrate his birthday anymore. Like mine, the day symbolized personal tragedy and loss for him, but still, it was his thirtieth birthday. And, of course, he was under no obligation to tell me of his plans. I should be grateful he hadn't invited his family to Carmel for me to wait on.

Crap. Crap. Crappity crap.

"He talks about you all the time," Marjaneh said softly.

Shocked by her boldness, I turned my head toward her instead of looking in the mirror. The makeup lady squealed and made me look forward again.

"He's always talked about you for as long as I've known him. You're very dear to him."

I blinked and blinked until my eyes no longer stung. The makeup lady would've screamed had I ruined my mascara with tears.

I didn't know what to say to Marjaneh, so I lied. "He talks of you, too, all the time."

I cannot express how glad I was to leap out of the makeup chair and hustle through the rest of my beauty treatments. Those went by fast and with much comedy and laughter, as befitted a gaggle of half-dressed women of varying ages in a stupendous hurry to look their best.

My outfit—not a sari, praise Khodai—was a floor-length silk gown of Indo-Western style in pale gold with pearl embellishments. It was another surprise gift—my husband's doing—as was the matching pearl and diamond jewelry set.

I felt like a princess.

Looked like one, too, according to Nirvaan. He flattered me with his debonair act as he helped me out of the limousine and onto a flower-studded driveway.

The mansion had undergone its final transformation while I'd been at the salon. A vanguard of trellises wrapped in vines of jasmine and lavender festooned the path to the party area.

Nirvaan looked like a prince, too, in his dark brown *jodhpuri* suit. My heart skipped a beat when he bent to kiss my lips, just like he'd done on our wedding day. I had to blink again. I wasn't going to cry. Not yet. Not just yet.

Behind him, Sarvar and Zayaan beamed at us like twin henchmen. Dashing henchmen. And there seemed to be a dress code. I looked around and found all the men in the immediate family in harmonized *jodhpuri* suits, including five-year-old Armaan. I couldn't help but smile. They were adorable.

The whole extravagant affair went off without a glitch. No rain dared to fall on this balmy second to last night of May. We could've done away with the tents, but we'd played it safe. We'd asked for an ambience of understated romance, and Neelu Patel had delivered it. There were candles and rose petals and bowls of chocolates everywhere. Electric lanterns swung from trees. And there were balloons, lots and lots of silver balloons. It was a birthday party, after all.

We put on our show, the entertainer sang and the DJ rocked the place. Once Zayaan spun Ba around the dance floor, her dance card filled up fast. The food was finger-licking good, and the bar was a limitless ocean. There were three cakes in three different flavors, and we each got a birthday song and a fistful of cake smashed on our faces. The speeches were emotional, but I'd been prepared. I had my tissues in hand.

When Nirvaan spoke, I didn't think there was a single dry eye under the tent. Images flashed on a huge screen behind him as he matched comments and pictures and memories, weaving them all into one wonderful bouquet of life. True to his word, he thanked every single person who'd come to celebrate with us. For many, this would be the last time they saw him.

He didn't thank his family. It wasn't because we didn't need thanks—we didn't—but because what he had to say to us was private. He thanked us instead through the pictures. They showed the world what we meant to him.

With the last photograph he chose to display, he revealed what was in his heart. It lingered there, longer than the others, and imprinted itself onto my soul. It was a recent one from our hiking trip. Nirvaan and I were sprawled on the boulder, holding Tickles together on my lap. Zayaan was on his knees next to us. I was looking at Tickles in awe. But Nirvaan and Zayaan were focused on me. Their faces wore identical expressions of admiration and joy as they gazed at me. They both looked so very much in love with me.

I loved my husband, but sometimes he made my life impossible.

14

I dreaded stepping out of my room the morning after the party. But I'd been summoned downstairs to say goodbye to the last of the guests who'd dropped by on their way to the airport or before their drive back to their hometowns.

Nirvaan hadn't come to bed at all. He'd tweaked my temper and wisely stayed out of sight. If he thought his mother would buffer him this morning, he was sorely mistaken.

I buried my face in my hands. How was I going to face his family? Everyone had seen the incriminating photograph— Marjaneh, too. I felt sick, recalling her face from last night.

After Nirvaan's speech, I'd dragged Sarvar up to my room. I'd paced and ranted and had two shots of whiskey. I'd been livid. Embarrassed. Horrified. I'd drowned in guilt and self-loathing.

Sarvar had tried to calm me. He'd said it wasn't the end of the world. It was only a picture, and he'd asked why I was making a big deal of it.

I'd shouted, *Why?* Hadn't he seen the picture properly? Hadn't he seen everyone's faces?

Enough was enough. I scrubbed my hands over my face, as agitated this morning as I'd been last night. I'd faced far worse things on my birthday and survived. I'd survive this, too. I wrapped a shawl around my shoulders and went downstairs.

It seemed my worry had been seriously misplaced.

The minute I stepped onto the foyer, Nikita and Armaan ran to me, screaming, "Happy birthday, Simi *mami*. We got you presents."

They bounced, hugging my waist and bestowing on me the most beatific toothless smiles. They dragged me into the living room, each child pulling one arm, where several gift boxes sat on the coffee table, waiting to be opened. They made me open theirs first—a handmade card with a pencil drawing of what appeared to be Eeyore wishing me luck on its cover and family tickets to Disneyland inside. Apparently, the Desais would be trolling the Magic Kingdom in the afternoon. I kissed them and their presents with due respect. Honestly, I could use a little Disney magic today.

"Happy birthday, wife," wished Nirvaan as his arms stole about me from behind, pulling me against his body in a hug. His voice was rough with too much talking, too much drinking and too little sleep.

I melted, like cheese fondue. Who wouldn't around this man?

But he had to be reined in.

"Good of you to remember I'm more than just a woman you love making a spectacle of." I turned in his arms to berate him but winced at the awful shadows under his bloodshot eyes. I ended up kissing him instead.

"I didn't mean it like that, Simi." He looked properly chastised.

I supposed his mother or Ba must have lit into him on my behalf. So, I forgave his lie.

I was too tired for anger. I needed a massage—we both did—especially in preparation for Disneyland or perhaps after.

He let me go as the family came into the room to wish me joy and luck on my birthday, each handing me a prettily wrapped box or envelope accompanied by a hug, a blessing, a kiss and a joke. I got jewelry—gold and diamond earrings from Ba, a tennis bracelet from Nisha and Aarav, a Patek Philippe watch from my in-laws. From Sarvar and Surin, I got investment bonds. I was a rich woman today and not only in the way of money.

My mother-in-law wished me happy birthday last but the hardest. We clung for more than a few minutes, gaining strength from each other's bones. Neither of us spoke as we hugged; we didn't even try.

At last, we went into a shockingly empty dining room where the housekeeper had laid out a hot Sunday brunch. After three days of constant hustle and bustle, this felt like an apocalypse.

"Did everyone leave already?" I asked, sitting down next to Nirvaan. I declined the juice offered and poured myself a mug of coffee.

"Yep. Radha *fui* and her family are off to San Diego. They'll be back late tonight, in case you're missing them already," said Nirvaan, shooting me a tired, and yet thoroughly provoking, grin.

I took a sip of my coffee, so I wouldn't have to answer. I didn't ask about Zayaan. I gathered he'd left for the LA sightseeing tour, and I figured we'd see him in Carmel later in the week.

But I was wrong. He brought his mother to the house. She wished to say goodbye to my in-laws and to thank them for their hospitality. My mother-in-law wouldn't let them leave without sharing a last meal with us.

Zayaan hugged me and wished me a happy birthday. We were back to feeling awkward with each other. I realized I'd always be awkward with him on this day. He looked tired, too. We all did. Maybe it was just the aftereffects of the party.

Maybe the silence at the table had nothing to do with the photo.

"Daddy, did you know that Nirvaan wants to sell the land Bapuji left him? And to that character Ram Ali? He sounds shady, if you ask me," said Nisha out of the blue.

Her voice was unnecessarily loud, like a gunshot in the night.

She turned to Nirvaan when her father made eyes at her to shut up. "I don't understand it. If you need money, why not borrow it from Daddy?"

Blame my poor reflexes on sleep deprivation, but it took me a while to react until I heard Nirvaan's, "What the fuck is your problem, Nish?"

I swept my gaze from a livid Nirvaan to a cheesed-off Nisha to my expressionless in-laws. Nirvaan and Nisha started a full-blown battle after that, which my father-in-law tried to referee with no success, no matter how loud he got, as well. Nisha's husband took his children out of earshot of Nirvaan's increasingly foul language.

"I'll do what the fuck I please with my own fucking land, understood?"

"I won't let you screw up the family holdings on some hero complex."

"Sister or not, you won't fucking tell me what I can or can't do with my property. Bapuji left it to me—"

"Exactly, with the understanding that it would remain in our family. *Blood* is family. Get it, Nirvaan? You've set up a substantial trust for your wife to maintain her current lifestyle. How much more does she need?"

Shame crawled through me. I stared, unseeing, at my clasped hands on my lap. I couldn't bear to look anyone in the face. This was worse than the photograph.

Nisha had been giving me the cold shoulder the last two

days since she'd found me wrapped in Zayaan's arms. Was this why? Did she think I was playing fast and loose with Nirvaan's legacy?

"Please, I don't want anything. Please, Nirvaan, don't fight. Please, just let me go," I whispered.

He did the opposite. He wrapped an arm about me and pushed my face into his neck. "Fuck you, Nisha. I didn't want any of you to know, but we're trying to have a baby."

I moaned when he said it. He'd promised not to tell until the IVF worked. We didn't want anyone to hold false hope. I wanted a back door to escape out of. Guilt stung my gut, and I wanted to puke.

No one shouted after that. No one spoke, either. I imagined they were all staring at us—at me—in horror. In hope. Oh, I couldn't bear to see the hope on my in-laws' faces.

"*Baba*, son, is this the right time for this?" Kiran Desai asked in a cool, calm tone meant to soothe.

I loved her for that alone.

"If not now, then when?" said Nirvaan, suddenly sounding deflated.

I shifted in my chair so I could look at his profile. Anger had made his skin sweat and turn pinkish. But his eyes...they'd gone pale in defeat.

"Simeen?"

I didn't want to turn to my mother-in-law but forced myself to.

"Do you want this?" she asked. There was no judgment on her face, only concern.

"Of course she does. We've already started the procedure," Nirvaan said in irritation.

"I'm asking Simeen. You will kindly let her answer."

"Oh, for fuck's sake, Mom. You should be happy for us. Don't you want another grandchild? *My* child? A part of me to hold on to? Or are you so used to not having me around that it doesn't matter?"

I sucked in a breath. My in-laws had left two small children in India when they came to America, and the next time the family had reunited, the children had been teenagers. Nirvaan and his sister had grown up as orphans, even while having parents. It didn't matter that Ba and Bapuji had been wonderful to them. Nirvaan had felt abandoned, and sometimes the issue would boil to the surface.

Nirvaan was hitting everyone below the belt, and I didn't understand why. He was getting his way in everything. So why was he angry?

Zayaan stood up and walked out of the dining room. He'd had enough, it seemed. I wished I had the guts to walk out like him.

"Here's where you live," said my mother-in-law, touching her breast above her heart. "Here's where you will always live, Nirvaan. And I speak for everyone who loves you. We don't need your child as a physical reminder of you. We won't forget you. We will never forget. But, at the same time, I think this should be Simeen's decision. Raising a child in a two-parent family is hard enough. Single parenthood will be a hundred times harder. Do you understand what you're asking of her, my son?"

I didn't deserve them. I didn't deserve this much love and support.

"I want to make sure you guys will be okay. I want to make sure Simi will be okay. That's all," said Nirvaan.

I assured everyone that I wanted this baby. And since the cat was out of the bag, Nirvaan told them the rest. That he wished Zayaan to be the baby's godfather. That he wanted to sell his grandfather's land, so his child and his wife need never worry about money again. That he wished me to have the freedom to live my life as I saw fit. He emphasized, "However and wherever she chooses to live." And he expected his family to support my decisions.

He apologized to his sister, asked if she thought he was wrong. She had nothing to say.

No one had anything more to say, and we sat there quietly, trying hard not to look at each other.

It had been an emotional weekend, and the confrontation had drained every sap of energy I'd preserved. I excused myself and went up to my room, promising the kiddos I'd be ready for Disneyland by noon. I'd barely closed the door when Zayaan's mother pushed it wide-open and followed me inside my bedroom. So much had happened this weekend that I wasn't even surprised to see her.

She accused me of all the things she'd always blamed me for. That I was a witch. I snared men in my web of deceit and destroyed them. I was responsible for Rizvaan's death. I was responsible for Nirvaan's ill health. Did I want to destroy Zayaan, too? I was a seething nest of bad luck, and I should do the world a favor and stay out of everyone's way.

"Zayaan has worked hard to rebuild our family's honor. He has made a name for himself in London. He has a bright future. Our community needs leaders like him. He's found a lovely woman he can proudly call his wife. You will destroy him if you trap him in your wiles. Think about his reputation. He cannot be responsible for you or your child. Hear a mother's plea, and release my son from this travesty."

She considered me an unlucky person. I probably was. But, right at this minute, I felt blessed beyond belief that she wasn't my mother-in-law and that Kiran Desai was.

"Don't worry. I want nothing from your son." I held up a hand when she opened her mouth to interrupt me, to call me a liar again. "I release your son from everything. You can tell him I said so. He's free to go back to London with you. I know you don't believe me, but I truly wish him and Marjaneh well." Then I asked her to leave.

My calmness surprised her. She'd expected me to defend myself, to care what she thought of me. She'd expected tears and explanations. She'd expected a repeat of what I'd done twelve years ago. But my cries had fallen on deaf ears then, and I was a quick study.

After the rape, I'd remained on Zayaan's bed, shaking like a leaf, while my limbs had turned to stone. Rizvaan had finished packing and left the room. I'd heard voices outside. I'd gone numb, and every word had sounded like gibberish, but I recalled people shouting outside. Then Gulzar Begum had come into the room. She'd been crying. She'd stood over me, looking down at me much like Rizvaan had. I'd stared at her without seeing her. She, like so much of that hour, was still a blur. Just a shadow in memory. She'd pulled me up and carried me to the bathroom. She'd washed me, dried me and made me wear someone else's panties.

By then, I'd started to regain my senses. I'd started crying. She'd held me to her, and we'd both cried. But when I'd begun to tell her what Rizvaan had done, she'd told me to shush. She hadn't wanted to hear it. She'd said no one would believe me because Rizvaan never came home. He'd run away. I'd been in shock, but I'd argued that it was not true. How could she make up stories? Finally, she'd told me to have mercy on her family. Her husband was dying. She'd never see her firstborn again. Did I want Zayaan to carry a stigma for the rest of his life? Did I want to shame my own family in front of the whole world? She'd said she would pray for my soul if I just kept quiet.

I'd told her I wouldn't say anything. No, I couldn't ruin Zayaan's life like that.

She'd helped me home herself—not up to my flat, just to the building's entrance. Sarvar had opened the door, and I'd burst into tears right there. Surin had been away on business, which was a good thing. If he'd been home, the night would've unfolded differently.

Sarvar called our family doctor for a home visit. I hadn't allowed the man to check me. He'd advised Sarvar to take me to a lady doctor immediately. Our cousin was a gynecologist in Mumbai, and Sarvar and I'd left on the first train out at dawn. He'd insisted I file charges. I'd refused.

I'd told him I never wanted to think of that night again. I never wanted to see Zayaan's mother again. I couldn't bear to face Zayaan or Nirvaan, either. They'd have taken one look at me and known the truth. And they would have torn the world apart for me. I would not let them destroy their lives along with mine. Sarvar had disagreed. But it wasn't his decision, was it?

I didn't know what I would've done if Rizvaan had lived, had the police not gunned him down in an encounter that night twelve years ago. I'd like to believe I would've found the courage to press charges, make him pay for what he'd done to me. But I couldn't be sure.

I'd taken a long time to stand looking at my reflection again. My body had healed with my cousin's help. My mind had healed with Dr. Asha Ambani's help. I'd grown strong in spirit because of my brothers' relentless faith in me. But it was Nirvaan who'd given me back my soul.

I waited until we were back in Carmel before I brought up Zayaan.

"We should let him go. Think of his poor mother. She can

barely manage without him," I said to my husband. It wasn't exactly a lie.

We lounged on the deck, sipping on coconut water. It was sunset, and the ocean looked as if it were on fire.

A fire burned inside me, too.

Did that old woman keep track, like I did, of the favors I did her? Did she understand how fragile her world was? That one word from me, one confession, and she'd lose her son forever?

Peace Is an Inside Job, read the sign on the parish church today.

I was struggling to make it true.

"Funny." Nirvaan quirked an eyebrow in amusement. "Gulzar Auntie told me that Zayaan could stay here for as long as I needed him."

He thought to call my bluff. But I was tired of bottling things up. I'd kept my cool about so many things this past weekend and I'd had enough.

"Be that as it may, he can't live with us anymore. It's unseemly. Tell him to go back to London with his family." Zayaan had to leave. He simply had to before the dormant volcano of our past erupted and set us ablaze.

A sigh rattled in Nirvaan's chest. "Can we please not fight about this? I made a mistake with the photograph and have apologized for it."

He tried to kiss me better. But I was spoiling for a fight.

"I don't want him here, Nirvaan. I don't want to be talked about. I don't want his help in any way, and you shouldn't want it, either. Send him away."

"I can't send him away. I won't." Nirvaan sat up on the lounger, shaking his head. "Put yourself in his shoes, baby. He needs to be here for his own sake as much as ours. He's not going to go even if we throw him out. You know Zai. You know he'll tell me to fuck off if I order him to leave."

I closed my eyes. I did know Zai. Even when I pretended I didn't know him anymore.

"Then have him move into a hotel, and we can take turns entertaining you," I said stubbornly. Nisha wasn't getting another chance to point a finger at me or call me stupid.

"Be reasonable, Simi. This is not his fault."

"I don't care whose fault it is. I don't want him here." I raised my voice to a shrill.

"Doesn't matter what you want!" Nirvaan snapped. He stood up, glaring down at me.

Now we were getting to the truth. *I'm not a dictator*, was it? "That's right. What I want has never mattered to you, has it?"

"Damned if I do, and damned if I don't," he shouted back, his frustration evident. In retaliation, I let all the venom that had been festering inside me for months, for years, pour out. I accused him of being a bully and a tyrant. I told him what I thought about his Titanic Wish List and where he could shove it. If manipulation or force failed, I pointed out his nasty habit of buying his friends' obedience. It was a side effect of his abandonment issues. My father-in-law had overcompensated his absence by showering his children with money. Until the cancer, Nirvaan had thought money could literally buy anything.

"You've always lorded over Zayaan with your money, and now, you're setting the same trap for me with the trust fund." I rubbed the Awesome Threesome in his face. "It's sick. Your obsession with Zayaan. The suggestions and innuendoes and nudges and shoves. It's ugly how you're pimping out your wife to your best friend. Say it. Just say it out loud, so there won't be any confusion about where you want our relationship to go."

Nirvaan let me shriek without interrupting even once. When I was finished, he was just as brutal with his comeback.

"Do whatever the hell you wish from now on. Have a baby,

or don't have one. Talk to Zai, or treat him like a leper. If you want to let a few nasty comments from narrow-minded people dictate your life, it's your prerogative. I'm going to enjoy what little life I have left on my own terms and to hell with social norms and you." He walked off to the beach then, leaving me to fume by myself.

Zayaan came back before the end of the week. And I got my period.

15

This happened to a body primed for a hundred-meter sprint. The gun shot off, adrenaline rushed through the system and the body sprang forward. Momentum carried it until the last hard push to the finish line.

My period was the starting gunshot for the in vitro athletics program.

I'd already begun a regime of prenatal vitamins and baby aspirin, as per Dr. Archer's instructions, and continued taking my birth control pills. Two days before my period, I'd started injecting a chemical into my stomach to suppress ovulation. This was so Dr. Archer could control and monitor my ovaries into maturity for a successful IVF.

In a way, keeping my mind occupied by medication schedules kept me from going bonkers around the guys. Both behaved as if nothing had happened last week, as if the last week itself hadn't happened—except they would make fun of random guests or bring up a funny incident I hadn't been privy to. Of the scandalous photograph or the argument with Nisha, neither one mentioned a thing.

Zayaan did not talk about his family or Marjaneh at all even though his mother had taken to calling exclusively on the home phone to reach him. To constantly remind me of her importance in her son's life, I supposed. So far, I'd been lucky. I hadn't been around the phone when she called. I hadn't been so lucky when Nisha called, and I'd been forced to make stilted conversation before handing the phone to Nirvaan. Of course, brother and sister had forgotten all harsh words exchanged, and all was well in Sibling Land.

As for my shouting match with Nirvaan—he'd clearly won that round, considering that Zayaan was still here.

It was enviable, the way Nirvaan and Zayaan compartmentalized their lives and feelings. Everything and everyone had a designated place, and somehow none of it overlapped. It made being with them easy. But with my hormones going crazy, I didn't want easy. I wanted a down and dirty fight, and they wouldn't give me one.

I spent the first day of my IVF cycle nursing my nonexistent cramps and existent angst. I read and napped and pouted and only stirred when I heard the guys giggling out on the deck. And, yes, they were giggling like a couple of schoolgirls would around Bollywood superstar Shah Rukh Khan.

I rolled off the bed, slipped on my flannel robe and walked out onto the moonlit deck. I blatantly looked for signs of debauchery and found not a single bottle of beer, Scotch, or Champagne lying around—birthday gifts we'd brought back with us.

"What's the matter with you?" I asked, glancing from one giggly man to the other.

Even behaving like asses, they were attractive to me. It had been a lovely, summery day, and they'd spent most of it shirtless and in the water. Apparently, they wished to spend the night like that, too. I sniffed and sniffed, and at last, I spotted the culprit in a dead skunk smell.

"You're both high." I planted my hands on my hips and tried to look unamused.

Nirvaan tapped his head. "Medical marijuana, baby. Good

for my brain bomb and the seizures, prescribed by the good ole doctor."

He grabbed me around the waist and pulled me onto his lap, smiling gruesomely like a Jack Nicholson Joker. I shuddered when he blew smoke into my face.

He offered me the pipe, and I gave him a stern look. Had he forgotten that I'd just shot myself with hormones so we could have a baby, or did he just not care?

Fantastic example of parenthood, I'd have said sarcastically, if I thought it would have any effect on him in this state.

"No, thanks." I raised my eyebrows at Zayaan. "What's your excuse?"

His smile was no less Halloween at midnight, all uneven teeth and bookish nose. "Whatever we do, we *dogather...thoo gether...too feather—fuck.*" The poetry-spouting octolinguist gave up on basic English pronunciation and guffawed.

As did Nirvaan, so hard that I was jostled off his lap. I couldn't help but laugh along with them. They looked giddy and happy and ridiculous. I took a page out of their easygoing biographies and adopted the attitude.

It was easy to forget the world when it was just the three of us in our cottage in Carmel.

"You guys are crazy," I said, stifling a yawn and the urge to ruffle the hair on their heads, little or abundant. "Okay, I'm going back to bed. One piece of advice, don't do anything I wouldn't do."

"Do...do...do...do...do...do..." Abruptly, Zayaan stood up and loomed over me, swaying slightly, his languid eyes round like dollar coins.

Nirvaan fizzed with laughter at the theatrics. "Do...do... what, *chodu?*"

Sometimes, getting high had this effect. You'd get stuck on a word like a broken record.

I slapped my hands on Zayaan's cheeks. Shock therapy might work. It did.

He stopped saying "do" and started saying, "Simi... Sim... Sim..."

I shook my head. I couldn't leave them like this. Well, I could've left Nirvaan. He was used to getting high—and not always medicinally. But it was obvious that this was a new experience for Zayaan. The bitchy part of my soul wanted to take a video and send it to Gulzar Begum with the caption, "Friends, drugs, and rock and roll."

"Up! Both of you," I ordered, pulling Nirvaan to his feet and wrapping a hand around Zayaan's bicep.

Whoa. His muscles were hard as tensile rope, and his skin was as warm as Surat in the summer. It took all I had to keep my palm where it was and not travel up the curve of his shoulder and down the hills and valleys of his succulent chest.

"Let's go for a walk." I herded them down the deck and hoped to God that the fresh air and exercise would help all three of us to regain our senses.

Our ménage settled into a different kind of rhythm in the following weeks.

When we were teenagers, the guys had been like parallel lines on a train track—running in the same direction yet maintaining autonomy. I'd squeezed in—first, as a third parallel line and then as the bridge between them, reveling in a sense of purpose when our lines began to curve and bend and merge. Three lines had turned into a single circle with no beginning and no end and no rough edges.

We didn't form a circle anymore. Nor could we go back to being parallel lines. I guessed we'd shaped ourselves into a triangle—three distinct lines joined at three sharp-edged points. If you shifted one from its place, the other two would tumble.

The IVF took over my life. On day three of my period, I had to go into the clinic for an ultrasound and blood work for a reproductive suppression check to make sure my cycle hadn't gone rogue. My ovarian stimulation, or stim cycle, began the next day.

From then on, I had to go into the clinic every other day for blood work and an ultrasound, so Dr. Archer could closely monitor my hormone levels and egg growth.

Twice a day, I'd inject my body with gonadotropins— hormones that would increase egg production and assist with ovulation. At the same time, overstimulation of my system was a no-no, and to counter it, I had to continue injecting the hormone-suppressing drug. The injections were administered subcutaneously into my stomach and were not at all painful, except one of them always burned when I pressed the plunger.

The guys escorted me to all my appointments. My umbrage on Nirvaan's radiation day had worked. He hadn't dared to play his separatist games with me again.

Zayaan could've chosen to stay home or wait in the car or in the lobby of the building. He didn't. And I didn't ask him to. Nirvaan certainly wasn't going to. As I'd feared, our three-some attracted some pretty inquisitive looks—never from any of the professional staff, though.

An incident happened today that should have upset me, but instead it struck me as unbearably funny.

As Zayaan was on the phone when we drove into the parking lot of the clinic, Nirvaan and I'd gone in first. The receptionist welcomed us as a couple, like usual, and we waited in the reception area for the ultrasound technician to come get us. Several couples, the women pregnant or potentially pregnant, waited with us, and we all exchanged those shy, blushy smiles patients would trade in such waiting rooms.

A goodly number of the potential dads had to give fresh samples of their semen, and at one point, there was a line outside the room demarcated for the deed. The looks on their faces were priceless when they came back to the reception area and their amused and/or anxious waiting wives.

I didn't remember Nirvaan's state of mind when he'd gone through the same process some years ago. I only knew we'd been filled with hope about so many things then.

To defuse the awkwardness of the whole act, one or another dad would invariably crack a joke and say, "Trust you did good?" or, "Had fun, did you?" And the room would burst into chuckles.

And on that note of merriment, Nirvaan and I were ushered into the ultrasound room.

After my tests, Nirvaan was escorted back into the reception area while I was taken into another room for my scheduled acupuncture session. I relaxed on a massage bed for forty-five minutes with needles stabbed into my forehead, stomach and feet to open my chi and allow for better blood flow through my body, especially my uterus. It was calming with scented candles lighting the room and soft rainy music filling the air. Once the needles were off, the acupuncturist massaged balm into my skin and sent me on my way. This was the only part of my IVF ritual I thoroughly enjoyed.

The guys waited for me by the coffee machine in the reception area, talking to a couple of the other men. I reached them, smiling and relaxed from the acupuncture.

As I slipped my hand in Nirvaan's and he bent to kiss my lips, one of the guys said, "Ah, good to see you again. Oh—"

It took me a moment to recognize the man. It was the little girl's dad from the other day, the one who'd seen me with Zayaan and assumed we were a couple.

To say a pin dropped around us was an understatement. The man—his name was Ryan, as I found out—stared at me and then at my hand clasped in Nirvaan's with his mouth agape. He eyed Nirvaan, side-eyed Zayaan and returned his bemused gaze back to me.

I shouldn't have laughed. But I was loose, body and mind, from my spa treatment. At the same time, I was itchy and wound up because of the ultrasound, which wasn't a great experience when your uterus was swollen with hormones. Laughter was a great de-stressor and it had felt good to stop caring, for a moment, about what people thought of us.

"LSKS," I mumbled and began wheezing.

Nirvaan joined in only seconds later, but Zayaan and Ryan didn't. They wouldn't even meet our eyes. Some of the people in the waiting area were on the same stim cycle as me and had been watching us for days, clearly wondering what was going on. Was I with this guy or that guy or both?

I'd never understood why civilized society tolerated, even accepted as human nature, extramarital affairs or rampant promiscuity as long as it was hushed and tacked on by appropriate amounts of remorse, but it wasn't okay for three people to openly love each other.

That was our naked truth. The three of us loved each other—without reservation, without malice. I wanted to know why it was wrong. Why were we kinky and deviant and different for accepting what was in our hearts and not trying to fit the mold? Life was enough trouble without shaming yourself and denying your nature, wasn't it?

"The same argument won't work from the other end of the spectrum," said Zayaan, throwing two candies into the ante pot.

It was poker night—in other words, stay-at-home night. We'd been out practically every evening for the past week, and I was ready for some downtime where I wouldn't need to dress up and wear high heels. I chilled in my pajamas, never mind that I looked three months pregnant already.

The fertility drugs were giving me terrible gas. Tonight was especially bad, and I blamed it on our dinner of vegetarian sizzlers—too much cabbage and broccoli. I kept moving out of range to relieve myself, but I was up to the point of not caring whether the guys heard me or not. It wasn't as if they'd care if I did something so totally organic in front of them. They did it in front of me and without apology all the time. But ladies didn't pass gas in public was one of my mother's etiquette rules.

"You wouldn't want a serial killer to use that justification, would you? 'It's my nature to kill, and I can't control it,'" Zayaan pointed out.

"I hate it when you make sense." I wrinkled my large nose at him.

"On the other hand," said Nirvaan, upping the ante with four candies for the second blind round, "yes, we should control the worst parts of ourselves, but why do we need to control the best? Aren't humans supposed to strive for and achieve the best within themselves?"

I flipped my cards faceup—an ace and two tens—and beamed. "Exactly. That is why I married you and not him," I exclaimed unthinkingly. I froze and then scrambled about in my head for some excuse and... *Oh, to hell with pussyfooting around this topic.* I gave Nirvaan an impudent grin. "Great minds, and all that jazz," I said instead.

"That is also why I married you and not him," Nirvaan deadpanned, flipping his own cards faceup.

I burst out laughing.

Zayaan, as usual, mumbled something rude, unamused to be the brunt of our jokes and his rotten luck at poker. I scanned the cards. Nirvaan had a king and two tens. Zayaan had the worst cards of the game. I was the candy queen.

Woot! I did a tiny twerk while sitting down.

"Let's play strip poker," suggested Nirvaan.

"Oh, no." I shook my head at my husband. "Not when I'm bloated and ugly."

Nirvaan argued that I wasn't bloated or ugly. Zayaan chimed in. I refused to thaw. Somehow, the *strip* got stripped from *poker*, and suddenly Nirvaan was all for skinny-dipping.

"We've never done that," he wheedled. "It's on the wish list."

"You've never skinny-dipped?" I called bullshit, scooting back in the lounger and crossing my arms over my stomach. For heaven's sake, I hadn't even shaved my legs since the birthday bash. *Ugh.* I was a hairy-legged farter. I was practically a guy.

"I have many times," he proudly claimed. "But you haven't." He waggled his brows, daring me.

Zayaan collected the cards and began shuffling the deck like a pro. "She has. With me," he said without looking up.

The statement left Nirvaan momentarily speechless, and I had to laugh at his gobsmacked expression.

"You're not the only daredevil here, you know. He's joking, though. We went dipping, not skinny-dipping. We had underwear on, tops and bottoms. Besides, I've gone real skinny-dipping with you. Don't tell me you've forgotten Ibiza?"

A few years ago, during a holiday in the Balearic Islands, Nirvaan and I had spent a day on a nudist beach. In most beaches in Spain, certainly most around the Mediterranean, nudity was commonplace, but Aigüa Blanques was an official nude beach.

It had been an edifying experience, to be sure, to come to the realization that whether a woman was fully covered, half-covered or stark naked, only a sick man would look at her in judgment and think of her as fair game. I would not say lust because I loved it when my husband lusted after me. I loved it when Zayaan's heated gaze warmed me in places gone cold.

"That was daytime. This will be night-dipping," Nirvaan quipped, swiftly recovering from Zayaan's admission.

Thinking of Aigüa Blanques heated me up in cold places, too. Sex had still been on the table back in Ibiza.

I snorted. "You, my honeybun, will say anything to get your way."

In most things, Nirvaan was like a bulldozer. He'd just steamroll your objections flat. Yet when it came to our sex life and my inhibitions, I didn't recall a single moment when he'd forced me to do something against my will. He'd taken time to change my mind. He'd persuaded me to his way of thinking with such tender nudges that I hadn't felt pressured. Most of the time, I hadn't even known I'd given in until it was done, like the nudist beach. *Given in or opened up to possibility?* I wondered now.

"Stop trying to convince her, *chodu*. There's a time for debate and a time for action." Zayaan put the deck in its box and set it aside.

I stretched luxuriously. "Finally, someone's on my side. But don't let me stop you. In fact, I insist you check it off the list without me. I'll be the designated videographer for the event."

If I'd thought Zayaan was on my side, I was so wrong. Too late, I noticed the unholy gleam in his eyes. And before I could even think to shut my own, they both leaped to their feet and stripped naked. They'd only been wearing swimming trunks, so it wasn't even some elongated striptease that I could've taken as a warning and looked away. One yank, and there they were, bare as the moment they were born.

"Oh, my God," I squeaked, burying my face in my hands. I desperately wanted to peek through my fingers, but I guessed I was a chicken tonight.

I shrieked again as Zayaan plucked me from my seat and threw me over his shoulder without even grunting while Nirvaan shouted encouragements.

I kept my eyes squeezed shut. "What is this? A reenactment of the barbarian and the captive? Put. Me. Down."

He didn't, of course. I felt like a sack of potatoes as he ran down the beach with me draped over his shoulder. Nirvaan whooped and hollered by our side. I opened one eye and caught a glimpse of his moonlit buttocks as he raced ahead of us and dived into the ocean.

Zayaan threw me in a second later.

The fun and games provided an asylum for the secrets we kept from each other.

We became the kind of people I'd always abhorred and hoped we'd never become. On the surface, we smiled and teased and laughed, but if we peeled the shine away, our demons would come out and play.

Trips to the fertility clinic or the hospice for Nirvaan's tests and consultations became a daily afternoon ritual for the better part of the month. The radiosurgery had gone well. The tumor had shrunk considerably, and it was a good bet it would keep shrinking. But Nirvaan's headaches had become frequent, and the doctors wanted to make sure no new tumors had formed anywhere. They changed the dosages of his medications, and he became sluggish and irritable. It wasn't a side of Nirvaan's I hadn't seen before, but my own hormone inductions made me far less sympathetic to his plight this time.

It seemed Zayaan did have a function in this house, besides being a thorn in my side.

My stimulation cycle was at its peak, and the hardest parts of the IVF process were about to start. I'd had an ultrasound the previous day to check if my eggs were ready to be harvested. Dr. Archer had supplied me with enough information, including live demos and instructional podcasts, that I felt ready to open up a fertility consultation business.

"You're up for the HCG shot tomorrow, honey. Don't worry. It's not as bad as it looks. Just remember to relax and breathe." Martha had tried to soothe me with some insider tips and motherly advice yesterday.

Human chorionic gonadotropin was an oil-based hormone meant to fool my reproductive system into thinking it was ready to ovulate. Essentially, it would artificially trigger the production of progesterone in the uterus and encourage the stimulated follicles to detach and attach to its lining.

I'd have laughed at the ironies of my current life—where not only me, but also my organs were in a pretend state. But even laughing had become uncomfortable these days. My ovaries were fairly blooming with eggs, and my lower abdomen felt like a hot-air balloon about to take flight.

"One of you needs to help me with this," I said, carefully preparing the trigger shot as I'd been instructed.

Attach the sterile needle to the plunger. Swab the drug vial with alcohol. Unscrew the needle cap. For a few moments, gaze in horror at the one-and-a-half-inch needle about to be inserted into my hip/ butt area.

The HCG trigger was an intramuscular shot, meaning the drug had to be released into my muscles and not my belly fat, as with the fertility drugs. I hadn't needed help with those injections, and after the first stomach stab, I hadn't even been nervy much.

When I looked up with the freshly prepared syringe in my hand, I found both Nirvaan and Zayaan staring at me in shock.

I took a deep breath and blew it out, trying to relax my body. "It's simple. Just stick this in somewhere within the circle Martha's marked on my muffin-top area and slowly press the plunger." I stood up from the kitchen stool and held out the injection. "Oh, and as in the demo, pull back the plunger a bit first. If you see blood, then you've hit a capillary or something. Take the needle out, and stab it somewhere else."

"Stop saying 'stab...stick...blood' and—fuck, I can't do it," said Nirvaan, shaking his head. "I can't do it. My hands are shaking."

I raised my eyebrows at Zayaan, daring him to be brave. He looked at the syringe with acute distaste.

"Fine, wussies," I said, shaking my head at the pair of chickens. "They showed me how to do this on my own. It's awkward, and I might hurt myself, but I can do it. Or I can inject it into my thigh, which they say is bloody painful."

Zayaan still looked constipated but took the injection from my hand. I turned around and leaned against the kitchen counter, sticking my butt out. I pulled my yoga pants down a couple of inches to reveal a smiley face. Martha had a great sense of humor.

Nirvaan's automatic "Woohoo! Striptease" sounded out of place and flat. He wanted all the fun and none of the pain. Typical.

"I think you should lie down," said Zayaan. He'd snatched a couple of alcohol swabs from the injection kit, and he was already moving toward the sofa.

I followed him. Nirvaan followed me. I lay on my stomach on the sofa, my head turned toward the open patio doors. The ocean sang its daily song. I focused on the call of the waves, the seagulls, the dogs barking close by, the tinkling chimes on the deck, the susurrating trees.

As if they'd synchronized the move, the guys went to their knees by me—Nirvaan at my head, Zayaan at my hip. Nirvaan began to run his hands through my hair, massaging my scalp. It felt so good that I hummed in pleasure. He murmured stupid, silly things as Zayaan tugged my pants down over my right hip. I tensed up. Nirvaan bent his head to kiss my nose. His hair had started falling out, the little of it that was left. He was going to shave it all off today.

I felt the cool lick of the swab, then a quick needle prick and a burning sensation.

Now for the worst of it…

"Breathe, baby. Breathe," muttered Nirvaan over and over.

My breath hiccuped, and I tasted the ocean on my tongue.

It hurt like hellfire as Zayaan slowly began to press the plunger, injecting the hormone into me. It wasn't quick, as the liquid was thick and couldn't be just shot in. It had to be administered slow and steady. Even so, it was done in less than thirty seconds. I started when a warm hand curved around my hip, and a thumb pressed on the site. Zayaan massaged the spot, round and round, exactly like the nurse in the demo had shown. It felt so, so good to be touched.

Zayaan was my pillar. I could either bang my head against him or use him to lean on. He was always the one I'd counted on, more so than Nirvaan back in the day.

My hip was sore for the rest of the day. If possible, I felt even more bloated than I'd felt in the previous week.

The next day, I went into the clinic for blood work, and pleased with the results, Dr. Archer scheduled the egg retrieval procedure for the following morning.

I was put to sleep for the procedure—a small blessing, I supposed.

When I came to for the first time, Nirvaan was slumped in an armchair by my bedside, sound asleep, with a magazine on his lap. I didn't have the energy to smile, much less call out to him to realign his posture so that he wouldn't wake up with a crick in his neck. My insides felt as if they'd been used as punching bags. I closed my eyes and fell asleep again.

The next time I woke up, both the guys were in the room, talking to each other in hushed tones. I looked down my body, covered in a hospital blanket, but I didn't see the IV connected to my hand. Dr. Archer had said I could go home as soon as my anesthesia wore off.

My in-laws had come that morning and would stay for a couple of days, so I could recuperate without worry. I was fed hot soups and easy-to-swallow comfort foods. My mother-in-law insisted Nirvaan massage my back every time I winced, which was every time I sat or stood or walked. I'd stopped feeling awful within a day but found I wanted to be pampered. I still had to take the progesterone injections above my butt. My womb had to remain in a state of artificial gestation.

Every day, the clinic gave us a fertilization report. They'd retrieved more than twenty healthy eggs from me and fertilized nearly all of them with Nirvaan's frozen sperm. The zygotes were thriving. Even then, they were closely monitored, and only the healthiest and chromosomally sound blastocysts would be used for implantation on the fifth day.

The most uncomfortable part of the embryo transfer was the amount of water I had to drink. My bladder had to be super full. Other than that, it was a five-minute procedure via a catheter to introduce the next generation of the Desai clan into my womb. We'd decided to transfer only one blastocyst— my youth really was a boon—and freeze the rest through a process called cryopreservation. If, at a later date, I wished for more children, I'd be good to go.

I snorted. I still wasn't sure about having this one, let alone some future brood.

I stayed off my feet for a whole day and had been advised to take it easy until pregnancy was confirmed. No strenuous activity, no Jet Skiing, no gallivanting about town on high heels and no hanky-panky. Not that sex was on the agenda anyway.

My in-laws left after my day of bed rest.

Nirvaan, Zayaan and I went back to being a well-oiled machine. We began spending a lot of time vegetating in front of the TV or lounging in bed. I was so bloated by this time, and my breasts were so sensitive to the slightest touch that I couldn't bear anything on my body, besides cotton tanks and elastic pajamas. I couldn't sleep on my back or my right hip. The area of skin and muscle Zayaan continued to shoot progesterone in was black and blue.

Nirvaan didn't leave my side. Zayaan entertained us with stories about his latest research and findings. He read passages of his writings and asked for our critiques, recited Rumi and Ferdowsi and paraphrased parts of *The God Delusion* by Richard Dawkins—a book I found reflected my own philosophy rather articulately. We had some interesting laughs and some abdomen-cramping disputes.

The night before I was scheduled for my first pregnancy blood test, I came out of the bathroom after a relaxing hot bath to find both Nirvaan and Zayaan fast asleep in my bed. All the room lights were still on. Nirvaan was on his stomach, one arm buried to the bicep under his pillow. Zayaan was sprawled on his back on my side of the bed. He clutched a thicket of papers to his naked chest, his other arm flung out and hanging off the bed. He was snoring softly.

It was hot in the house. June was coming to an end, and it

hadn't rained in ten days. Nirvaan had stripped down to his boxers, but Zayaan had kept his pajamas on. My nightgown was made of breathable thin cotton for the same reason. The house didn't have air-conditioning, and the floor fans we'd installed were a bigger bother than help, tripping us up. So, we'd pushed them out of the way and into corners.

It looked like the guest bedroom for me tonight. I covered Nirvaan up to his waist in a summer quilt, and then I carefully took the papers in Zayaan's hand and set them aside on the nightstand. I stood by the bed for a long time and just watched my guys breathe. The queen-size bed looked tiny occupied with twenty-four square feet of masculine skin, bone and muscle. Even unhealthily thin, Nirvaan filled his side of the bed. The other half was engulfed in Zayaan's powerful, thick body.

Emotions welled up in me, shooting up my bloodstream, dancing and delighting, lighting me up inside out.

I picked up the mobile phone charging on the nightstand and clicked a picture that would be framed inside my heart forever. Then I switched off the lights.

There was barely any room between them, but I crawled in anyway. The right side of my hip and buttock was sore. I'd been sleeping on my left side or on my stomach for days. I dug my back and butt into Nirvaan's side, pulling a bit of his pillow to rest my head. He grunted without waking and rolled automatically to curve his body to mine. He smelled of Tiger Balm. His head had been hurting earlier, and I'd massaged it for him. His arm snaked around me, pulling me closer, as his elbow settled low on my stomach and his hand cupped my breast. I used to feel constricted when Nirvaan spooned me, but I'd had years to get used to him, years of his slow steamrolling to mold me into shape and open me up to his will.

I sighed with pleasure, loving his hands on my sensitized body.

Zayaan stirred, and a soft tension gripped his prone form—mine, too, when he came awake to find me next to him. He apologized for falling asleep in a voice gruff with dreams and made to get off the bed. I hesitated only for a heartbeat before I laced my fingers through his and stopped him. He turned to me, his heavy-lidded eyes questioning.

"Stay," I whispered. "There's plenty of room." Though there wasn't. Not nearly enough.

He raised our joined hands to his lips and kissed my hand. Then he tucked my hand against his chest, right above his heart, and went back to sleep in seconds.

The smile on my face threatened to crack my cheekbones. It stayed there till I fell asleep.

16

If I hadn't been so involved with the IVF and the demands of my own body, I'd have noticed Nirvaan's apathy sooner.

I woke up with an awful feeling in my gut. Had I rolled onto my bruised hip in my sleep? But I was on my stomach. I rolled onto my back, relieving the pressure on it and my bladder.

My eyes snapped open when it struck me I'd rolled in bed. If I could roll then I was alone. I squinted at the bedside clock. It was 3 a.m. I'd slept for five hours, not nearly enough. Both Nirvaan and Zayaan could survive on just four to five hours of sleep per night, had for years. I listened for them and heard nothing. But I wouldn't if they were in the den or Zai's room, would I?

I sighed, drawing the quilt over me, wondering what they'd thought of waking up in bed with me between them. Had they made anything of it? Like my acquiescence to certain hints? Probably not. We'd had sleepovers in Surat, too, so that was nothing new. It'd mostly been at my house, with the door open and with Surin wandering in and out of the room as he pleased. The one sleepover at Nirvaan's was the one that stuck out in my memory. We'd been hanging out in his room, watching movies and playing Uno. It'd gotten late, and we'd dozed off—me on the bed, Nirvaan on a beanie bag and

Zayaan on the window bench. Nisha had walked into the room in the morning and angrily shaken me awake. She'd told her mother about it.

"I'm not saying you've done something wrong or that the boys don't need to care about their reputations, too, but you're the girl, *beta*. If something happens...not that it will...but if it does, you'll be judged harsher than them," Kiran Desai had sat me down and lectured. "You're like a daughter to me. And both those boys are lucky to have you for a friend, but you must be careful about these things."

I wondered what my mother-in-law would say about to-night.

A whisper of a moan seeped out of the bathroom, making me start.

Nirvaan.

My heart began to pound. I shot out of bed, and in three steps, I was at the bathroom door. He moaned again. I heard him clearly through the door. I knocked, but he didn't answer. I didn't bother knocking again. I turned the knob. It was locked, but the locks were a joke in this house. I snatched a hairpin from the dresser and poked it into the hole in the middle of the round doorknob. It immediately clicked open.

Nirvaan sat on the toilet with his head in his hands, his moans continuous and torturous.

"Headache?" I went to him, touching the nape of his neck.

His skin was sweaty and jittery. He leaned into me, his head on my stomach. I had to breathe through my mouth. His stool stank so badly.

"Diarrhea?" I kept rubbing him from neck to lower back and up again. I tried to think if he'd eaten something bad or if it was just the treatments and his condition.

"Nirvaan?" I whispered again, my heart speeding up, my thoughts racing for answers.

But he kept moaning, his head pressing into my middle like he wanted to drill a hole with it. I wondered what to do, what I could give him to stop the motions or the headache. The second I tried to step away to call his doctor, he screamed, and all the hair on my body stood on end.

What the hell was this? It had never happened before.

He screamed again and again. I yelled for Zayaan but kept my hands on Nirvaan's shoulders. He jerked under my hands, like someone had shot him, and suddenly he was on the floor, shaking from a seizure.

I fell to the floor next to him, holding his shoulders down. Yet, his body flapped so hard that his head bounced against the floor. I let go of his shoulders and grabbed his head before it bounced again and cracked itself open.

"Zai!" I screamed. He was too big for me to hold down by myself.

Nirvaan shook. Spittle flew out of his mouth. His eyes were open and staring at the ceiling. He passed motion again, and… dear God, it was black. He was passing blood.

"Zai!"

Zayaan dashed into the bathroom. He had his headphones on and was barking out our address into it. "I called nine-one-one." He threw the headphones away and grabbed towels and napkins. He stuffed a napkin into Nirvaan's mouth and literally sat on Nirvaan's legs to stop them from thrashing.

The epileptic fit lasted for two minutes.

Two lifetimes, I thought with a shudder, loosening my hold on Nirvaan's head.

He curled into a ball on the bathroom floor and started crying.

"Can't see. Hurts." His words were softer than a whisper. They scared me to my bones.

I didn't know whether to clean him up before the ambulance got here or drag his head in my lap and rock him till he quieted. I took him in my lap, digging my fingers into his scalp to ease some of the pain.

Zayaan got off the floor and started the shower. He came back to kneel by us again. "*Chodu*, think you can stand for a minute?" He put his hand on Nirvaan's back.

Zayaan waited, but Nirvaan didn't answer or move, just kept his head covered with his hands, so Zayaan picked him up, as if he weighed nothing, and stepped into the shower. I helped as much as I could, but the shower wasn't big enough for the three of us.

I got more towels and wiped Nirvaan down once he was clean. Zayaan carried him to the bed, and we managed to dress him in pajamas and wrap a shawl around him. He wasn't shaking anymore, but his hands and feet were cold. Zayaan went into his room to change, and I called Nirvaan's doctor to let him know what had happened. I didn't leave my husband's side till the paramedics came.

Once they came and took care of Nirvaan, once they left with Nirvaan and Zayaan for the hospital—I stayed behind because I was no good for Nirvaan until I stopped shaking—once Dr. Unger assured me he was being treated in the emergency room, I sat on the rocker on the porch and let myself fall apart.

I was ready but not nearly as composed as I'd have liked when Sarvar came to fetch me at seven in the morning. He didn't want me to drive myself to the hospital. I agreed simply because my hands wouldn't stop trembling even now, four hours later.

I should have followed the ambulance. I should have been inside the ambulance with Nirvaan but as usual my courage had failed me. Then Zayaan had called to tell me that Nirvaan was stable and was sleeping and there was no need to rush to the hospital.

I'd filled the hours with chores. I'd cleaned the bathroom, run two loads in the washer and dryer, changed the sheets on the bed and made breakfast, which I'd packed to take to the hospital with me.

Sarvar kissed my forehead and held me in his arms for several minutes. He simply held me. I told him I was okay, and he needn't worry about me. We needed to worry about Nirvaan.

"It's not a good sign," I remarked once we were on the way. "I shouldn't have let him dismiss his headache this morning. He's lost weight. I should've noticed that he hasn't been eating well the past week. How did I not see how much weight he's lost?"

How would I have seen it? I angrily asked myself. I'd been too busy moaning about my hormones and bloated stomach. I'd been too busy lusting after Zayaan when I should've been watching my husband.

Gulzar Auntie was right. I was born under an unlucky star.

"People die around me." I closed my eyes, resting my head against the car seat's backrest. "Sam, Mumsy, Daddy, Zai's dad and brother. Now Nirvaan. I should lock myself away. Stay away from people. You should stay away from me."

As good a listener as my brother was of my woes, he scolded with similar forbearance. "If you're quite done with your pity party, I suggest you pinch your cheeks and get some color on your face. Forget causing people's deaths. You look like death itself. You don't want your husband to wonder if he's married a zombie, do you?"

"Har, har, har, Sarvar. Death jokes? Really?"

But his words did what he'd meant for them to do, and by the time we walked into Nirvaan's hospital room, I'd managed to gloss my lips, too.

Nirvaan was his typical rapscallion self, lording over his hospital bed. He flirted outrageously with the two nurses standing on either side of his bed, checking his vitals. They discussed the best way to administer a penile catheter—not that he needed one this time, but for future reference.

Only my husband, I decided with a sigh. Only Nirvaan could bounce back from an epileptic fit in this way.

"Baby." His face lit up when I walked into the room. "Meet Tina and Sorcha. My wife, ladies." He infused *wife* with copious amounts of innuendo. "I gotta come clean... Tina and I spent the morning *nekid* in the sponge bath. Didn't we, sweetheart?" He waggled his eyebrows, eliciting a barrage of giggles from Tina.

"Ah. No wonder she's giggling, honey, if she's been handling your parts," I said, winking at my husband.

He barked out a laugh and pinched my cheek. I took his face between my hands. I wanted to smother him with smooches but contented myself by pressing my mouth to his. His lips were dry, abrasive and cold. Luckily, I always carried a pot of Vaseline in my bag.

The nurse duo informed us that his vitals looked good, and they'd be taking him for full body scans soon, encouraging several lewd comments from Nirvaan before they left. Except for an IV drip on the back of his hand, he wasn't connected to any tubes. Even so, I put the protection bag into a drawer next to the rolling table by his bed. It was more out of habit than a belief that Ahura Mazda would come charging in on a white horse and change the inevitable, but I still felt soothed with the ritual I'd forged five years ago.

The cloth bag held my *sadra* and *kasti*—a divine armor and girdle of sorts, in the form of a sacred blouse and thread all Parsis who'd been initiated with *navjots* into the Zoroaster religion were meant to wear at all times. Much like the thread

ceremony for Brahmins or communion for Christians, the *sadra*
and *kasti* were symbols of faith and were supposed to keep the
faithful safe from evil. I'd stopped wearing mine the day after
my parents' funeral. But I'd kept them—out of superstition
or hope, I didn't know.

"You guys must be starving." I noticed Nirvaan's food tray
sitting, untouched, on the table.

He found hospital food insipid. But if he'd been hungry,
he would've eaten it.

"I brought your favorite breakfast, sweetie. Oatmeal *upma*."
Without waiting for an answer, I opened my basket of goodies
and filled a small paper bowl.

Nirvaan protested being fed like a child. He really wasn't
hungry, he said, but I cajoled a few bites into him with inde-
cent promises and jokes. Zayaan and Sarvar served themselves,
and within seconds, the hospital room began to smell like a
coffeehouse. I'd brought two thermoses of coffee and one of
tea. I'd brought enough oatmeal porridge, chutney sandwiches
and cut fruit for ten people, knowing my in-laws would arrive at any moment. I'd called them as soon as the ambulance
had left the driveway.

Sure enough, they were there just before the attendant
from Radiology wheeled Nirvaan away for his tests. My in-
laws went with him, insisting Zayaan go home and rest for
a while. He looked completely worn-out. But he refused to
go, alternatively pacing the room, looking out the window
or sitting restlessly in a chair, only to get up a minute later
and pace again. Sarvar took him out for a walk and got him
out of my hair.

"He's had too much coffee," I said, pouring a small cup of
coffee for myself. I was floating on too much caffeine and too
much adrenaline myself. Keeping busy helped. I really had

cooked too much food, I realized, staring at the piles of foil-wrapped packets and thermoses on the hospital's rolling tray.

I asked Ba if she wanted tea. She did, and I handed her a steaming hot cup.

After our stomachs were warm but not settled—I wondered if my stomach would ever feel settled again—she said, "He'll need you, Simeen *beta*."

I sighed. "I know. I'll make sure he doesn't overdo the fun. That he sleeps and eats on time. No more gallivanting about town and bouncing on Jet Skis. And definitely no more beers."

Nirvaan's doctors hadn't forbidden him from drinking, but they'd cautioned that alcohol sometimes adversely influenced anticonvulsing medication. Nirvaan was always careful about the amount of alcohol he consumed, but our birthday party and recent nights of clubbing obviously hadn't been good for him.

"I don't mean my grandson. Anyone with eyes can see how well you take care of him. I meant Zayaan. You'll need to be strong for him, too."

I took an extra-large gulp of coffee so I wouldn't look as dumbstruck as I felt. First Nirvaan and now Ba?

"Zai? Why, Ba, he's the strong one. He's been so good for us...for Nirvaan. He's our rock."

I told her how he'd handled the seizure, how he'd been handling Nirvaan these last months.

Zayaan had always been tough. At eighteen, he'd stepped into his father's shoes, borne his responsibilities with extraordinary maturity. Nirvaan had kept me updated about Zai and himself whether I'd shown interest in their lives or not, whether I'd replied to his emails or voice messages or not.

No, Ba was mistaken. Zayaan could handle anything—death, disease, breakups. It was me who couldn't handle life. It was me who was weak and useless and forever needy. Look how I'd fallen apart this morning. Zayaan hadn't. He'd known exactly what to do right up to climbing into that ambulance with Nirvaan.

"Your *bapuji* and I spent more than seventy years together, you know. It was a nice life. I won't complain. But he had an ugly temper and not enough luck. In our times, families were large. Not this *amey bey, amara bey* or two-point-five children limit. I had six sons and three daughters. I lost some before I lost your *bapuji*." Ba's brittle smile spoke of a long life and too much grief. "The point is, I've raised men and been married to one. So I know for all their bluster and stoic fronts, they're like babies when things go wrong. They need their women to hold them and nurture them and show them life might be a lot of trouble, but it can be good."

I wondered if all women past a certain age talked this way as my mother had said something similar to me a long time ago.

Your father used to bottle things up when we first got married and blast like a soda bottle when shaken. It took work, but eventually, I showed him that a good emotional release every now and then was good for the soul. I hope Suri and Savvy find women who'll under-stand them, my mother had said.

Surin had been dating a twit, in her opinion. That had been in his first year of junior college. And it'd turned out that my mother was right. I thought my mother would approve of Surin's wife, Parizaad, and the way she handled my brother.

Scrunching my nose, I asked Ba the same question I'd asked my mother. "Why is it a woman's responsibility to show a man the way? As intelligent grown men, shouldn't they know their own natures?"

Ba laughed heartily. This time, her eyes laughed, too. "They should, but nature is as nature does. They are not nincompoops, *beta*. They just need to be reminded of that from time to time."

She patted my hand. "You're like me. You have strong instincts. You'll know what to do."

I shook my head. I wasn't strong and my instincts—if I had any—were worthless. They'd issued no warning about Riz-vaan's evilness. They'd failed me completely where my parents were concerned.

"Do you remember the Indiana Jones movie we watched years ago with the disgusting tomb of vipers? My stomach feels like a pit of writhing vipers. I'm scared, Ba. I am so scared for Nirvaan." I wasn't ready. I wasn't prepared to let him go at all.

She patted my hands again. "Indy faced his fear by closing his eyes and diving into that pit. I don't want you to do anything that dramatic. But, *beta*, things are never as bad as you anticipate them to be."

The absurdity of our conversation should've amused me. Everything sounded funnier in Gujarati. But I was too worried to laugh. And whether it was fear or instinct goading me, I knew that I had to maintain my distance from Zayaan. I didn't want to tempt fate again.

Several hours, doctors and tests later, we were informed that Nirvaan would be in the hospital for three days. The MRI and CAT scans showed that two new miniscule growths had popped up around the first one, which was shrinking but not fast enough. He needed more radiation. Whether it would be whole head or targeted was being discussed.

The team of doctors warned the epileptic seizures might get more frequent or less frequent. They just didn't know. "The brain is such a complex piece of machinery, Mr. and Mrs. Desai."

If the seizures became worse, surgery was an option. But surgery came with its own set of risks. There'd be brain damage. Nirvaan could suffer anything from amnesia to mood swings to muscle or neurological dystrophy, which could cause blindness at best, or at worst, he'd go into a coma. They just couldn't predict.

Nirvaan was adamant that he didn't want a chunk of his brain cut out. He wished to live a fully cognizant life or die. There was no middle option for him.

Before I took Nirvaan home, I suspected that I wasn't pregnant. But I didn't break the news for another week until I'd confirmed it.

Brain tumors weren't like other cancers. In a sense, a patient could be well enough to go skydiving one week—not that he should—and in the next, he could wind up dead. Sometimes, you couldn't even tell that the person was sick, more so in younger and relatively healthier people like Nirvaan.

"All in all, I'd rather die from a brain tumor than the lymphoma. Death by tumor seems a bit more graceful, not to mention dramatic," said Nirvaan, contemplatively, about two weeks after the epileptic seizure.

While he spoke of dying, I admired the living panorama before me.

We were out on the deck again—our official lounging space—playing rummy during a particularly pale sunset. The sun was like a scoop of orange sorbet liquefying into an orangey puddle. It was obvious that California and not Florida should be the Orange State. A sprinkling of clouds and birds, smudging the sky like caramelized nuts, completed the natural sorbet. That's it. I was going to sign a petition for California to become the Orange Sorbet State.

I was a teensy bit high, I realized, as my musings turned prosy and bizarre. I'd only taken one puff of Nirvaan's prescribed pot pipe—at his insistence—but it had been enough. I was now in a happy orange state.

The sunset made me vividly happy. A profound conversation made me happier and giddy with nostalgia.

I couldn't remember the last time I'd spoken to the guys from my heart. *When was it? Oh, yeah. Twelve years ago. No, no, don't think of that night. Always messes things up.* I waved goodbye to the past and shut the door in its face.

"I second that," I said, spreading my cards out like a fan in front of my face. My nails looked awful, bitten. Then I blinked as my mind caught up with my mouth. "I mean, I don't want you to die at all, but if you are going to anyway…this is better. No hospitals. No tubes going in and out of your body." I shuddered, recalling how he'd looked during his lymphoma treatments. "This is much better. Here today, gone tomorrow. Poof."

Did I really say that out loud?

"I'm glad the two of you are on the same page about this," said Zayaan drily.

Luck was on his side tonight—he was better at rummy than at poker. I tried to sneak a peek at his cards, but he drew them close to his chest. Also, he hadn't puffed on the pipe and was behaving oh so snooty toward me.

"Meanie." I stuck my tongue out and fizzed with laughter.

He shot me a shiver-worthy glare with his dangerous, gorgeous eyes.

"*Ooh*. The killer-look kills me every time. *Uff.*" I fell over on the lounger and spread my arms wide, wondering if I looked good dead.

Zayaan shook his head. "She's lost her mind."

"Little Bo Peep!" I exclaimed, sitting up. "Let's find Little Bo and enlist her help to find it…my mind. Find my mind." I thought it a brilliant idea.

Zayaan groaned, and Nirvaan chuckled.

"Honey, I love your laugh. Laugh some more," I sweetly begged.

Nirvaan laughed again. "Nope, *chodu*. She's finally telling the truth."

Truth, truth, truth, I mulled it over. *Mustn't tell the truth. But why not?*

I scratched my fat, bumpy nose, staring at a cobweb on the latticework on the porch's ceiling. *Bad, bad thing—the truth.* I bolted to my feet, and promptly forgot why I'd stood up.

"What the fuck?" yelped Nirvaan, grabbing hold of the flimsy deck table I'd almost toppled over with my sudden spring jump.

Both the guys stared at me in shock.

I found their slack-jawed expressions hilarious. I doubled over with laughter. "Oh, God…your faces. Priceless. Crap. I have to pee now." I dashed into the bathroom, shed my jeans and underwear, made it to the commode on time and let go. "*Yes.* That feels…so good."

I did my business and washed my hands. While at the basin, I splashed cold water on my face. I hadn't really inhaled much smoke from the pipe, but it had been enough to shoot straight into my brain. Not for long, though. My high was already coming down. I still felt an absurd urge to giggle, but I'd regained enough control not to give in.

I walked back out into the living room, flapping my hand at the guys to indicate I was fine. I didn't go out on the porch. Instead, from a closet by the main door that housed the washer and dryer units and the cleaning supplies, I selected an extra-long duster. I went outside then and set about to annihilating the cobweb I'd spotted on the deck.

I'd always been compulsive about keeping a spotless home, but it had become an obsession of late. I hated insects in the house or dust or anything that might cause illness or an allergic reaction. Cobweb and its resident black widow spider—not really—dispatched to the netherworld, I returned to my perch on my lounger to find the poker chips and cards replaced by an empty Coke bottle on the deck table.

Coke from a glass bottle tasted crisper than from a plastic bottle or a can. Coke in Europe tasted a lot less sugary, hence better, than it did in the US. I didn't know why I noticed such things, but I did. We only ever bought glass-bottled Coke in this house because I was the only one who drank it.

"Using a Coke bottle as a curio for deck furniture is innovative, to be sure. Did you fish it out of recycling?" I kept my focus on Nirvaan. I was trying hard, very hard, not to look at Zayaan, directly or indirectly. *Dear God, did I really blurt out loud the effect his killer eyes have on me?*

Nirvaan's mouth drooped into a pout of immense disappointment. "You're not high anymore. Damn. Your system's good. Don't know whether to be upset or proud."

"Why, thank you, honey. I live to make you pot proud. But what's with the Coke bottle? Please don't tell me you're going to try bonging or whatever with it. And, whatever it is, count me out."

"Bonging?" Nirvaan burst out laughing.

"You know what I mean. That thing with the weed and a bong or bottle." My knowledge of bonging existed purely from movies and vicariously from Nirvaan's confessions about his wild college days. I pursed my lips, expectantly raising my eyebrows.

"Spin the bottle, baby. I thought the game would be perfect since you were high." Nirvaan shrugged as if it had been worth a try. "But this is better. Rules are as before, a kiss or the truth."

There remained enough pot in my system to make shock

feel like a power charge running through my veins. I wasn't at all sure bonging wouldn't have been a better option.

"That doesn't sound fun. Oh, I know. Let's catch the new Dracula flick at the theater," I said as if I'd just had the best idea.

"Too bad you said we should stay home tonight. And you're right. 'The flickering lights of a big screen could induce a headache.'" Nirvaan parroted my earlier words with a wicked rascal smile.

Crap. Those excuses had sounded genius this afternoon.

I finally glanced at Zayaan, hoping he'd be the voice of reason. Long and lean, he was stretched out on the lounger with his dangerous dark eyes closed. I was getting vastly irritated by the torso flashing going on around me. Nirvaan, I got. My husband loved to flash skin, always had. But since when had Zayaan become okay with nudity—partial nudity? And when in the name of Ahura Mazda did he find time to muscle up between doctorates?

"Zai's sleeping. And I need to start dinner." I was lying. I'd already made dinner this morning.

"I can multitask," said Zayaan, sounding amused. He opened his eyes. Glee danced behind his black-as-coal irises.

"I hate it when you gang up on me." I was sick of it, in fact. Both of them needed to be brought down a peg or two.

"We're not ganging up on you," said Nirvaan, giving the bottle a sideway spin test. "We're trying to loosen you up."

"I don't want to loosen up. I want to be…" I bit my tongue before "free" flew out. That just showed they didn't need to loosen me up. Apparently, I was loose enough tonight.

Nirvaan clapped his hand on the spinning bottle, abruptly stopping its motion. He looked up at me as I stared him down. I was very aware of Zayaan watching us.

Zayaan was the base of our triangle—strong, steady, immovable. I wondered what would happen if he shifted his stance. I mentally willed him not to.

"What do you want, Simeen?" asked Nirvaan, suddenly very serious.

In the fifteen years we'd known each other, he'd called me by my full name maybe a dozen times, no more. It startled me.

"You never tell me what you want anymore. You used to in Surat, all the time. You'd demand things from us, demand our time, our undivided attention, but for the past eight years, you've never once expressed a desire for something...anything. You've never shown me what is in your heart."

My cheeks grew hotter with every word, every observation. I was dismayed that Nirvaan had seen through my silence. Horrified I was such a bad actress. And embarrassed that Zayaan sat between us, once again a witness to the inner workings of my marriage. But at the same time, I was glad he was listening. He needed to know where this could never go.

"You're being silly, Nirvaan." I smiled it off, like I had for years. "I haven't asked you for anything because you always anticipate my needs. You've always known what's in my heart."

Nirvaan twisted his mouth, as if he'd tasted something sour. I'd disappointed him. Again. "Fine, have it your way. Let's play the game. But first, promise you won't cheat. Promise me when we ask you a question, you'll give us the truth."

Many months ago, Nirvaan's doctors had apprised us on what we'd be facing over the course of the next year. *Maybe a year. Maybe less, maybe more. We can't predict time frames with any certainty with tumors.*

We should expect seizures, headaches, incontinence, loss of appetite—thankfully, Nirvaan's appetite was back with a vengeance—disinterest in life, discussions about death or meaning of life, making sure the family affairs were in order, balance and time-lapse issues, confusion, anger. Not all together and not always, but we had to watch for these symptoms, which would get progressively worse as the cancer ate Nirvaan's mind. We'd gone through most of these symptoms at least once.

My husband wished for a peek into my heart, so I gave him the unvarnished stark truth. "You want to see into my heart? Into my soul? Here's a glimpse. I want you to live. I want you to fight for us. *For me.* I don't want you to let go of me so easily."

I wasn't only talking about the cancer, and my husband quickly got it. So did Zayaan. No one had ever accused them of being dumb.

"I chose you, Nirvaan. To be mine, as my mate. Now, you can either choose to be noble, or you can choose me back."

17

There were more good days than bad in our household during the following months, but it was the bad that stuck in our heads.

During one of our phone sessions, Asha Auntie asked me to plot out my life. I regularly phoned her these days and not only at Sarvar's insistence. But I wasn't sure how much it helped, talking to her or to Sarvar. Most days, I felt like a pressure cooker ready to blow.

"Imagine someone has asked you to write a memoir," she prompted.

Immediately, I listed all the bad events that had marked my life and in detail. But the good moments—and I'd had plenty of those if I chose to gush over them—I only skimmed, as if protecting the memories.

I felt like, if I mentioned the happy moments out loud, Khodai would set His evil eye on me again. Asha Auntie had tried to repair my relationship with God once before, but I wasn't ready to forgive Him.

Summer passed in the blink of an eye, yet time flowed with excruciating slowness.

It was hideous, waiting for my husband to die. But it was what I was doing. It was what all of us were doing, really.

Some days, Nirvaan couldn't see properly. He would see

two of everything. The first time his vision doubled, he'd been looking at me. He'd joked about his ultimate fantasy of having two of me in bed come true, but I could tell it scared him.

As his mind failed, his anger and frustration began to manifest in odd places. One day, he loved us—Zayaan and me and his family—the next day, he wished us all to hell.

We'd fought again this morning. It wouldn't have upset me so much had his sister not witnessed it.

It wouldn't have happened at all had she not been there, I thought uncharitably.

Nisha and her family had come up from San Diego for a two-week visit at the end of the kids' summer vacation. By the second day of their visit, Nirvaan and I had fought three times already.

I hadn't discussed the failed IVF with my husband at all. The week after Nirvaan's first seizure and subsequent hospitalization, I'd gone to the clinic for a pregnancy blood test, and when it had come back negative, I'd told Dr. Archer and Nirvaan that I didn't have the strength to go through it again. End of discussion.

I supposed it was Nikita and Armaan who'd brought children back on Nirvaan's mind. They were sweet kids but a handful, and I was tired and petulant from constantly picking up after them. Nisha was used to an untidy, kid-friendly house. I wasn't.

On their second afternoon in Carmel, the kids, Zayaan, and Nisha's quiet and stalwart husband, Aarav, were off Jet Skiing, leaving the odd triangle of Nirvaan, Nisha and me behind. I had just finished setting the living room to rights when Nisha told me I shouldn't have bothered.

"It's just going to get littered with toys again. You should leave the cleaning for the evening when they are tired and will fall into bed," she said as she brewed a pot of tea for herself, trailing a different kind of mess around the stove and sink in her wake.

Of course, it aggravated me that she said this after she'd seen me slop it up for the past half an hour. Leaving aggravation aside, did she not see that if I didn't bother to clean up, her brother, who couldn't see as well anymore, might trip over the toys and land on his head on one of them? Was she stupid? I also didn't mention the potential of spreadable infection in an unhygienic house and that we couldn't afford even one dirty dish lying in the sink, attracting germs that might or might not attack Nirvaan's compromised immune system. I held my tongue in all ways. She was Nirvaan's sister and I didn't want to fight with her.

But when Nirvaan said, "You'll need to show Simi how to be a mother, Nish," I just lost it.

What did he think I'd been to him for the past five years, for I sure as heck hadn't been his wife? I realized he might have said it in jest, but I was in no mood for pokes or jokes.

"I don't need to be shown any such thing. Picking up after you has taught me well. And, for the record, I'm never having children, Nirvaan." *There.* It was out in the open. The peek he wanted into my heart wasn't so agreeable, was it?

"Oh? The IVF didn't work?" asked Nisha, as if she hadn't known, as if she couldn't see that I wasn't pregnant. Why did she hate me so much?

She came to sit on the armchair, sipping her tea, while Nirvaan and I faced each other down across the coffee table.

I was on my knees, checking under the table for wayward toys. Nirvaan was sprawled on the sofa. I waited for Nisha to bring up the trust fund that had been set aside for the child and me—*child* being the operative word. I hadn't asked Nirvaan if he'd sold Bapuji's land. I didn't want to know. I planned to refuse any and all financial help from his family once he… when Nirvaan was no more.

Nisha didn't bring it up. Instead, she said, "I think you need to try two or three times before an IVF works."

Nirvaan pounced on that immediately. "Exactly. They said the same thing at the clinic. We should try again. You've had two months to recover."

"No, we shouldn't," I said firmly. "You said it was up to me. And I've made up my mind. I don't want a baby."

Needless to say, Nirvaan didn't appreciate my honesty. He flayed me with his meanness. "It's probably your negative attitude that made you miscarry. You never wanted our baby."

"It's not called a miscarriage if the zygote didn't attach to my uterus at all!" I shouted, outraged that he'd say such a vile thing to me.

I would've stopped there, but Nirvaan made an exceedingly distasteful comment next.

"Oh, baby, baby. Why yo womb reject my love, baby?" he rapped like a punk, hiding an accusation behind a joke. Everything was reduced to a joke or an order with him.

His words made my heart bleed, and I wanted to hurt him back.

"Maybe it was your deficient genes that made an imperfect, chromosomally abnormal zygote. Maybe it's your sperm that can't do its job properly, so stop making me the villain when it's your own inadequacies that have failed you."

An hour later, when the jet riders came back home, we were still fighting. The general consensus was that I needed a break. I'd wound myself too tight. Nisha suggested I go visit my brother while she was in Carmel.

"I'll hold the fort down here, so don't worry," she offered generously.

I dug my heels in. I would not be separated from Nirvaan.

What if something happened to him while I was gone? What if I never got to fight with him again?

I refused to go until Nirvaan made me.

"We both need a break, Simi. It'll do us good," he said, hurting me some more. He was giving up on me. I could see it on his face.

"Fine, I'll go. But a day is plenty to clear our heads," I said.

The next morning, I gave my husband a *Mean Girls* wave before driving up to San Jose. I was adamant I'd be back by nightfall the next day.

Let me be the first to admit that the break had been a great idea.

Sarvar's town house was as spotless as the beach house, so I had no need to run about, brandishing a vacuum hose. I didn't need to cook as we ate out mostly. And it was the weekend, so Sarvar devoted all his time into knocking sense into me.

"I was relieved when the IVF failed," I confessed to my brother. "I don't want a child, so why am I upset?"

We were having dinner at an Ethiopian restaurant, which always struck me as incongruous. If you thought about it for a minute, a country known for poverty and mass deaths of its citizens by starvation had its own food culture. I guessed it was a God-has-a-dark-sense-of-humor type of thing.

"I like this restaurant. Ethiopians might starve, but their cuisine flourishes on other continents," I said, pushing the platter of food toward Sarvar.

Ethiopians shared their meals. They dug their fingers into a common platter and ate it together, like certain sects of Muslims. Like Zayaan's family had done on special occasions. I'd shared the *thaal*, the common platter, with them once. I'd loved the intimacy of the act, the laughter that had ensued when hands bumped into each other as you accidentally reached for the same food.

"I feel awful about the failed in vitro. That *I've* failed Nirvaan, failed to accomplish the one thing he asked of me." I was grieving for a baby I hadn't wanted. I took a deep breath, counted to ten. I was grieving for a life that was no longer mine. "I don't want to want Zayaan. I *can't* have him. So why can't I stop thinking about him? Stop wanting him?"

It didn't matter that Nirvaan had all but given his blessing. It was wrong to want Zayaan. It felt wrong.

Sarvar swirled his glass of wine and took a sip. "Is it wrong because of what people will say, or do you feel you're being unfaithful to Nirvaan?"

"Either. Both. Khodai, I can't process my feelings anymore." I sat back in my chair with a heavy sigh. I couldn't seem to gather the energy to go into the restroom to wash my hands. I'd eaten with my fingers, *desi*-style. "I never felt guilty for wanting them both before. I didn't care what the world would make of it. I'd wanted them both, and I went after what I'd wanted."

It had been more than some childish dream or daring act. More than love even. I had been hurting when I met the guys. The loss of a parent could destroy you. Being an orphan changed you. I'd been so close to my mother. To fill her void, I'd latched on to the guys like a puppy to a teat. I'd grown closer to Zayaan because we'd both been in Surat—accessible to each other at any time. And if I was being completely honest, Zayaan and I'd connected in a way that Nirvaan and I never had, never did. If I allowed that connection to form again, would it mean I'd used Nirvaan simply as a means to an end? That I'd trapped him with my lies and then killed him?

The nest of vipers in my belly hissed at me. I felt sick.

"Simeen, look at me, love." Sarvar's quiet request broke through my thoughts.

I grimaced because I knew what he was going to say. He'd been telling me the same thing for years.

"Talk to Nirvaan. You know you must come clean about all of it. It's the only way you'll stop feeling like shit."

When you'd fashioned your whole life around a secret, it wasn't so easy to give it up.

Every day, I made excuses for not baring my soul to my husband. First, there was Nisha and her brood. Then my in-laws came to stay. How could I disrupt their family time by monopolizing Nirvaan? This was not a conversation we could have in passing. I needed time with him. Time alone with him to explain, to defend my actions, and to beg for his forgiveness. I refused to consider what revealing my secret would do to Zayaan or the chaos I'd fling into his life. I only hoped Nirvaan would understand why we couldn't tell him.

Two days after my in-laws and Nisha had left, the vipers continued to writhe. I found a million things to keep us busy, so I wouldn't have to confess the truth.

We spent the day at a museum, looking at the vanished world of the Mayans. Some of the artifacts predated the birth of Zarathustra himself. I couldn't help but compare the time-tested stone figures—now chipped and ravaged but still there—to my husband. I wondered why God hadn't given stone a soul but had given fragile man one.

On our way home, Nirvaan asked Zayaan to pull the Jeep into a roadside viewpoint on a cliff. We got out to take in the vista of water and sky, cliffs and beach. All familiar. All similar. A thousand other places across the world had the same view, but it didn't stop us from admiring it. I took pictures of a bunch of surfers riding five- to six-foot waves with pizzazz but not a lot of skill.

"I know Nirvaan surfed in his college days at Malibu Beach," I said, training my phone's camera on the guys now. "Have you?"

Zayaan shook his head. "Have you?"

"Nope," I murmured as I kept my finger pressed on the clicker while moving the camera from the left to the right in a panoramic shot.

"You guys should," said Nirvaan. "If you can stay upright on the board, riding the waves feels glorious. But if you slip, its like you're Pinocchio being swallowed up by a whale of a wave."

He slid his hands into the pockets of his jeans that were much too big on him now. He'd gone down two sizes, and he wouldn't let me buy him new clothes. I didn't want to think about why.

"Want to try it, baby?" he asked, halfheartedly.

"There are some things strictly meant for my starstruck observation...like surfing and Stephen Amell's abs," I replied, trying to lift Nirvaan's increasingly pensive mood. Something had been bugging him since morning.

He smirked, as I'd known he would. He pulled me flush against him and, together, we watched surfer after surfer try to break a wave. Only some managed. And when it happened, we hooted and catcalled, and the guys whistled in appreciation.

"I'm going to miss this," Nirvaan murmured. He tilted his head to the sky and inhaled in a long breath. "Do you think I'll be able to see all of this from up there?"

I sharply turned my head to look at my husband, but the wind whipped my hair into my face. Suddenly, I didn't want to smooth it away, scared of what I'd see on his face. I did it anyway—not because I was brave, but because I was determined to capture every one of his expressions. I didn't remember my parents' faces anymore, not fully, and I had such few pictures of them. I would remember Nirvaan's face forever.

He seemed calm, happy even, gazing at the world. The sockets around his eyes were prominent, despite their steroid puffiness—because of the angle of his head or weight loss, I didn't know. He had a rash of acne along his bony underjaw. I stretched up to kiss his cheek.

"Fuck, I'm going to miss this life. Miss my wife. Miss this *chodu*, too." He elbowed Zayaan in the stomach, making him grunt. "Miss the starry skies and seething oceans…the first hissing flavor of Mummy's *undhiyu* casserole on my tongue. Miss the pain of an ingrown toenail."

"Nice," said Zayaan.

The two idiots high-fived each other, making me roll my eyes.

"Miss squeezing a pair of double-D silicon melons and—"

"What?" I squawked in shock, interrupting my husband. "Whose fake breasts have you squeezed, and why don't I know about it?"

"No one's. And, now, I never will," he bemoaned.

I slapped his arm, hard. He'd joke even in death.

He yelped. "Shit. That hurt."

"Good. And if you're done kidding around, I want to go home." I turned toward the car, but Nirvaan caught my arm and stopped me.

His bony face was alight with life and hope and a thousand unfulfilled promises. "Promise me, you will laugh every day. Fight every day. Do you know how beautiful you look when you're angry?"

"Nirvaan…" Pain squeezed my heart. I wanted to die.

"Promise me, you'll learn to cuss, learn to love again. Live again. Open your heart to a million possibilities. Promise me, you won't give up on each other," he said with urgency now.

Nirvaan hadn't pitted Zayaan and me together since the night I'd asked him to choose me.

My voice full of sorrow, I promised my husband what he'd asked of me, knowing full well I would break my word.

We went home, and by evening, the wind was howling, and waves were crashing onto our shore. Rain wasn't expected. It hadn't rained at all this month. How was it already the end of September?

Nirvaan remained unusually quiet. He didn't have a headache. He wasn't tired. He simply didn't feel like yakking. Or playing video games or strip poker or teasing me or doing anything Nirvaan-like.

It was too squally and chilly to sit out on the deck, and for the first time in many weeks, I closed all the windows and doors around the house and lit the fireplace. The sky was a cloudy dark mess, and the sun was completely hidden. There was a lighthouse a few miles south of us, and if you looked closely into the stormy gray ocean, you could see the faint cast of its light over the water. Perhaps it was a lifesaving beacon for the daredevil surfers who'd be out riding the waves.

Our phones had beeped the standard emergency warning not to go into the water until after midnight tonight. Along certain sections curving the Monterey Bay coast, the warning said not to even venture onto the beach, especially nearer the surf. There was a strong possibility of sneaker waves sucking people miles into the sea.

I switched on the TV after an early dinner to watch a *Law and Order* marathon. Nirvaan stretched out on the sofa next to me and rested his head on my lap, shutting his eyes. I drew my fingers over his stubbled scalp, pressing acupressure points for migraines and sinus headaches. Behind us, Zayaan had spread his paraphernalia across the breakfast bar and settled down to do some work. For anyone looking in from the outside, we made a pretty domestic picture.

Nirvaan's sudden melancholy worried me. It wasn't as if he'd never sounded off before, but I decided I would call Dr. Unger and apprise him of the change. Maybe it was a reaction to his new medication.

Halfway through the episode, just when a second murder victim had been discovered in a Dumpster, Nirvaan sat up. He rose to his feet, stretching.

"Do you need something, honey? Want to go to bed?" I asked, watching him closely for signs of pain.

He answered with a shake of his head, his eyes on Zayaan. A chill ran down my spine as his features congealed into an imitation of the masklike Mayan stone figures we'd seen that afternoon.

"I have one last favor to ask of you," he said in a clear, solid tone.

No, no, no, no, no! I shouted in my head. What did he mean by 'one last favor'? What did he think was happening to him?

"Anything for you, *chodu*," Zayaan answered promptly.

But his voice sounded tense to my ears, too. I didn't look at him to confirm it. I couldn't. I couldn't take my eyes off my husband.

"Nirvaan—" I began, only to be shushed. *He couldn't mean...*

"I've made a living will and given you power of attorney," said Nirvaan, blowing my fears to smithereens.

Was it selfish of me that my first thought about this new form of morbidity my husband had introduced into our lives was to thank God that it wasn't me he'd chosen as the executor?

"I don't want to live on a respirator. I don't want to live in a vegetative state. I don't want to live in a fucking wheelchair with drool dribbling down my face," said Nirvaan, walking toward the kitchen where Zayaan sat.

I slowly got to my feet and finally turned to look at Zayaan. I'd expected him to get angry, and he did. He argued with Nirvaan for some time. His face grew flushed and not just because of anger. Tears fell nonstop from his eyes.

For the first time, I allowed myself to ackowledge just how badly Nirvaan's impending death was affecting Zayaan. I'd purposefully kept my distance from him, building a wall of guilt and anger between us. But the thing about triangles was, there were three bases and three combinations of points coming together in an apex.

Tonight, Zayaan and I made the apex—we had the common ground of grief holding us together—and Nirvaan was our base.

"You can't ask this of me," Zayaan choked out, his voice hoarse and devastated.

Tonight, I realized how little my husband had asked of me.

"Who else? I don't trust my family or Simi with this." Nirvaan shot me an apologetic glance. "They'll get emotional, and I won't suffer for their sentimentality. I need someone who will ask the right questions of the doctors and make a good judgment. A humane decision. I need you, man."

Zayaan kept shaking his head. He pressed a fist to his mouth and stopped a howl from spilling out.

I realized how free I was. Free to cry. Free to grieve and rage and bitch and moan at Ahura Mazda and Nirvaan and fate. I was free.

And Zayaan was not.

"And you think I won't get emotional? That I have no heart? I can't do this, Nirvaan. I'm not that strong."

But Zayaan was that strong. He had to be. He simply had to be for Nirvaan's sake. And for mine.

"Look, man, I'll try to die on my own. This is just in case I don't do a good job of it. I know. Shocking, huh? Me? Not doing a good job with something?" Nirvaan tried to make a joke, but his words hitched on his own sobs.

He reached for Zayaan just as Zayaan stood up, and they both met each other in a fierce hug. Crying and cursing each other.

I stayed where I was, imprinting the sight of them into my brain. They were beautiful.

I had no doubt I would love them until the end of time. Just as I had no doubt they would always break my heart.

18

It was my turn to cringe in the spotlight.

After a final thump on Zayaan's back, Nirvaan turned to me. His jolly mask was back in place. The guys might have composed themselves, but I was ready to shoot off to the moon, colonize it and never come back to Earth.

"You'll have the baby," Nirvaan said, like it was a fact.

"Didn't you leave it up to me?" I retaliated, my breath coming in bursts.

I hated the bones sticking out on his face, the hollowness of his cheeks, the unnatural whiteness of his skin.

"If I left things up to you, nothing would ever get done." My husband was not a pleasant man when he was crossed.

I could've brushed the words aside with a shrug had he meant them in jest. But Nirvaan's tongue was coated with bitterness, and they pierced my soul, spreading their poison.

"Leave her alone, fucker."

I didn't need Zayaan to defend me. I didn't want him to.

"I won't," Nirvaan said, refusing to relent. "And neither should you. Grow a pair of balls, *chodu*, and go after what you've always wanted."

I fisted my hands, so I wouldn't hit my husband. "Why are you doing this? Why are you pushing me…us together? Are you testing us? How many times do I have to tell you that we don't want each other? We don't want to live in some version of a life you've dreamed up, however wonderful you might think it is. I don't want him. I don't want to be with him. I *can't* be with him," I blurted out.

"Why not?" asked Nirvaan, his head cocked to one side.

I rocked back on my heels in shock. *Why not?* That question and in that tone and with that strange light in his eyes. He…knew. He was challenging me to confess the truth, I realized with crystal clarity. *He knew.*

I glanced at Zayaan wondering if he knew too and quickly looked back at my husband in relief. He didn't.

"Aside from the fact that you're not dead yet, your ghost will always come between us. Zayaan is not you. He won't be able to accept me loving you. It's against his nature. Then, there's Marjaneh. And I can't stand his mother. And I'm not a Muslim, and I will never convert. Should I go on?"

It was my standard laundry list of reasons why Zayaan and I could never work. I'd had years to come up with it, perfect it, add to it, subtract from it, for my own sanity. The thing was, none of those reasons mattered but for one. The one I still didn't have the courage to voice.

Denial was a handy thing. It fooled oneself into believing that pumpkins were carriages.

Zayaan walked out of the house before I even finished spewing my venom. He shoved open the patio doors, letting in a gust of wind that blew his papers all over the kitchen floor. I dashed to save them. Nirvaan dashed out onto the deck, shouting at Zayaan to come back in and hash this out. It was unsafe out on the beach. Zayaan ignored all warnings and disappeared into the night.

Nirvaan stood on the deck, watching him go. Letting him go at last.

So there, I'd broken the Awesome Threesome once and for

all. We weren't even a triangle anymore. We were just three people stuck together in a really bad situation.

Finally, Nirvaan slid the doors closed but didn't lock them and came to help me with the papers. Once collected and weighted down on the coffee table, he pulled me down to sit on the sofa. His mask had slipped into a frown, a desperate confusion. I smoothed his eyebrows, clearing it away. His eyes, they used to be big and round and black as night. Now the right one was smaller than the left, and the skin around them—where his lashes should be—was perpetually rimmed in red.

"Why didn't you tell me?" I asked softly. Had the truth always been present between us? Had I willfully denied my instincts to serve my own purpose? "Why didn't you ever tell me that you knew what Rizvaan had done?" Why had he let me lie to him all these years?

With a last frown directed at the spot where Zayaan had disappeared, Nirvaan relaxed into the sofa, tucking me under his arm so that my face rested in the nook of his neck. I kissed the underside of his jaw.

"I figured you'd tell me when you were ready. I waited for you to tell me, but you never did," he said, chuckling self-deprecatingly. He began fiddling with my hair, twisting it around his finger. "I should've known you wouldn't trust me with anything serious."

"I trust you with my life." I placed my hand over my husband's heart. "I started to tell you a thousand times, but the timing always sucked."

"Yeah, I know."

Something in the way he agreed made me push back and look at him. "You think I don't trust you?"

He heaved a sigh, letting my hair go like a spring. "If you could have, would you have told Zayaan?" I started to say "no" in reflex, but he cut me off. "Don't lie to me, Simi. God, we should be so past glossing over things by now."

"I don't know," I said after a couple of heartbeats. But because he deserved my honesty, I added, "I probably would've told him if they—his father and brother—hadn't died. He just deals with things differently than you. You're volatile. I can't predict how you'll react. Zai is...I don't know...solid. Sober."

"Sober." Nirvaan crumpled his face as if the word was without flavor or favor.

"Well, he is...in all ways." I couldn't help but smile.

"Where's the fun in sober?"

I didn't allow him to distract me. I asked him who'd spilled the beans—my brothers obviously—but which one and why, so I wouldn't guillotine them both. Imagine my surprise when it turned out to be neither.

The night of the rape, Nirvaan and Zayaan had come back to Zayaan's residence and caught Rizvaan sneaking out the back of the house. They'd caught him in the garden in front of the *jamaat khana*, toting a duffel bag and a gun. Kamlesh Uncle was still with the police, forming a game plan on how to best help Rizvaan.

"Zai confronted him. Told him to come to the police station and sort things out. He didn't listen. He threatened to blow his brains out. We let him go. But he said something before he left, and it didn't click until the next morning when I came to see you and found you gone."

I forced myself not to think of the gun. "What did he say?"

"Wasn't what he said, but the way he said it. He wished Zayaan and you bliss in your future nuptials. He had this smirk on his face when he said 'nuptials.' I thought he was jerking Zayaan's chain, like he always did where you were concerned. He left then, after threatening to shoot us if we followed him. We called Daddy, who informed the police, who, in turn, were preparing to raid the warehouse where all the shit exploded."

The police had surrounded the warehouse at the docks where Rizvaan and the rest of his cronies had holed up, waiting for a boat to take them out of India. There'd been a shootout, and Rizvaan had become one of the casualties.

"We waited with Daddy several yards away and heard the gunfire clearly. When it was over, Zayaan didn't want to go back to his house or the hospital. He was a mess that night, Simi. He didn't know how to tell his mother. He felt..." Nirvaan blew out a breath, cutting off the story.

I twisted toward the deck, half expecting Zayaan to be standing there, watching us through the glass doors, listening. He wasn't.

Turning back, I finished Nirvaan's story for him. "Zayaan felt shitty for turning Rizvaan in, right? He would've wanted to save his brother."

No matter what nasty things Rizvaan had done, Zayaan would've felt like he'd betrayed his brother and his family. That was Zayaan in a nutshell—overly responsible, overly protective, overly possessive.

Nirvaan cupped my face between his hands. "He wasn't thinking straight. He didn't hear the insult in Rizvaan's words. If he'd known...if we'd known what that bastard had done to you, we'd have gutted him. Castrated him and fed his dick to him. Roasted his balls and fed them to the street dogs while he watched."

"I know." I tried to smile, but Nirvaan was squishing my cheeks. I probably looked like a chipmunk.

He kissed me hard, fast, and I clung to him.

"I know," I said again, tears blurring my vision. "That's why I left. I didn't know he'd died. I didn't want to..." I stopped to gather my thoughts, wondering how to explain my frame of mind in the aftermath of that night. "I wanted him punished in worse ways than you've described, but I realized that to punish him, to expose him, would've shamed Zayaan, too. It would have destroyed Zayaan, no?" I wanted Nirvaan to validate my reasons for keeping quiet all these years. I needed him to tell me that I'd done the right thing by running away, by shunning them both. "He wouldn't have been able to get past it. He would've let his scholarships rot. Wouldn't he have?"

Zayaan would've married me, not for love but out of responsibility and horror and shame, and we would've ended up hating each other.

I started crying when Nirvaan agreed with me. He told me that I'd done exactly right by Zayaan. It was proof positive that my actions hadn't been in vain. My husband gathered me in his arms and let me weep, giving me all the comfort I'd craved for twelve years but denied myself.

When I calmed down some, he reached for the tissues on the coffee table and helped me blow my nose.

"Tell me the rest." I wanted to know everything.

Nirvaan had come looking for me first thing in the morning but found my apartment locked. He'd tracked Sarvar down and gotten an earful for his effort.

"That's when it sunk in that the bastard had done something really bad for your brother to have spoken to me like that. Really fucking bad." He wiped my tears away with a fresh tissue. "What happened that night, baby?"

"He threatened me…with a gun."

It was my turn to come clean. Every other sentence I uttered, Nirvaan interrupted me with a foul curse. It sounded so invigorating that I envied his flair with cussing. I left nothing out or almost nothing. I left out Gulzar Auntie's part in it. I didn't know how Nirvaan would react to a living, breathing nemesis, and I didn't want to find out. Besides, I knew, as surely as I knew the sun rose every day, that Zayaan's mother would answer for her actions, in this life or the next.

"I have another confession to make," Nirvaan sheepishly said.

I smiled encouragingly, unburdened of my secret at last. I'd done it. I'd told my husband the truth, and the sky hadn't fallen on our heads.

"Asha Ambani is a distant cousin of Daddy's. I've been in touch with her all along."

My jaw dropped, and I gaped at my husband. "You know Asha Auntie? What? But that's impossible. My cousin recommended her...right? Or did you tell my brother about her?"

"No. It was a coincidence. Can you believe it?" he said, looking as incredulous as I felt.

At this point, I was ready to believe anything. He told me the rest.

Ignoring Sarvar's and Surin's decrees to stay away from me, Nirvaan had finagled information of my whereabouts out of Surin's secretary. He'd fully intended to follow me to Mumbai the very next day.

"But it struck me that you might be scared, and if I barged in, demanding answers, I'd upset you even more. I called Asha Auntie, the famous psychologist in the family, and asked for advice. She didn't know it was in reference to you. And it was before you were her patient. We didn't put two and two together until much later—a couple of years later. She told me to give you time to heal. That I should leave you alone until you initiated contact again. But I ignored that bit of advice. It didn't feel right, letting you vanish from my life. It didn't feel right, Simi, for you to suffer this alone."

I kissed him once, twice, long and deep, with love brimming over. "I'm glad you ignored Asha Auntie and me. I'm so glad you didn't give up on me." Neither had Zai, until I'd gotten engaged to Nirvaan.

"I'll never give up. I want you to know I'd have stepped forward, if you were pregnant, and married you. Zai would've, too," he said gruffly.

"I know." I sighed. I'd never doubted them. I'd doubted my own worthiness but never them. "My cousin is a gynecologist in Mumbai. She immediately put me on the pill. There was no danger of a child."

"Is that why you don't want children?" Nirvaan asked softly.

I laughed at my husband. I couldn't help it. "Now you ask? After seven-plus years of marriage and fights and drama? No, Nirvaan. I don't know if I *don't* want a baby." I closed my eyes and then opened them again. My thoughts were beyond muddled about this topic. "I only know that I don't want another person I love to die on me."

Life held no guarantees. Sometimes, children died before their parents, like my brother Sam. Like Nirvaan. Did I have the strength to bear another cross on my soul?

A bone-deep remorse clouded Nirvaan's eyes and his face was a canvas of shattered dreams. "I'm sorry for putting you through this. So fucking sorry for getting fucking cancer. I would sell my soul to change it all. You know I would. That's why I want—"

The patio door slid open, cutting off Nirvaan's words, and Zayaan whooshed into the house along with the wind.

That's why I want you to have a baby? Or have Zai? If I had to guess what my husband had been about to say, I'd pick the latter.

Without acknowledging us, Zayaan strode past us and went into the hall bathroom, shutting the door with a smack. No, life hadn't been and wasn't going to be easy for any of us. Not ever again.

"Zayaan is not yours to give, Nirvaan. He's his own person and makes his own choices. And believe me when I tell you, I. Do. Not. Want. Him." I made my stand very clear. But was I convincing Nirvaan or myself?

"You did before. You chose him before. I was a fluke, Simi. Had that night not happened—"

I pressed my fingers against his mouth to shut him up. "But it did happen. And I don't want to discuss this anymore."

We went to bed, exhausted by our talk, and I fell into a dream-filled sleep. I dreamed of horses galloping on the beach, of gods and goddesses brandishing thunderbolts and tridents and lovers and swans, of humans cowering in fear under their wrath, of the first scene in the movie *Troy* in which Brad Pitt roused between two naked bodies.

I bolted up in bed, my heart pounding. I looked about for naked bodies and thunderbolts but found only my pajama-clad husband beside me. I pressed a hand to my racing heart, not sure if I was relieved or disappointed. I slid off the bed and padded into the bathroom where I took care of my morning business. I brushed my teeth and my hair and went to wake up my own Brad Pitt.

I blew into his ear. No reaction.

Nirvaan used to be ticklish around his neck and ears. Now parts of his body weren't exactly desensitized so much as slow to react to stimuli.

I bit his earlobe and got the reaction I wanted.

In one smooth motion, he started awake, pulled me down, rolled and had me pinned to the bed. I squealed with laughter. His muscles might be weaker than before, but they were still harder and larger than mine. I was well and truly trapped beneath his sleep-warm body.

"You want to play, huh?" Sleep had deepened his voice into a growl.

"I woke you up to watch the sunrise, but since you asked so cutely...yes," I replied before licking a path across his collarbone.

He rolled off and sat up on the edge of the bed, his back to me. I tried not to feel rejected.

Oh, to hell with it. I knelt behind him, wrapping my arms about him. "Please, don't say no today." *Please, choose me today.*

He stood up and, giving me a slanted smile, he stepped toward the drawer where his little blue pills were. He took one out, popped it into his mouth and dry-swallowed it.

"Open the curtains, wife. I want to watch the sunrise, too," he commanded as he strode into the bathroom, scratching his bum.

I gave a triumphant "Whoop!" and danced to the windows to draw the curtains open. Back I danced into the bathroom to watch Nirvaan race through his morning ablutions.

I admired the turn of his wrist as he brushed his teeth and gargled and spit. The way his pecs—softer now than a few months ago—jumped when he splashed water on his face. At the last minute, he detoured into the shower and thoroughly washed himself. I smiled, guessing what he wanted from me.

I made him sit on the closed commode as I dried him. I rubbed him down, dabbing water from inside his ears, under his armpits, between his legs. I would have gone to my knees right there, but he took my hand and led me back to our room.

He sat down on the edge of the bed, drawing me between the V of his legs. I stood, looking down at my handsome husband. I drew my fingers over the arch of his forehead, down his cheekbone, and rasped the rough skin on his jaw and lip with my thumb. I leaned in to lick his lips, but his eyes shifted to the damask curtain posing as our bedroom door.

MY LAST LOVE STORY

I turned my head, knowing Zayaan would be standing there. It was time to watch the sunrise, wasn't it? I closed my eyes. I couldn't bear the thought of him watching us now. I used to love him watching us before when I had no fear or inhibitions or guilt or shame. I had no words for what I felt right now. The past and the present collided inside me. A simple yes from me, and they would merge.

I opened my eyes, and the curtain was drawn closed, swaying slightly, as if a breeze and not a gentle hand had trifled with it. I sighed, wishing Khodai would stop playing games with me.

Nirvaan caught my hand and brought it to his lips. He firmly held me to him, as if he expected me to bolt.

Bolt where? Out there? To Zayaan? *Ha.*

"When you came back to Surat after three years in Mumbai, I thought... I hoped you were ready to let go of the past. I called Zayaan and told him to get his ass to India. We were both coming to see you. He booked his ticket before we'd hung up the phone. But his mother fell ill, and he had to cancel at the last minute. He didn't even get a refund on the ticket. He wanted to come, Simi. He doesn't know about the rest. I haven't told him." He took my face between his hands and forced me to look into his eyes. Love, anguish, regret, hope, it was all there. "It wasn't my place to tell."

"Thank you," I whispered. It hurt so much. All of this. All the time. It hurt.

"He believed Surin," Nirvaan went on. "He thinks your brother was correct in trying to protect you from gossip. He stayed away to save your reputation. His family was tainted by scandal, and he wanted to cloak himself in respectability before he came for you. He wanted to make you proud of him, not be ashamed to be with him. He was going to ask you to wait for him, to marry him as soon as he was on his feet. He loves you, Simi. So very much. He loves you more than I do."

To shut him up, I kissed Nirvaan harder than I'd meant, and our teeth clashed. "Don't. Don't you dare say such a thing. Don't you dare measure and compare your love."

"It's the truth, baby. And you love him more than you love me. And here's another truth. I don't mind. I love that about you. I loved how bold you were at fifteen. How willing you were to step outside the box. Zayaan used to be like that, too. Don't you remember?"

Our eyes clashed as our teeth had. I knew what my husband was asking. I wanted it, too. I always had.

"Used to be, Nirvaan. You said it yourself. We were children. We didn't know whether we were coming or going."

"But we're adults now, and we do know what we want." Sometimes, Nirvaan was like a predator, biding his time in the bushes, and when his prey drew close, he pounced.

Was a threesome what he truly desired? Why wouldn't he just come out and say it? Why was he driving me crazy with innuendo?

"Fine. If that's what you really want," I said as I withdrew from him.

His mouth fell open at my sudden capitulation. I was thrilled by his reaction and had to clench my jaw tight not to laugh or even smile. Not so gung ho now, was he? Not so open to possibilities?

I strolled out of the room, and I would've whistled had I known how. I had my answer, and I knew what I had to do.

My eyes adjusted quickly to the darkness of the living room. Sure enough, Zayaan was standing in front of the patio doors, looking out at the wakening beach, his prayer book in his hand.

As well be hung for a sheep as a lamb, my father would've said.

"Zai," I called out, my voice as soft as the sound of his name.

His shoulders stiffened before he slowly turned around. Tension wafted off him in such thick waves that I could've sliced it off with a butcher knife. I'd never been more grateful for the dark. I couldn't see his eyes or expression. I didn't want to know if they held curiosity or hope or arousal or all of it. It was enough that I felt it all. It would have to be enough.

"Can you please pray later?" I asked of him. "I want you to go for a walk. Don't come back for two hours."

I didn't wait to see if he went. I knew he would.

I went back to my husband and explained something to him. "Imagine I'm an ocean. You are the bright sunlit part of me, and Zayaan, the darker depths. I need you both to be who I am. I love you both. Always have. Always will. But, Nirvaan, you are my last love story. I don't want another one."

Then I pushed my husband down on the bed and stripped off my nightgown.

Maybe it was our confessions. Maybe it was that I'd clearly chosen Nirvaan when I could've had both. Maybe we both knew time was running out. Whatever it was, for the first time in years, our lovemaking was free of expectation, free of ghosts and, therefore, it was spontaneous.

I explored my husband's body, slowly and thoroughly. His body wasn't a surprise to me. When you'd nursed a man through an illness, his body wasn't a secret from you. I had bathed Nirvaan in showers and in tubs, sponged him off when he was too weak to lift a finger. I'd fed him food, cleaned his sores, wiped his bum, and buzzed wild hair from his nose and other places. So, yes, I knew his body intimately.

But sex was a different kind of intimacy. It wasn't one-sided. It was pleasure, given and taken. A mutual gratification of love and promises, shared and renewed.

Except for the first few times we'd made love, Rizvaan's ghost had never climbed into my marriage bed. Zayaan had. I'd thought he always would. But he didn't come into my mind this morning. Or, he came but he didn't stay. Nirvaan loved me so thoroughly that I had no room to think of anyone else. My senses could only moan and demand and gasp.

"Again," I begged. I was utterly spent, I could barely talk, but greed was something that could never be satisfied. There was a time limit to my greed, so I was ravenous.

My husband said nothing. Did nothing.

I opened one eye. It was all I could manage. The wicked, wicked man sat cross-legged by my hip, grinning down at me.

"You've always liked that, haven't you?" He raised a rakish brow, looking very much like a pirate in front of a treasure chest.

"Again. Please?"

My good husband didn't make me beg a third time. He swooped down and, ever generous with his pirate's bounty, he gave me what I needed.

I left Nirvaan sleeping to get coffee. I'd slept, too, and woken up with a pounding headache. Orgasms could cause headaches—the good doctors said so—but I thought mine was due to caffeine withdrawal.

I filled my Eeyore mug with coffee, took a couple of sips, blew on it, took a couple more sips and felt partially human again. The sun was up. The day had dawned. We'd not exactly seen the sunrise, but we'd done an in-depth study on the variegated effects of sunrays on body parts. I grinned and took another gulp of coffee. We planned to make it our morning ritual.

My eyes fell on Zayaan's prayer book discarded on the lounger and I sighed, my grin fading. I supposed I owed him an apology. I shouldn't have come out in that state and thrown him out of the house. He wouldn't have dared come into the room after peeping in once. But I'd wanted to make a bold statement. I hoped I had.

But why wasn't he back? I'd asked for two hours of privacy. It was now past three hours.

My eyes scanned the beach and caught his windblown figure standing thigh-deep in the waves. There was something about the stark picture he made—his posture, his banishment—that tugged on my heart.

Before I knew it, I'd set the mug down on the coffee table, and I was flying down the beach, my robe flapping at my ankles.

"Zayaan, what are you doing?" My gut pushed an apology to my throat, like the waves pushing at the sand beneath my feet. Quick as a wink, it receded—the wave, the sand beneath my feet, the apology stuck in my throat.

He turned to me. He was wet from his head down, his white *kurta* pajama transparent against his body.

"Did you go swimming with your clothes on?"

Zayaan was a strong swimmer. He'd swum out to the light-house and back once, the whole expedition taking a couple of hours, while Nirvaan and I'd trailed him on Jet Skis.

I shook my head in disbelief. Zayaan was pragmatic, not stupid. He wouldn't have gone swimming without a chaper-one. So, why was my gut writhing like snakes again?

He pushed through the lapping waves, coming at me. The sun hit him full on the face, flaming him up. I should've run. I should've broken his pursuit of me—and it was a pursuit even though I was standing still. If it wasn't broad daylight, if I didn't know Rizvaan was dead, I might've panicked. Zayaan looked fierce. Enraged. I wanted to run.

Liar, liar, pants on fire.

The second he got close, Zayaan pulled me into his arms and kissed me like a man starved. He didn't give me room to panic, to think. A steely arm banded around my waist. An unyielding hand palmed my head, holding me immobile. Tongue, mouth, lips were all I could feel of us. His stubble abraded my skin.

Zayaan was passion and fire, for all his stoicism and calm. Nirvaan was tenderness and finesse, despite his zest for life. I'd always marveled at their differences, within and without.

I would not be ashamed or lie that I kissed Zayaan back.

I knew what this kiss meant for both of us. It meant good-bye.

He thrust me away before I had a chance to memorize the taste of him on my tongue, the warmth of his skin against my mouth, the strength of his shoulders beneath my hands or the solidness of his body against mine. We were both breathing hard when he stepped away. My heart felt battered and fragile. Unreliable.

He looked at me with a face devoid of expression once again. "We're done," he said. Then he stalked past me and into the house.

I wrapped my arms over my stomach and wheezed out a cry, a laugh, a sob. I didn't know what.

We were done. Finally.

19

I had a full month of what I would always remember as the second wind in my marriage before Nirvaan lapsed into a comatose state.

It'd happened gradually even though it felt sudden to me.

"He was fine just this morning," I sobbed into the phone when I called his parents from the hospital.

If fine was a thirty-year-old man spending more time in his pajamas than out of them.

If fine was not remembering his name and not caring he didn't.

If fine was sleeping for so long that his wife had to shake him awake just to make sure he would wake.

I considered all those scenarios fine because once those bouts of lethargy and confusion were over, Nirvaan still looked at me with his wicked rascal eyes and smiled.

Everyone came that very afternoon or soon after—my in-laws, Nisha, Aarav, Ba, Sarvar, aunts and uncles, cousins and friends. The Desai clan laid siege on the hospital waiting room, and though we spoke in hushed whispers, the sheer number of us made it sound like an infestation of cicadas on hot summer days. They'd all come to be with Nirvaan even though only a handful of us were allowed to go in to see him.

Nirvaan was in the intensive care unit. The pressure in his

brain that had caused the coma had been relieved immediately. He was breathing on his own. *Praise Khodai*. His heart was beating strong. He was connected only to a catheter and an IV.

We all waited for him to wake up…or die.

As most things in life, comas were a gray area, and Nirvaan's doctors could not predict what might happen with any certainty. It all depended on the patient.

Leaving their children with grandparents, Surin and Parizaad flew in, too. For me. I cried when Surin bumbled into the hospital's waiting room, his eyes wide behind his thick, boxy spectacles, searching me out. I ran to him, and when he enveloped me in his clumsy bear hug, I blubbered into his chest. I clung to him, this man who was my parent by default. This man who'd promised he wouldn't let anything bad happen to me ever again the night our parents had died. Surin's was the last hug I accepted or gave back willingly.

As the first week stretched into two and the unpredictability and uncertainty surrounding Nirvaan's condition showed no sign of relenting, the crowds began to thin. But I'd already begun to freeze them out.

I realized most people meant to offer comfort when they said stuff like, "Whatever happens, happens for the best," or, "It is God's will," or, "Have patience, dear," or, "At least he isn't suffering."

I especially hated when they patted me on my shoulder, as if that brief stranger's touch was going to spread eternal sunshine through my soul. It took all the strength I had not to jump up and shout, *Nothing bad happens for the best. And best for whom, assholes? And there is no God. If there were, He wouldn't do shitty stuff like this. And are you suddenly a neurologist because how in the fuck would you know Nirvaan isn't suffering?*

There was a lot of cussing going on in my mind all the time.

Cussing was a liberating franchise, and at the same time, it was to the point. No wonder Nirvaan loved to cuss so much.

I felt a sudden urge to see him then. I'd already had my turn that morning, but I asked my father-in-law if he wouldn't mind waiting a bit more for his turn. It would've been his right to refuse me. There were six of us who sat with Nirvaan for an hour each in rotation, and he'd not seen his son today. But I'd long since stopped being surprised by Kamlesh Desai's generosity.

The intensive care unit was one large room divided into twenty smaller patient rooms with glass doors and a fully staffed monitoring station right in the middle. I disinfected my hands and waited in front of Nirvaan's patch of the barren white ICU meadow.

Nisha was inside. She was singing to her brother or praying, but I couldn't hear her out here. We tried not to leave Nirvaan alone, except at night when ICU rules wouldn't allow us to stay.

Even when they fed him, Zayaan stayed with him. I couldn't. I didn't even attempt to be brave about it. I didn't want to watch the attending nurse insert a funneled pipe into Nirvaan's mouth or nose, alternatively to avoid internal lacerations, and pour a thick liquid down his throat. They would do this twice a day.

Nisha noticed me, and after only a mildly questioning look, she kissed Nirvaan on his forehead and came out. She touched my shoulder as I removed my shoes, and she stepped into hers. I stiffened, but I nodded, acknowledging the commiseration, and then I didn't think about her anymore.

He looked as if he were sleeping. As if all I had to do was shake his shoulder or blow in his ear, and he'd grab me with strong hands and pull me down on top of him, tickling me till I screamed for mercy.

"Please, baby. Please open your eyes and look at me. Grab me. Tease me. Tell me I look ugly when I cry." When he didn't answer my summons, I picked up his hand and pressed it to my lips. "Fine. You don't want to answer, then let me update you on the latest gossip. It's about your cousin Reka's husband…"

I relayed the scandal and some other choice stories that had been making the rounds in the waiting room. It amazed me how resilient life was regardless of death, ill health, trauma or terror. Here, Nirvaan was in a coma, fighting for his life, and out there, a bunch of women from his family were tittering over how a husband had given an STD to his wife.

"Fucking morons, all of them. Your aunts, Reka, her fucking husband and the bimbo he's fucking. Oh, by the way, I know why you curse so much. I'm getting rather fond of several four-letter words, too. Mumsy's going to be quite disappointed in me…but I'd rather her than you."

His hand felt warm on my cheek, and it made me feel better. Extremities getting cold wouldn't have been a good sign.

"They keep a wide berth from Zayaan. He's not doing well, baby. He doesn't talk except to discuss you. Doesn't eat until Ba or Mummy force him to."

Ba had picked up Nirvaan's mantle, and every day she found new ways to nudge Zayaan and me together. *Give him a glass of buttermilk, will you, beta? Can you ask him what he wants for lunch or if he needs anything from home?* It was official, the Desai clan's penchant to amuse and irritate me at once.

I ran my eyes up and down Nirvaan's body. The swelling on his forearm with the IV in it had gone down a bit.

"I'm trying to be a friend to him, baby. But he's the one pushing me away now. I'm…" I paused, shuddering in a breath. "I don't think we can be what you want us to be."

I was numb where Zayaan was concerned. I spoke to him

by rote. I looked at him and felt nothing. No, that wasn't true. I felt sad when I looked at him. I felt sad all the time.

"People are wondering why he's the one in charge. Why the doctors speak to him first, even with Daddy and Mummy and me around."

Not that Zayaan left any of us out of the loop, especially since two teams of doctors were deliberating over Nirvaan's condition. But the extended family couldn't fathom why he had power of attorney and never failed to make sly and snide comments about it.

"He's Nirvaan's brother from another mother" had become my standard reply. I didn't care if I sounded facetious.

"They aren't all awful, you know. The women are always bringing food. The guys, especially Manish and Deeps, have been running all over town—doing grunt work, making sure the cars are gassed up and the house is in order, and taking care of the rest of the clan spread out in hotels from here to San Jose. I didn't think much of them for a long time, you know. I hated the way your friends had abandoned you when you fell ill. I thought very badly of them then. But they're here now. Do you hear me, Nirvaan? Everyone is here for you. Everyone is waiting for you to wake up. Please, baby, wake up."

I had to stop talking and look away for a bit. I pressed my fingers over my eyes and took deep breaths in and out, in and out, until I was composed once again.

"Oh, before I forget, one of your aunts made the Surti *undhiyu* you love so much. Now she's trying to convince the nursing staff to puree it as your next meal. Would you like that, honey?"

I talked until my father-in-law came to relieve me. I didn't want to say goodbye to my husband, but I had to...just in case I never saw him again.

★ ★ ★

That evening, I felt Nirvaan's finger twitch. No, I wasn't being fanciful. I might seem like a person whose head floated in the clouds, who wasn't there in the here and now, but I was solidly grounded in reality. If I weren't, I couldn't have survived all the traumas I'd faced. If I wasn't, I would let Zayaan back into my life.

At first, I thought my own nerves had made the finger twitch. I didn't think my hands had stopped shaking since we brought Nirvaan to the ER two weeks ago. But when I felt the tiny pressure of his pinkie nail on my palm, I jerked in shock.

I had the nurse page the attending ICU doctor. Dr. Rhonda checked the monitors in the room and Nirvaan's eyes for a cognitive response. She tickled his foot and held his hand but nothing. We sat vigilant. I was aware of her pitying looks, but I knew what I'd felt. She left after a bit, and Nirvaan's finger didn't twitch again.

But the incident was a thorn under my skin and kept me awake all night. I didn't know what to do. Should I tell the family, the doctors? What if I was mistaken? What if I was being fanciful? I couldn't raise everyone's hopes for nothing. But how could I not say a word? My God. What if Nirvaan had really moved?

I cursed him then, for trusting in Zayaan and not trusting me to act in his best interests. I cursed myself for even thinking to take a back seat in this. Yes, I would probably be emotional about Nirvaan's health, his life. If he'd thought Zayaan would be any different...*ha*. I would never forgive myself if I didn't speak up.

But what if I was wrong?

Fuck.

The next morning, I willed Nirvaan to move his finger again but to no avail. I spoke to another staff doctor at length, and then I made sure he spoke to Nirvaan's doctors, so they'd do whatever tests needed to be done. Every day, they monitored his brain functions with EEGs and CT scans and functioning MRIs. The point being, he was still exhibiting brain function. He was breathing on his own. His nervous system was functioning without external aid. He was doing really well under the circumstances. The only question was, how long would it last?

Zayaan sought me out while I lunched with Ba and Nisha in the hospital's atrium. He pulled me aside.

"You felt him move?" His eyes bored into mine.

I would've walked away if he'd sounded even remotely skeptical or given me a she's-gone-crazy look. He didn't. He listened to my explanation. His face gave nothing away. When had he learned to master his emotions so well? Or had he always been like this—unreadable, unreachable—and only Nirvaan and I had been privy to his softer side?

I demonstrated what I'd felt. I placed my pinkie nail on his palm. "I was holding his hand in both of mine. His fingers were straight, and then his little finger curved into my palm. I swear, I'm not making this up."

"Nirvaan moved his hand? Why haven't you told us?" gasped Nisha from behind me.

Crap. She'd snuck up on us.

My first instinct was to take the back seat again, let Zayaan explain it to her, to everyone. But I owed it to my in-laws to tell them myself. I sat them down, even Nisha and Ba, and told them everything. Just as I'd feared, it became a big deal—which it was—but the hope reflected on their faces curdled my belly.

Khodai, please don't let me be wrong, I prayed over and over, all day long. I couldn't be mistaken about this, for their sake. And Nirvaan's...and mine.

★ ★ ★

I wasn't wrong, but I hadn't been right, either.

It had been an involuntary movement, which wasn't nothing, as any movement exhibited by a comatose patient was considered a good sign, explained Nirvaan's doctors. They said Nirvaan was in a deep coma right now. He was a three on the Glasgow Coma Scale, which was as bad as it could get. But involuntary movement was a sign of improvement, not deterioration.

I took heart in the prognosis as I let myself into the beach house, parking my roll-on bag and tote by the washer and dryer. I'd been sent home early with instructions to take a sleeping pill and knock myself out for the night. And I would as soon as I dealt with some of the dirty laundry I'd brought back from the hospital. I loaded the washer, started a cold cycle as I couldn't be bothered to sort out coloreds or delicates, and had almost grabbed the vacuum when I noticed that the house was in pristine order. Even the kitchen. Some helpful family fairy had come in and cleaned my house sometime during the past week. I hadn't come home, not even at night, since Nirvaan had nudged me with his finger. I should be grateful, but I felt like a stranger in my own house now.

Right. More time to read and relax in the bath, then.

In the bathroom, I screwed open the tap and water rushed into the tub as I twisted my hair into a braid and pinned it up. I went to fetch my e-reader, upending the tote when I couldn't find it. I searched every pocket of my empty roll-on before I acknowledged that I'd left it at the hospital. Suddenly, tears gushed down my cheeks. I couldn't even handle packing my own shit without flubbing it. I crumpled on the bed I'd shared with my husband and hugged his pillow to my chest. I missed him so much. Every breath was a challenge without him.

As my tears ran their daily course, the jingle of the wind chimes drew my attention to the windows. The setting sun glared at me in reproach. I hadn't paid attention to the sun's movements in a while. Suddenly, I didn't want a bath. I wanted to feel the sand beneath my feet and the ocean on my tongue. I zipped Nirvaan's sweatshirt up to my chin—I wore it all the time now—and hauled my ass down to the beach after closing the bath's tap.

Almost immediately I noticed a black blur zipping across the water in front of the giant ball of orange hovering over the horizon. I blinked at it, stared until my mind processed it as a Jet Ski. I twisted around to squint at the beach house. The carriage house that housed our Jet Skis was open. And Nirvaan's orange-and-black wetsuit was missing from the hook on the porch. I stalked to the carriage house and saw that Nirvaan's Jet Ski had disappeared, too.

My heart flip-flopped inside my chest when I realized it was Zai out there.

Anger bubbled up in me. How could he ride the waves on Nirvaan's Jet Ski in Nirvaan's wetsuit when Nirvaan was in a coma? How dare he even pretend to enjoy life right now? I ran up the porch, grumbling at Ba under my breath. No wonder she'd forced me to come home to "relax." I stripped off my jeans and sweatshirt and put on my wetsuit over my T-shirt, and then I ran back out to the carriage house. I chased Zayaan down on Lady Periwinkle, my Jet Ski.

"What are you doing?" I shouted, bringing the bike to a stop next to Zayaan's. He'd cut off his engine in the middle of nowhere and was bobbing in the water.

He flicked a lazy grin in my direction. It looked out of place between us. He hadn't smiled at me like that in forever.

My anger froze when a particular skunky scent wafted my way.

"You're getting high?" I was beyond shocked now. "What is wrong with you? I can't believe you're getting high when you should be…when you need your brain to be the sharpest it's ever been."

What in hell was he thinking getting stoned instead of coming to a decision about Nirvaan's health?

"Give that to me." I leaned over and tried to smack the cigarette out of his hand. It accomplished nothing except my Jet Ski bumped hips with his and we bobbed apart and then bumped into each other again.

"Relax, Sims." He stretched his arm up and away from me when I tried to grab the joint again. "I am trying to sharpen my brain by relaxing it. I can share, if you need to relax, too," he offered magnanimously. He wasn't giggling, so that was something.

Khodai. We were all going mad. I quickly realized that yelling at him or fighting wasn't going to work. Had it ever worked on Zayaan? What worked was freezing him out. I should ride off and leave him to brood like he clearly wanted to do.

I didn't. I waited for him to finish the cigarette. I even took a few puffs of it myself. It did not relax me, so that was a complete waste. We huddled over our bikes in sync with the silence of the ocean inasmuch as an ocean brimming with life could be silent. Far out in the distance, gulls shrieked and ran circles over the water. Below, whale-watching boats were out to show the tourists a good time, and if I squinted just right, I caught the Vs of the tails of a pod of humpbacks as they dove for their food.

There's this feeling I got when I wasn't on solid land. When I was surrounded by the arrythmic sound of waves. A feeling of floating in space, of being part of something that was bigger than me, bigger even than this world.

"Where did you get it?" I asked as Zayaan tucked the used stub into his pocket.

He took a deep breath, inhaling clean ocean air instead of unhealthy smoke. "It was the last of Nirvaan's stash," he answered without looking at me.

It hurt that he was done with me even though I wanted it so. It hurt that he was hurting. For Nirvaan, because of Nirvaan. Because of me.

"If you want to talk, I'll listen." I offered him an olive branch. I didn't know if that would make us hurt less or more in the end.

Zayaan looked at me then, his eyes heralding the storm he was struggling to gain control of. I didn't look away.

A lot of it I knew already, but he began to tell me what troubled his heart.

The main obstacle was the tumor, which would kill Nirvaan if left untreated. One team of doctors suggested we cut all of it out to save his life, as repeated radiation would be worse for him in the long run. The other team explained, if we cut out that much of his brain, he might remain in a comatose state or shift into a vegetative state, which might eventually improve to a semifunctional state with therapy, medications and luck. Or might not.

Nirvaan had disdained any option that would leave him an invalid. His living will was proof of it. But if there was a chance, the slightest chance of him waking up, of recovery, then how could we squander it?

"I've gone over it and over it and over it. Besides the doctors here, Daddy and I have consulted with the best neurosurgeons in Paris, Germany and Mumbai. No one, not one of them, will tell us with any certainty what the outcome of the surgery will be. All they offer are probabilities," he said, sounding confused and angry at once.

I'd been present during those discussions. I hadn't offered an opinion or asked questions then. I hadn't wished to confuse Zayaan or my in-laws. My husband had freed me from this responsibility, and I refused to feel guilty about it.

"Daddy is wondering if we should fly to New York and get a sixth opinion," he said.

"What do you think?" I'd started to shiver a bit. There was a chill rising in the air and my wet hair was freezing my scalp. It was still light out, and I saw indecision glitter in Zayaan's eyes. I didn't wait for him to answer. "Look, I've been silent because I trust you to make the right decision. Nirvaan trusted you. Daddy, Mummy…everyone knows you'll do what's best for Nirvaan."

Apparently, it was the wrong thing to say, because Zayaan growled out a string of curses. "Yeah? Well, maybe you should rethink that. I've wished for his death, do you know that?" Zayaan broke off to curse again. Viciously. "The day you got married, I wanted to kill him. Every time I thought of you and him together… I've wished him to hell—wished you both to hell. And then, when he fell ill…all I could think was…I did that to him."

I'd stiffened at the start of his tirade and by the end of it my stomach roiled. Now we were getting to the bottom of Zayaan's pit of vipers.

"You didn't jinx Nirvaan," I said gently. We'd both become so good at the blame game.

"Didn't I?" I couldn't tell if he was crying because his face was wet from the ocean spray. "Nirvaan shouldn't have asked this of me. He shouldn't have trusted me. I can't be trusted, don't you see?" He broke off, his chest heaving as he fought not to cry.

I wanted to climb onto his Jet Ski and into his lap. I wanted to take him in my arms and smother him with kisses until his jealousies and self-reproach were put to rest. But I couldn't do that because of my own guilt and culpability, so I reminded him about the kind of man his best friend was.

"But he did trust you. Even knowing that you were jealous and had very probably wished him ill. Nirvaan trusted you. *Trusts* you. He loves you, Zai. He knows you will do right by him."

There were only two options really: remove the tumor or let it kill him very slowly from a brain herniation. There was also a chance Nirvaan would die of aspiration pneumonia if he stayed unconscious too long.

Removing the tumor had three possible outcomes: there was a 40 percent chance that Nirvaan would wake up with some indeterminate brain damage that may or may not leave him completely impaired; a 40 percent chance that Nirvaan would remain in a coma and develop further complications; or a negligible chance of the surgery leading to his immediate death.

The statistics weren't encouraging, to be sure.

"Fuck, Simi, I don't know what to do. Tell me what to do."

What could I say? That we shouldn't do everything in our power to save Nirvaan? That we should let him die like he'd wanted—with grace and dignity? That ship had sailed.

"You know Nirvaan's heart better than anyone else, Zai. I am here if you need someone to talk to. But I cannot—I won't make this decision for you."

I wasn't that brave.

Nirvaan had been in a coma for six weeks when the doctors gave Zayaan the ultimatum. It was now or never to remove the tumor. The dissipated friends and relatives began to flock to the waiting room again. People began arriving from out of the country. Zayaan's mother came, offering solace to my in-laws and a shoulder to her son. I kept out of her way.

The surgery was a success insofar as the bomb inside Nirvaan's brain was defused and he was still alive. The day he
opened his eyes, we all cried—not in joy or relief, but in remorse. Nirvaan had opened his eyes, but he recognized no
one. He'd opened his eyes to oblivion.

The doctors explained that it was normal, that it would
take some time for his brain to recondition itself and relearn
how to process and transmit data. Nirvaan exhibited adequate
lower-brain function, which regulated his breathing, heart
rate and sleep cycle without external aid. He exhibited some
upper-brain-stem function, which allowed him to open and
shut his eyes. After a few months of therapy, he might also
manage to make sounds.

"Not speak, mind you," said Dr. Unger.

That would take years, if ever. He warned us to manage
our expectations. With cutting-edge Alzheimer's medication,
they hoped to boost the healthy neurons in his brain to com-
pensate for the ones that had been damaged or cut out. But
only time would tell how much of his memory remained in-
tact, and how much of it he'd lost. Only time would tell how
lucky he was. Nirvaan would be in the hospital for another
two months or until he could walk on his own. He could go
home then—under strict care and vigilance, of course.

"He'll need to be fed, bathed, walked, washed and supervised at all times, just like a baby."

It was official. Through the noblesse oblige of the healthy,
we'd made Nirvaan into the very thing he'd dreaded the
most—a vegetable.

Grief was an ocean inside me. Some days, it would well up
in my body like high tide, crashing against my self-possession,
pouring out of my eyes and mouth and nose in salty rivers.

Other days, it would lap at my insides—quiet, familiar, sooth-ing, a little condescending.

He isn't dead, my conscience reminded me, *so quit behaving like a widow.*

Everyone left within a week of Nirvaan's awakening. The world hadn't stopped spinning while he was ill. There were things to do, businesses to run, bills to pay and families to think of.

Eventually, only my mother-in-law, Zayaan, his mother and I remained by Nirvaan's side. They'd moved him into his own room with his own twenty-four-hour nurse. Bea-trice was a wonder, and miracle of miracles, she'd be coming home with us as Nirvaan's live-in nurse.

The Carmel beach house had undergone a major renovation during the months Nirvaan was in the hospital. It was fitted with ramps for wheelchair access and an invalid shower, ex-panded to fit a couple more bedrooms than it had originally boasted. I didn't know how my father-in-law had finessed the purchase from its previous owner, but I guessed he'd paid an arm and a leg for it.

Had I mentioned lately what a blessing money was? If I hadn't, I'd been remiss.

That we could gut the house and make it habitable for Nir-vaan or afford a twenty-four-hour caregiver or do a million other things to improve his quality of life made the guilt of what I'd done a little easier to bear. After all, if I hadn't felt him move, things might've worked out differently.

I didn't know why I'd decided to stay on in Carmel-by-the-Sea and not move to LA and in with my in-laws. I just knew I wanted to be alone with my husband, cocooned and trapped in our miniature snow-globe world.

I didn't know what Zayaan was going to do now that things were settled and I had Beatrice. I hoped he'd go back to London soon. I'd made sure he wouldn't come home with us. A few times when Nirvaan's aunts had lorded over the waiting area, I'd offered a ghost of a scandal to their ears.

"Are you coming home, Zai?" I'd ask aloud in their hearing.

To the gossip queens, the question had taken on a vulgar cadence. They'd stared at us, and they hadn't stopped staring since. I was sure we painted a picture—the wife and the best friend—always together, united in our desire to care for Nirvaan and in our guilt for gambling with his health.

Imagining what they whispered behind our backs had become my pastime.

Haw. *Look at the chit. Husband in a coma, and she's worried about Zayaan's dinner.*

Did you notice how he looks at her and how she looks back?

Best friend, shmest friend. Lord knows what goes on in that house when no one's looking.

Zayaan got the message, though, and he made sure he was never at home at the same time I was.

The very next day, I got my answer with regard to Zayaan. He would be leaving for London with his mother within the week.

"Sana's wedding is next month, and I need him there. There's so much still to be done," Zayaan's mother explained to my mother-in-law.

"Of course, Gulzar, he needs to be there for his sister. Zayaan *beta*, don't worry about anything. Nirvaan is doing well, and Simeen and I are here. Your poor mother can't do this alone. Your family needs you. Weddings are a lot of work, *beta*," said my mother-in-law.

What else was she supposed to say?

Zayaan argued that he could fly there the week of the wedding and fly back right after, but both mothers were adamant.

"Life must go on," my mother-in-law said to him.

And there was no need for everyone to sit around in the hospital.

He glared at them. He scowled at me. "I thought we were past this. I thought we were...friends."

"We are friends," I agreed. I didn't have another word for what we were to each other. "We'll always be friends, no matter where we are." But I refused to save him from his mother. That was not my fight.

Frustrated with my answer, he said he'd think about it.

There was a life truth that I'd come to realize all on my own. That the vices we abhorred in people we hated became virtues in the ones we loved.

Feroza Batliwala had been a possessive mother. She'd judged and found lacking a good chunk of my brothers' and my friends. She'd always had a thing or two to say about Surin's and Sarvar's girlfriends, and I was positive she would have had issues with Nirvaan and Zayaan, too. No one had been good enough for her beautiful and clever babies.

Gulzar Begum was no different. But the difference between her and my mother was, my mother wouldn't have allowed an atrocity to occur in her home.

Somehow, I found myself alone with Gulzar Begum inside Nirvaan's room that afternoon. I would've walked away, but I didn't want to leave Nirvaan alone with the witch.

"Are you happy now?" she began without preamble, confirming my suspicion that she'd planned for us to be alone all along.

Happy? She thought my husband in such a state made me happy?

I sat at the foot of Nirvaan's bed, massaging his feet, like the physiotherapist had shown me to do to strengthen circulation. I cursed Beatrice for taking her tea break at this very hour.

"You need to assure him that you're fine. He has a lot of

things to take care of back home," she said, unconcerned that I hadn't replied or that I wasn't even looking at her.

Zayaan's "I'll think about it" had been too ambiguous an answer for her. I also understood her insecurity. Her precious son had looked to me for guidance instead of agreeing with his beloved *ummi*. Oh, she must be seething with hatred for me.

Did it make me a horrible person to be dancing with glee inside?

"His sister needs him. Don't you see?"

The woman was persistent, wasn't she?

"He'll be there for Sana. Sofia, too. Zayaan knows his responsibilities," I said so she'd leave. And if he dared forget, Ummi Dearest would remind him, surely.

"He used to know his responsibilities before he came here. Now I see he can't even take care of his own self. He's lost weight. He looks sick. This is not good for him. Don't you see?"

I heard desperation in her words and hated the twinge of sympathy in my gut. In another universe, I would've empathized with this mother whose only son, the only support raft she had left in the world, seemed to be drifting away from the shore she was standing on.

"Let him go. Don't you have any compassion in your heart? You have a husband. Take care of him. Be happy in that. What more do you need?"

I lifted my eyes from my husband's unresponsive face, staring daggers at Gulzar Begum.

What more do I need? Had she really said that to me? How about a whole husband? How about my virginity back that your devil spawn had taken from me? How about my self-esteem, my pride, my parents?

I could've told her that she needn't pitch a fit because Zayaan and I were done—in one respect, at least. I could've eased her agony and assured her that her son was hers and hers alone.

I didn't.

She was right. I wasn't a compassionate woman.

Not with her.

But Gulzar Begum had never learned to retreat while ahead. "I should tell him about Rizvaan and you. Maybe then he'll know what kind of person you are."

She'd destroy her own son to teach me a lesson? What kind of a mother was she?

I stared at her jowly face for one second too long. "Be my guest. Let's see which one of us he despises the most then," I said. Then I turned back to massaging Nirvaan's feet, dismissing the nasty woman and her empty threats.

When the day came, I didn't say goodbye to Zayaan. I made my mother-in-law wish him and his mother a safe journey back to London because I was afraid that if I saw him, I'd ask him to stay. And that was about as generous as I could be with that family.

Sorrow and loss touched everyone. They came at the unlikeliest of moments, robbing us of breath and speech, our souls even. But it was in such moments that we faced our true character. It was in these moments that we manufactured our best courage.

Ba died before we brought Nirvaan home from the hospital.

She died with grace and dignity. She went to sleep one night and never woke up. If Khodai would grant me one wish, I'd wish such a death for all the people I loved.

I'd miss her. Of course I'd miss her, but I was tapped out of tears and had nothing left to drum up for her. I was past my grief, past anger, past helplessness. I was blessedly numb.

And knowing Ba, she'd have tut-tutted anyone who'd lament a life long and well lived.

If a ninety-eight-year-old dosi isn't meant to die, who on earth is? I imagined her saying.

As soon as we received the news, I drove my mother-in-law to the airport to catch the next flight out to LA. I didn't attend Ba's funeral. I wouldn't leave Nirvaan. I didn't want to even if we had Beatrice. And I told my mother-in-law not to hurry back.

"We'll be fine. He'll be in the hospital for another month. And there's Beatrice."

"I know he'll be fine," said Kiran Desai, giving me a watery smile.

She'd aged in these last months. Lines of fatigue and worry crowded around her mouth and eyes. Even my father-in-law, who hadn't had a single gray hair on his head, had a line of them sprouting along his temple and sideburns. Time was catching up with all of us.

"It's not only him I worry about, *beta*."

She meant me. Another hot poker of guilt stabbed me in the stomach, letting me know I wasn't completely numb, after all.

"Don't worry about me, please. Nirvaan and Ba both believed I was strong. And I am, you know." I crossed my fingers, hoping I hadn't jinxed myself.

"I know you are, but that's not what I meant," she said as I pulled into the county airport.

I parked the Jeep in the lot and rolled my mother-in-law's bag into the terminal for her. It didn't take us five minutes to check in. The flight was not full, but the airport was small enough to feel full even though there weren't many passengers checking in, in the afternoon. I bought us two cups of coffee, and we sat side by side on the plastic chairs before the security gate.

My mother-in-law blew into her coffee cup, which I'd left lidless to cool faster. "Eight years ago, I didn't take the news of your engagement too kindly. I thought it was a mistake for the two of you to marry." She gave me a sideway glance, much like her son used to.

My heart squeezed tight, and I willed it to stop aching. He'd looked so stunned when I'd proposed to him. He'd been happy, nervous, confused. He'd argued I should wait for Zayaan to fly down from London, wait until all three of us were together again before I made any decisions. I'd refused to wait, and I'd given Nirvaan no choice but to answer me that day.

"Because I wasn't Hindu?" I guessed tentatively.

Community standing meant a lot to my in-laws, and as a rule, Gujarati Hindus tended to marry within their community—or at the very least, into similar belief systems. Nirvaan's friends had openly expressed shock and envy that he'd married a Parsi woman without his parents going ballistic.

"That was one reason. Another was, you were too young. Nirvaan was a foolish young man. A flibbertigibbet. Brash. Insensitive. I didn't think he was ready to settle down. Ready to focus on one person or be a husband. But there wasn't only one person, was there?"

I choked on my coffee, and my mother-in-law obligingly thumped my back. "Sorry?"

"You forget, *beta*, I've seen the three of you grow up. I know you love my son, and he loves you, but you feel something for Zayaan, too. And I don't know what it is between those two boys, but it's more than friendship." Suddenly earnest, she twisted her compact body toward me. "I don't know what happened between you and Zayaan, but if you think it's us… that we won't approve…that's not true. Nirvaan would want you to be happy…both of you. We do, too, *beta*."

"What...what do you mean?" I stuttered, aghast by what I was hearing.

"Twenty-eight years ago, I didn't trust my feelings, and I let your father-in-law convince me if we had enough money, all our troubles would end. I left my children in the care of others. I didn't see them again for eleven years, and by then, they were not my children anymore. I will regret leaving them for the rest of my life. What I'm saying is, relationships matter, *beta*. All relationships. But the special ones matter the most. Don't live in regret, Simeen. It's not worth it."

First Nirvaan, then Ba, and now my mother-in-law. The Desais just didn't quit, did they?

After we hugged goodbye and cried buckets, she went through Security. I sat in the car until her flight took off, watching it fade into the clouds.

I wondered if Nirvaan had put Ba and his mother up to nudging me into action in his absence. I wouldn't put it past him. I didn't know if I could live without regret in this life, or do half the things my husband expected of me, but the fact that my mother-in-law cared for me like my own mother had was enough to make me weep.

I was surrounded by brave people, had been all my life. I couldn't insult them by being less. I'd been afraid for an eternity, not truly living life but just waiting for death to happen. I'd always considered myself an unlucky person, Khodai's least favorite human, but now, I thought—no, now, I knew I was the luckiest person in the world. Lucky to have known my parents and Ba and *mukhi saheb*, lucky to know the Desai clan, my brothers and, yes, even Nisha. But most of all, I'd been so very, very lucky to have known and loved Nirvaan.

Suddenly determined to prove their faith in me, I blew my nose and strapped on my seat belt. Setting the gear to D, I drove back to the hospital via the fertility clinic. I wasn't going to be scared of this thing called love anymore, no matter its risks.

I was going to have Nirvaan's baby.

20

Life once again became a triangle between the hospital, the beach house and the clinic.

My IVF cycle was shorter this time. I didn't have to ovulate and retrieve eggs or even wait for my oocytes to be fertilized. My frozen zygotes were ready to be inserted into me as soon as my womb was ready for gestation.

I was put on the daily dose of progesterone again, and I steeled up and shot myself in the upper thigh daily. It was infinitely more painful in the thigh muscle, and my skin bruised, as if I had gangrene, but I persevered with loads of ice and gritted teeth.

Sarvar would drive down to Carmel every weekend to keep me from becoming an island unto myself. I didn't quit my daytime vigil at the hospital, but on weekends, with Sarvar, I learned how to chill again.

Ba's funeral became the talk of the community. The entire world, it seemed, had shown up at her wake—or what the Gujaratis called the *oothamnu*. Following it, for thirteen days, hordes of people came to the mansion to pay their respects and mourn with the family.

Hindus cremated their dead and scattered the ashes over a body of holy water or a place dear to the departed one. We Parsis were a bit more macabre with our death customs.

We simply dropped the body into the *dakhma*, the Tower of Silence—which, ironically, was a waterless well dug deep into the ground of the cemetery—and let vultures swoop down and devour the dead. Something to do with the cycle of life, a convoluted form of the ashes-to-ashes and dust-to-dust theme, I believed.

"I think I prefer cremation myself," I told my brother one late December evening as I lounged in bed, encouraging Tickles the Zygote to take root in my womb. I was meant to relax for twenty-four hours, but I was playing it safe, and it was nigh coming on thirty-six now.

Sarvar had been with Nirvaan all day these three days, giving me the peace of mind I needed to get pregnant.

"Unnecessarily morbid, Sissy," he said, arranging a Christmassy scarf around his neck before pulling a knit cap over his head.

He was driving back to San Jose tonight for Zeus's holiday party. I was sad to see him go, but I guessed not everyone enjoyed being a recluse.

"Well, under the circumstances, can you blame me?" I was surrounded by death and disease. Only the life growing in my womb—please, Khodai, let it have taken root—kept me from floating away like a ghostly waif into the beyond. I needed Tickles to anchor me to this world.

Sarvar turned from the mirror in my bathroom. "Will you be okay?"

"Yes. I promise I won't jump into the car and drive to the hospital as soon as you leave. I talked with Beatrice, and Nirvaan is already down for the night. I'll wait until tomorrow to bounce in—well, not bounce, but you know what I mean. Go to your party. Have fun. Have a shot of tequila for me. Besides—" I picked up my e-reader and waved it at him "—I have my sexy new book boyfriend to keep me company—a tall redheaded highlander in a kilt, no less."

Solitude didn't bother me. And this was a good kind of alone. My in-laws were in India to scatter Ba's ashes over the plot of land Bapuji had married her for, as per her wishes, and weren't due back for another couple of weeks. Ba had been an Indian citizen, and there were formalities to be completed, a charity to be set up in her name. I hoped to give them some good news on their return.

Smiling, I ran a hand over my stomach, wondering if Tickles liked being inside me. No, I wasn't alone anymore.

"I'd feel better if you came with me," my brother reiterated.

I groaned. "Quit treating me like a child, and get going."

Sarvar kissed my forehead and my nose, which he possessed a twin of, and then he stood around, looking reluctant again. I literally pushed him out the door then. Shaking my head and grinning, I locked up behind him.

Not fifteen minutes later, the doorbell rang, and I rolled my eyes, feeling both cherished and irritated at the same time.

"You just can't help hovering, can you?" I scolded, opening the door.

I'd expected Sarvar. I was beyond flabbergasted to find Zayaan on my stoop.

A zillion emotions, beginning with shock, saturated the entirety of my being with the force of a typhoon. I grabbed the door for support and hoped I wouldn't get washed away, like so much debris. I wished for Nirvaan then. I yearned for the bright sunlit strength of my husband's love to keep me from drowning into the depths of the past.

Zayaan couldn't know about the baby. Sarvar had promised he wouldn't tell.

"You look terrible." I released the door and walked into the living room. I didn't want to do or say anything I'd regret, even though regret between Zayaan and me was as inevitable as Nirvaan's passing.

I wasn't surprised by the visit itself. I'd expected him to come back to see Nirvaan. Of course I had. Plus, his things were still here—some of his clothes, his papers, his nifty work gadgets. And I knew he'd return when he heard about the baby. Zayaan would be Tickles's godfather. I'd made peace with that promise, too.

The timing of this visit surprised me, though. Wasn't his sister's wedding next week? I wondered if his mother knew where he was.

"You could've let me know you were coming." I sat down on the sofa before my legs gave way beneath me.

The door whispered shut. Without a word or explanation, Zayaan walked across the living room to stand in front of the patio doors, which remained closed at all times now.

I didn't go out onto the deck anymore. I couldn't. It held too many ghosts. But I watched the sun rise and fall through the glass every day.

Right now the sleeping water and the sickle moon made an interesting backdrop, and I focused on it rather than Zayaan's confusing reappearance in Carmel. I wasn't prepared for this visit. I needed more time to sort out my feelings for him.

"I'm surprised you cleared Immigration," I remarked, half in jest, half in terror. Dear God, I totally, positively wasn't prepared to deal with him right now.

Scruffy and dangerous, he gave the impression of a bomb about to go off. His hair was overlong and curled over his nape, and he had a full thick beard on his face. He mustn't have shaved in days. His jeans and sweater were limp, and the scarf around his neck seemed more like a hangman's noose than protective gear. In short, he looked like his brother.

The good part? I didn't panic. I was calm. I wouldn't let the writhing snakes anywhere near Tickles's home in my womb.

"Are you hungry? There's plenty of food in the fridge," I said when I got tired of measuring the width of Zayaan's shoulders.

He turned around, shaking his head. His eyes fell on the game controllers on the coffee table. All four were labeled— N, S, Z and G for guest. Zayaan flinched visibly and I hurt for him. He carried so much pain on his strong shoulders, and so much of it I had placed there.

"I ate with Nirvaan when I stopped by the hospital from the airport."

Of course he had.

"He looks better," Zayaan said starkly.

I nodded in agreement.

Nirvaan's eyes would follow movement about the hospital room sometimes. I liked to believe they fixed on me more than Beatrice or Sarvar or any of the hospital staff. His doctors agreed that if there were no more setbacks, I could bring him home in a month.

"Why did you push me away?"

My skin pebbled into gooseflesh, as if I were standing on the beach on this cold winter night, even though I sat close to a raging fire. I closed my eyes against the naked anguish on Zayaan's face.

I didn't want to have this conversation tonight. I couldn't be tense tonight. Why had he come tonight of all nights?

"What are you hiding?" A bite of rage colored his voice.

I opened my eyes to gauge his meaning. What did he think I was hiding? Who had he been talking to? A million likely scenarios ballooned in my head. I'd never believe his mother had fessed up her sins. Nothing was making sense tonight.

"Surin said we should talk...come clean with each other. What did he mean by it?"

"My brother Surin? When did you speak to him?" I asked, my shock palpable now.

"I went to Surat for Ba. I couldn't make it to the LA funeral, so I..." His throat convulsed—on a curse or a sob, probably both. "I met Surin there. He invited me over for dinner."

As if that explained anything. "So you had dinner with my brother and then you came here. But what about your sister's wedding? Isn't it next—"

"Fuck the wedding!" he shouted.

I flinched, which seemed to enrage him further. He went electric, fairly sparking like lightning bolts. I sat up straight.

"Fuck you, Simeen. Fuck you for destroying my life. For not waiting. For letting me think... God. You don't know what I've thought all these years. Fuck you for not trusting what we had."

His chest heaved up and down. So did mine. Our breaths were coming in bursts, as if we'd climbed a huge mountain to the summit where the air was thin and our fall certain.

Suddenly, Nirvaan wasn't the only link between us. Zayaan and I had a history quite separate from Nirvaan—a history that, in my most fanciful moments, I'd traced back to Persia. A history I'd ripped to shreds the night I was raped.

Zayaan was right. I hadn't trusted him. More tellingly, I hadn't trusted my love for him. I hadn't believed that our love was strong enough to survive the horror of what I'd suffered at the hands of his brother and his mother. And I'd pushed him away. For his sake and mine, I'd run away.

He didn't know of the rape. I was sure of it. My brothers wouldn't tell him without my consent. Nirvaan, by his own admission, hadn't told him. And Gulzar Begum didn't have the guts to tell her son the truth. But I had to tell him. I owed him the truth.

Zayaan closed the distance between us in two strides. He grabbed my shoulders and pulled me to my feet, shaking me. He wasn't rough. But my body recoiled on its own like a bad habit that would not break.

"Damn you for fighting me. Damn you for bringing religion between us. For leaving me when I needed you the most."

He yanked me close and put his mouth on mine. His tongue plunged in—hot, abrasive, unbelievably erotic. His arms banded around me, squeezing me hard, and I whimpered. My body was ultrasensitive tonight. He ripped his mouth from mine and backed up so fast that I was left hanging on to a phantom kiss. His face was as white as the moon behind him.

"I'm sorry. I shouldn't have...fuck. I don't know what came over me. Bloody hell. Simeen, don't look at me like that. I know you don't want me. That you find me crude and needy and...just not good enough." He stepped farther and farther away. "I shouldn't have come. I'm sorry," he said. Then he spun on his heel and stormed off. He was out the door in seconds.

I was frozen in place. I was shocked, elated, cold, hot, relieved and devastated all at once.

How long would I let Rizvaan rule my life, my choices? How long would I blame Zayaan for his brother's sin? He wasn't responsible for my rape any more than I was responsible for Nirvaan's cancer. Wasn't it time I stopped punishing us both?

I raced after him, shouting, "I do want you!"

Zayaan stopped on the steps and turned around. But he didn't climb back up. He was waiting...allowing me time to come to my senses, to reject him again.

"I never said that you're not good enough. And I want you

so much that I tremble with it. You make me crazy with wanting you." God, I wanted to touch him. I wanted him to touch me so badly. I was through with denying myself this man.

I'd shocked him. It stained his face, glazed his eyes. He hadn't expected me to come after him, to say what I'd said. He'd expected another lie.

I held my arms out to him. "Make me tremble, Zai. Make me forget everything but the world we'd once made for the two of us."

I laughed when he leaped up the porch steps and hugged me tight. For a long time, we just stood there, wrapped in each other's arms. My face pressed to his chest, I sobbed.

When I quieted, he picked me up, as if I were a fragile and precious thing, one of his ancient scrolls of Persian poetry, and he strode into the house, into my bedroom. It didn't escape me that he'd first taken a step in the direction of his own room, but then he'd stopped and deliberately turned toward mine...and Nirvaan's.

There were so many things I had to say to him, to ask of him, but I didn't know where to begin. And, honestly, I didn't want to talk or think right now. I only wanted to feel.

He placed me on the bed I'd shared with my husband, never taking his eyes off me. His hopes and desires, guilt and self-loathing, were naked on his face, and for the first time in a dozen years, I allowed myself to drown in the feelings he evoked in me.

If Nirvaan were here, he'd have made the love-was-a-dish-best-served-naked comment. He and my father were right. There should be no lies, no secrets, not even clothes between lovers.

I started with my clothes. "Get naked, Zai."

His eyes flared with heat at my command. I kneeled on the

bed and pulled my granny nightgown over my head. I wasn't wearing a bra, and I left my white cotton panties on—for now.

Zayaan shucked off his shoes and socks. He slowly unwound his scarf and threw it aside. He flicked open the buttons on his jeans, every flick deliberate, devastating, delicious. The tease. His hands toyed with the hem of his sweater until I raised my eyes to his face.

"We need to talk," he said.

"We will. But I want to make love to you first." *Before I tell you the truth and shatter your faith again.*

The heat in his eyes turned into a conflagration as they journeyed over my nearly naked body. An answering blaze crackled through my belly when his eyes touched the blue-black spots on the outer curve of my upper thigh where I'd injected myself, and then they backtracked over my swollen belly to my ripe pink-tipped breasts and to my flaming face.

"You're doing the IVF again." It wasn't a question.

"Yes." I sat back on my haunches, or I'd have fallen over. My knees were shaking so hard. I placed a hand over my belly. "I had the embryo transfer yesterday morning."

His throat convulsed. "You could be pregnant." Another statement.

"Yes," I said with hope and dreams beaming out of every part of me.

Would he stay, or would he go now?

He sat on the bed, facing me, his striptease forgotten. I wasn't half a foot away from him, but suddenly, I felt as if a great gulf had opened up between us. He'd brought me into Nirvaan's bedroom. Was he okay with the rest, too?

"Is this a problem?" I asked quietly.

It was one thing to be an honorary uncle to your best friend's child. It was another to be…what? Exactly what was

I asking him to be? A father? A stepfather? A godfather? An uncle? None of the above? No wonder he looked dazed.

I reached for him, to reassure him, and his arms came to rest on my hips at the same time.

"I won't let it be a problem," he swore, bringing his mouth down on mine.

Elation robbed my breath, and I moaned into his mouth. He was so warm. I couldn't get enough of kissing him, touching him, needing him. I was burning, and he willingly fanned the flames.

He pushed me back against the pillows and rolled on top of me. The glorious full weight of him settled on me for a second before he raised himself, planting a hand on either side of my head. I arched into his kiss. He nipped my lips, sucked on my tongue, licked my mouth, as if it were candy. I was still nearly naked, and he was still fully clothed. I tried to balance the equation.

I pulled his sweater up, shoving at his shoulders to get it off. He wouldn't let me, and when I whined against his mouth, he bit my lower lip.

"Patience," he murmured.

He kissed my throat, the ridge of my shoulder blade, making me forget what I was about. I forgot my own name. He got me drunk on soft, soft, feather-like kisses. The quick tiny darts of his tongue and teeth on my skin drove me crazy. A fingertip stroked against my panties, teasing me to the edge faster than I'd ever experienced before, only to ease off when I strained against his hand. He nuzzled my nipple with his nose and beard to calm me when I couldn't take it anymore, only to make me wild again with his hot, hot mouth.

I shivered as he pressed my breasts together and sucked one and then the other, over and over. Moaned when he ground his pelvis into mine. Begged for more, more, more than just his hands and mouth on me.

"Stop torturing me, Nirvaan," I gasped without thinking.

Once, I'd read on some agony aunt column that accidentally addressing your current lover by your ex's name was common and natural. It had to do with habit and how *into it* you were with the new guy. As in, it was a good thing. I'd slotted the column as a big pot of hocus-pocus—until now.

We both froze when I said Nirvaan's name. I was extremely conscious of my hand inside Zayaan's jeans, curved along the shape of his bum. My first instinct was to snatch it back and push him away. Zayaan's hand trembled with indecision on my breast.

"Don't, Sims…" He sighed, his breath painting a hot blush across my chest.

I'd kept my husband out of this bed, deliberately out of my mind, once I stripped off my nightgown. I didn't know why I'd thought it might work when Zayaan had never stayed out of the bed I'd shared with Nirvaan.

I loved two men. I should be used to mental threesomes by now.

"Don't, what?" I asked.

If he said, "Don't say Nirvaan's name," I'd ask him to leave. Didn't he understand Nirvaan was a part of us?

"Don't hide from me…not your thoughts, your desires, your fears. Don't hide anything," he requested in earnest.

Tension drained out of me. I put my face against the curve of his shoulder and began to laugh. After a second or two, Zayaan joined in. When we finally got ourselves under control, he raised himself on an elbow, still grinning. I slapped a hand on his chest when he leaned in for a kiss.

"One more thing," I said.

He quirked a rakish eyebrow.

"Quit going all Nirvaan on me."

He raised his other eyebrow as high as its rakish twin. I wanted to laugh again, but what I had to say was too important to be taken in jest.

"He's the one with the slick bedroom moves. Not you. At least, you never used to have those. What I'm saying is, just be yourself. I…I've missed your intensity… I've missed you."

Still, he took his time to jog up the pace. He lit candles about the room and switched off the lights. He revived his striptease and wouldn't let me do anything but lie back on the bed and enjoy the show.

For months, I'd felt guilty for admiring his body when Nirvaan's was failing. For taking pleasure in the musky, masculine scent of a healthy man when Nirvaan's sickly, sweet smell would make me gag. I was not going to feel guilty anymore—not tonight, at least.

Zayaan came to bed, both of us naked, at last. We aligned ourselves on our sides, heads on pillows, staring into each other's eyes, as our hands roved and touched and mapped our bodies to memory.

The hair on his chest, armpits and genitals was neatly trimmed, and I wondered briefly if it was hygiene or religion that had made him manscape. Whatever the reason, he looked clean and appetizing. I raked my nails across the ridges of muscle on his chest, making him hiss.

He grabbed my hand, tugging me on top of him. He pushed my hair off my face, not letting me hide anything from him. His hair-rough thigh slid between my smooth legs, and he anchored us together—mouth to mouth, chest to chest, groin to groin.

"Yes," I hissed as my body hummed with excitement.

There was the passion he had been hell-bent on leashing. I

wanted it unleashed. I wanted to be swept away in a tidal wave of pleasure. I wanted to be burned alive so I could be reborn.

I used my teeth down his chest, sank them into a hip blade. He reared up with a shout and grabbed my shoulders. Shrugging his hands off, I roused him to a fever with lips and teeth and tongue, dipping lower and lower. I was on a mission, and it wasn't one of mercy. He flopped back with a groan when I took him in my mouth.

Zayaan was cut where Nirvaan wasn't, long where Nirvaan was thick. They tasted the same—salt and tart and heat—yet I knew their differences. I would always know and revel in their differences, my twin knights. I stroked him, teasingly at first and then with purpose. Zayaan's hands fisted in my hair a little too tight, and I welcomed the pain.

When you felt pain, it meant you were alive. I was learning the same about joy. I was giving life a chance.

I wasn't numb tonight. I wasn't dead or frozen or unfeeling. I was alive. In this bed. With this man. And as long as I was alive, Nirvaan's baby would thrive inside me.

The tide turned, and Zayaan flipped me onto my back. Not a slick move. He wasn't thinking now, and it made me smile. He explored every inch of my body, as if I were data to be studied, weighed and consumed. It was my turn to groan and break into gooseflesh. Every part of me seemed to be connected to every part of him, every fiber, every follicle, every delectable taste bud.

"I want to see you. All of you." Zayaan manacled my wrists in one hand and stretched them up over my head. His other hand hooked under my knee, and he pushed my leg wide-open.

"Zai, please," I begged. I was half-embarrassed, fully aroused when he stared at that part of me. I wanted him to touch me.

"Know your voice," he said, using the same gruff inflection he reserved for poetry recitation. *"Recognize you when you first come 'round the corner."* Rumi again.

I had no breath left to giggle.

His hand began to read me like braille. He licked between my breasts.

"Sense your scent when I come into a room you've just left."

He shifted his body to kneel between my thighs. He picked up one foot and pressed soft kisses on it.

"Know the lift of your heel, the glide of your foot."

I slid my other foot along the back of his thigh, his calf. I married our soles together.

"Become familiar with the way you purse your lips, then let them part, just the slightest bit, when I lean into your space and kiss you."

He kissed me then. Khodai, did he kiss me.

I moaned into his mouth and wished...wished for so much. I arched into his hand, willing him to hurry up and join our bodies, but he tightened his hold on my hands until I lay flat again.

"I want to know the joy of how you whisper 'more.'"

"Dear God, Zai. I can't whisper 'more' unless we finish the first round," I groaned. I was at the end of my tether.

He snorted, but he released me.

Suddenly, I was a buoy bobbing in a sea of nerves with no anchor. And before I had time to grumble or tell him how much I wanted him, Zayaan rolled off me, and our eyes locked together.

We were sweating, both of us. Sex was a strenuous business and, if done right, not for the faint of heart. We were neither fainthearted nor out of shape. But we were cautious—at least, Zayaan was.

"I don't have a condom." He looked ready to bang his head against the wall.

My lips twitched. "You're clean, disease-free. Healthy... obviously. I'm clean, healthy and possibly pregnant. And if I'm not..." I left the rest hanging.

If the IVF failed like last time...

If I couldn't hold Nirvaan's baby inside me for whatever reason...

Zayaan didn't look away from me. Not even when doubts and reservations sprang across his face again. He held my heart in his hands until, not ten seconds later, a mask of decision fell into place.

He covered me again, from head to foot, and slowly pushed into me. He was bare. I was ripe. If I wasn't pregnant with Nirvaan's baby already, there was a good chance I'd get pregnant with Zayaan's. This was a commitment we were making to each other and to Nirvaan.

"I love you," Zayaan whispered as he slid inside me to the hilt.

I started to say that I loved him, too, so, so much, but my gasp swallowed up my words.

It was indescribable when you experienced something you'd only dreamed about. It was overwhelming and life changing. It was sudden and shocking, and it was over much too soon because it didn't even take half a dozen strokes for us to explode in orgasm together.

"That's not fair. It was too fast," I cried the minute I caught my breath.

"Don't cry because it's over; smile because it happened," quipped Zayaan as he rolled off me, tucking me against his trembling chest.

"Rumi again?" I teased, secretly ecstatic he was quoting the love poet so much.

"Dr. Seuss," Zayaan deadpanned before he dissolved into a fit of moronic laughter.

I smacked him on the chest and left him in bed with the giggles to wash up in the bathroom. I didn't need to look in the mirror to know I was smiling like a fool, too.

But I looked because I had old ghosts to exorcise.

It was still dark even though a slit of pinkish predawn had ripped open the night.

I walked onto the deck for the first time since Nirvaan had woken from his coma. The waves hailed me with gentle growls, and I greeted them back, breathed them in. The chilly ocean air tried to defeat me, but I stood my ground. I would not run away ever again.

Zayaan sat on the lounger, head bent in *sajdah*, probably adding Nirvaan and the baby to his daily *dua*. And me.

We'd made a commitment to each other last night, and I meant to keep my word. I wondered if he could, after all was said and done this morning.

I had to tell him of the rape. I didn't want any secrets between us.

I frowned, pulling the blanket tight around me, to keep the shivers at bay. I hadn't bothered dressing myself when I'd woken to find Zayaan gone. For a second, the snakes had come back disguised as panic, and I'd realized they hadn't really gone away. They'd simply been sleeping.

I sensed more than saw his shoulders shake. He couldn't be laughing, and Zayaan was never cold. I went to my knees before him and took his face between my hands.

Soundless streams of tears tracked his face.

"You were right to push me away. I would've dragged you down with me. I couldn't save Rizvaan. He was not a nice man...but he was my brother...and I betrayed him. I failed to protect my family. I would've failed you, too... God help me, I would've destroyed your life. Look what I've done. He trusted me to care for him, and look what I've done. Oh, God, Simi, look what I've done to Nirvaan. It's my fault…my fault."

I went with the instinct Ba had credited me with. I pressed his face against my shoulder to stop the babbling and allowed him the release he so desperately needed.

For the first time, it struck me what Nirvaan had been about these last few months. I wasn't the only one he'd been trying to fix in this house.

I realized something else, too. Zayaan wasn't ready for the whole truth. Maybe he'd never be. That night was my burden and I had to carry it alone. But it didn't have to stop me from living my life or being happy.

"It's not your fault. *Hush*. You are not responsible for the choices your brother made. You are not responsible for Nirvaan's condition. You—*we* did the best we could under very bad circumstances. Hush, sweetie. Please."

It took him a long time to calm down. Time enough for me to set aside fear and remorse, degradation, disease and death. I gave love the reins and let it wander as it pleased.

As the sun broke over the horizon, Zayaan pulled me onto his lap. He molded my body to his, murmuring first shock and then appreciation as he grasped that I was stark naked under the blanket. He wanted me. Again. I smiled through my tears. Again.

Here, on this deck, I'd kissed my husband at sunrise and made impossible promises over sunsets. Here, we'd made little paper boats of our dreams and set them adrift on love's vast shore. So, here, I turned in our lover's arms and told him I loved him.

"Will you stay with us?" I asked, our mouths touching.

"Always and forever," Zayaan promised with a kiss.

Here, in our house in Carmel-by-the-Sea, there was no right and wrong. It just was.

Life & Lemons...

I wish I could tell you the Awesome Threesome rode off into the sunset on Jet Skis, raiding the high seas, brandishing scimitars and water pistols. That the rest of our lives were filled with laughter and love poetry like we'd imagined before we'd turned eighteen. Don't get me wrong; some of it was. But a lot of it was sheer work and a continuous juggling act.

Making a marriage work between two people was hard. Making a ménage work where one partner was in a severely vegetative state and the other with no legal ties, save for a promise and a limited power of attorney, was beyond difficult.

There were days when I'd doubt my own shadow. Days when Zayaan and I'd fight as hard as we made love, scaring Beatrice to the point where she'd feel compelled to kidnap Nirvaan and visit a friend so that he wouldn't have to hear us shout—correction, hear me screech. Zayaan didn't shout. He held his tongue, schooled his expression and rode out the storm.

I told him, in no uncertain terms, his mother was banned from our home forever. He was free to visit her in London as often and as long as he wished. I had no desire to come between mother and son, but I would not entertain her power games in my house. I had no wish to poison the son against his mother, but I had to draw a line. His sisters and their families were more than welcome, and that was the extent of my largesse toward the Khans.

I hated seeing Zayaan hurt or torn between his responsibilities, but I wasn't a mouse anymore. And I needed all my strength to care for my husband.

Nirvaan's health remained an ongoing battle and was not always uphill. When he slid down, the results were disastrous, and it shook us up. My world would tilt off its axis until Nirvaan was better again.

The Desais and my brothers were my bastions. Even Nisha ultimately decided that I wasn't a leech—or not as big a one as she'd assumed. With them behind me, I could face the world and its myopic judgments. It wasn't easy. Dear God, it wasn't easy to ignore the sneers and the questions.

Zayaan bore the brunt there, too. He wasn't my husband. He wasn't our baby's father, not legally and not in the eyes of the world, even if he was Daddy and Nirvaan was Papa. He bore it all for love, and I worshipped him for it.

Marjaneh didn't disappear from my life like Sandwich Anu. She was Zayaan's friend and a colleague and remained one whether I liked it or not. I got used to her. I didn't have a choice.

As for me, I learned to get along with Ahura Mazda. I came to believe He'd had a plan for me—for us—all along. He'd meant for us to be a unit—Nirvaan, Zayaan and me. Why else had He brought us together on Dandi Beach on our birthdays? Why else would we feel incomplete without the other or compelled to rescue one another?

On the days I was being fanciful, I would weave a tale of a soul with three bodies who made one baby.

Yes, we had a daughter. A little angel with a smile as wicked as her Papa's and eyes as enigmatic as her Daddy's. She had my complexion and chestnut-brown hair but, thankfully, not my nose. Her every laugh, her very existence made our lives worthwhile and our choices sacred. She was our soul.

We named her Nirvi, after Nirvaan. But we called her Tickles, for love.

★ ★ ★ ★ ★

Acknowledgments

When you do things from your soul, you feel a river moving in you, a joy.

—*Rumi*

First and foremost, I have to thank Jalāl ad-Dīn Muhammad Rūmī for the wonderful words he gifted to this world. His words helped me through some of the roughest patches of writing this novel. There were tears. There was anger. There was sorrow. There was grief. And there were memories—new ones, old ones—all moving through my soul like a river of joy.

There are many, many souls who helped me make this book what it is in myriad different ways. Lisa, Sharon, Trupti, Sejal, Komal and Pallavi for helping me shape the bones of the story. Jovana Shirley and Deb Nemeth for showing me the right amount of muscle it needed. To Preeti Singh, Ritesh and Mukti for your generosity and support. To Seema Mehta Mehringer for excavating your IVF memories with me.

To my editor, Allison Carroll, who understands the soul of this book. Thank you from the bottom of my heart for championing S, N and Z beyond my wildest dreams. Thank you to the team at Graydon House. I love every step of the journey we're taking together.

To Andrea Somberg, my agent, for making difficult things

possible. And to Dana Kaye, of Kaye Publicity, for extending that world of possibilities for me.

The themes *My Last Love Story* touches on are about love, relationships and internal strength. So, lastly, I thank all the people who give me that and more—always, every day and in infinite ways. My family, my friends and my readers, I am because we are.

With much love,
Falguni

Questions for Discussion

1. What was your overall experience while reading *My Last Love Story*? Were you engaged immediately and throughout or the opposite?

2. Which character did you like the most? Which one did you like the least? Why?

3. Consider the meaning behind the novel's title. Whose last love story do you think it refers to—Simeen and Nirvaan's, or Simeen and Zayaan's?

4. Read aloud a passage from *My Last Love Story* that stood out to you. Explain why.

5. Did you learn something new by reading this book? Has this book changed your views of the world in some way?

6. Discuss some of the themes the story touches on.

7. Simeen was orphaned during her formative years. How do you think, if at all, the need to fill this parental void impacted her choices in life?

8. In Simeen's shoes, how would you have reacted on and after your eighteenth birthday?

9. To many, Simeen's running away to Mumbai might seem like a cowardly act, but do you agree with Simeen about keeping the trauma a secret in her situation? What do you think would have happened had she told the truth?

10. Discuss the same for Nirvaan.

11. Discuss how Zayaan would have reacted had he known the truth.

12. Part of the story took place in India and part in the United States. How did the cultural differences and societal mores impact how this story unfolded and the options available to the characters?

13. Do you think it is possible for three people to love each other equally?

14. Had the traumatic events in the story that broke up the Awesome Threesome never occurred, would Zayaan and Nirvaan be as accepting of each other in Simeen's life?

15. What kind of man would Nirvaan have been if he had not had cancer? What about Simeen and Nirvaan's marriage? How would it have fared without the cancer?

16. Compare the two mother-son relationships narrated in the novel.

17. Nirvaan's mother essentially gave the green light to Simeen to live however she chose, in complete contrast to Zayaan's mother's admonishments. Do you think Simeen

would have had the courage to choose as she had without Nirvaan's mother's approval?

18. Did Zayaan's mother protect her own interests by forcing Simeen's silence in Surat, or did a mother simply protect her cubs?

19. Was Nirvaan right in trying to arrange Simeen's life to run smoothly when he was gone? Why did Simeen call him a bully for that?

20. Zayaan, while a good friend, was also, in many respects, Nirvaan's rival. Why did Nirvaan put his medical decisions in Zayaan's hands and not in Simeen's or his parents', which would have been the conventional pecking order?

21. What are your thoughts and feelings about Zayaan? What do you think he knew or suspected about the past?

22. What feelings did reading the last line invoke in you?

23. If you could change something about *My Last Love Story*, what would it be? And why?